APES OF THE WILDFIRE

AN "ANIMAL EYES" STORY

JUSTIN MORGAN

Paws
On
PUBLISHING

ISBN (paperback): 978-1-7399570-6-3
ISBN (digital): 978-1-7399570-7-0

Published by Paws On Publishing

I really hope you enjoy this book.
If you do, kindly consider leaving a review or rating online.
Even one word is a big help!
Sincere thanks,
Justin

For my big brother, Lee, who stayed forever little.

CONTENTS

PROLOGUE: THE BIRD KING

INDONESIAN BORNEO
1985

ALONE IN HIS NEST, high in the canopy, an orang rubbed the sleep from the corners of his eyes and took a breath of humid air. The day wasn't yet dawned, but already the cicadas were protesting the heat, as they shrieked their dreary drone from the trunk of every ironwood.

Today the monsoon would come. It *had* to. Heavy clouds had hung above the trees for weeks, low and dark and filled with promise. Yet not once did they burst, and now vegetation everywhere was as parched as heathland. Rainforest needed rain – or else, what kind of forest was it?

Hooking his fingers over the side of the nest, the orang peered cautiously down. Something had come trudging below in the dark hours, prompting fitful dreams. Relieved to see it was gone now, however, and certain he was safe, he hauled himself over the edge and dangled from a bough, savouring the whiff of figs that drifted up into his nostrils.

The orang's hunger grew sharper. He intended to travel across to the basin today to catch a glimpse of the twins, but with his mind now focussed on spiky, smelly jackfruits, he decided he'd first pay a visit to the orchard.

He dropped to a lower branch, meeting the passing gibbons who eyed him blankly as they swung by on their ludicrous arms, hooting their song of dawn. Licking his lips in anticipation of finding snacks on the ground, the orang suddenly remembered the noises that had disturbed his sleep, and thought better of it. Safer for now to remain in the mid-trees, at least until the sun's rays reached the forest bed.

Hand over hand, the orang swung away from his nest, smiling as he thought of the twins. They were growing so fast! It was incredible, really, the speed at which little things became big things. He recalled what his own mother said when he was still nursing at her breast. 'You'll be all grown up before long, son, and then it will be time for you to make your own way through the forest.'

It had made his heart hurt to hear that. 'But I want to stay with you forever, mama,' he said.

There was tenderness in his dear mother's eyes, yet she offered little solace. 'No child stays with their mother forever, Dama. Tree-men like you must feel thankful to get as long with your mamas as you do – most creatures manage only a few monsoons with theirs. But I'll grow another child soon, and when my stomach starts to swell, you'll be good and ready to move along and find a life of your own.'

Of course, his twin sons weren't twins in the true sense, since they were born of different mothers. But since he had sired both, and since sisters Effie and Ivie had delivered them on the same day – very nearly at the same time, if accounts were to be trusted – it was natural to think of the boys this way.

Dama's smile grew wider. Becoming a father for the first time was still a source of amusement to him. He couldn't quite believe just how right his mother had been:

it seemed he'd no sooner left her side than he was obeying a new set of instincts.

Would his babies be like him when they grew up? Dama's own cheek pads had developed early on, rounding out his face to catch the attention of all the forest's females. His sons' might, too. But then it was just as likely their faces would stay lean until twelve or thirteen monsoons had passed, and that was a heartening thought. Why shouldn't a couple of boys simply enjoy their childhoods, free from the fear of conflict and rivalry?

With the heat of the day rising, the low-lying mist was beginning to burn off, making more routes visible to Dama through the mid-trees. At a steady pace, he whipped along the limbs, and as he journeyed into the brightening horizon, a faint gurgling caught his ear. It was just the sound he'd hoped to hear.

Below, water was running down the face of the rocks. Opening his fingers wide, the orang fell out out of the sky, catching hold of a limb which pivoted him across to the stream. Clinging to a vine with three of his appendages, he used his free hand to drink, letting water pool in his palm before sucking it up through pursed lips. Cool and sweet with minerals, he sloshed it around his parched mouth, happily.

Birds were waking now. Around him, the dawn had come alive with warbles and trills and strident yelps where a party of scruffy-crowned hornbills were passing overhead. Then, from high in the sky, another kind of call sounded, and even though Dama was still thirsty, he leapt away from the stream as quickly as he could.

He climbed into the canopy silently, breaking through the topmost skin of leaves with caution. Throwing back his head, he saw a bird passing above him, and his heart began to thump.

The kite's neck and breast glowed white, made radiant by the rays of the dawning sun. The black tips of its wings were angled, and its body plumage was much the same shade of reddish brown as Dama's own shaggy hair.

There was no doubt about it.

It was Lang, the Bird-King.

He had returned.

Dama held his breath as he watched Lang soar. The kite dipped to the side, flying the first of many circles before issuing another wail over the treetops, this one lengthier than the first. At this, even the cicadas fell silent a moment. Did all the forest's creatures know the significance of the coming of the kite, or was it just Dama's own kind?

No matter: for the orang-utan – the people of the trees – Lang's return meant only one thing.

The time of peace had come to an end for this corner of the mighty forest.

❦

Still the dark clouds failed to slake the land's thirst.

Not a drop of rain had fallen, and now the breezeless, broiling atmosphere was squeezed into an even narrower sliver of air. Dama had covered half the distance to the basin, but with the day gone to dusk, his energy was so low he could proceed no further.

Even making a nest was an ordeal. Sat in the three-way fork of an ironwood, he languidly reached out for twigs, pulling them into his body and snapping them across his foot. He then lay each fractured piece across the fork until a pocket of branches enveloped him, and wearily collapsed into it.

He let out a big burp, pungent with the scent of jackfruit. He'd found the orchard without much fuss, though was dismayed to discover ants had already stripped away much of the tastiest flesh. Luckily, though, plenty remained within the core of the spiky husks, so he spent the afternoon in the shade of the trees, eating his fill and napping. With any luck, the ants would leave him something for the return journey, too – and if they didn't, he'd gobble them up instead.

While all around birds were returning to the trees, the sky was growing ever busier with bats as they poured out from their hidden caves, and when one came flitting madly over the side of the nest, he threw out a fist and caught it. Holding the little animal in his hands, Dama leant close to study it in the grey half-light of dusk, pulling out the leathery skin of its wing.

How startlingly like a hand it was! Each bone was really just a strange kind of finger! The creature's chirruping, however, soon grew bothersome, and Dama let it go. And just as it vanished from his field of vision, a smell wafted into his nostrils. But this wasn't fig, or jackfruit.

This was burning.

Below, a rustling sounded. Dama kept very still. Something was down there. Perhaps it was the same sort of thing that had passed beneath him last night?

The smell grew more acrid, and the shuffling continued, and after a while, when he was sure it was too dark to be sighted in his nest, Dama braved a glance down to the forest floor.

There was nothing to see, at first. But then a light flickered, and a perfect point of orange heat shone, and in the radiance of that glowing circle, a face was revealed.

It was a land-orang! He wore coverings on his lower half, but his torso was bare, and completely free of fur. A small white stick was hanging between the odd creature's lips, and from it smoke came curling up into the dark night.

After some time, the land-orang moved away. But Dama quietly stalked him from on high, wondering what business such a creature had here, so deep in the jungle, at so late an hour?

Nearby were more bare-chested ground-men. Spying on them behind the trunk of a mangowood, Dama winced at the dreadful noise of their tools. Yet, as uneasy as these made him feel, his curiosity was simply too strong, and he edged lower.

To his surprise, the trees began to disappear. In the time it took for the moon to reach the apex of the night sky, a huge gap had opened up. How had it happened? In the same way that they grew, trees usually took their time to come down – yet they lay now perfectly flat upon the ground.

The land-orangs completed their work, and everything went quiet. But then the peace was disrupted in the most bewildering of ways.

It began in the north, with a whirring in the clouds. At first, it was so faint that Dama put it down to imagination. However, it soon grew into such a cacophony that he was forced to shelter his ears with his hands.

A great wind began to blow the boughs – he was afraid he might be sent toppling out of his nest – but Dama couldn't tell just where all this commotion was coming from. Then he noticed that the ground-men were shining bright lights up into the sky; following their beams, his eyes settled on a bird of gargantuan proportions.

As it hung in the air above the fallen trees, Dama's bewildered mind raced. How could so solid a thing remain where it was, when no wings appeared to be flapping? How did its own weight not pull it back to the ground?

The underside of the vast bird then opened up, and several strands, like vines, came dangling down, sending the ground-men scurrying away into the western tree-line. Then, as if that weren't odd enough, a new group of land-orangs – ones whose whole bodies were wrapped beneath coverings – emerged from *out* of the bird.

Dama watched, frozen with terror, as the creatures lowered themselves down the vines and crawled over into the cover of the trees to the east. The terrible bird rotated, whipping the palm fronds with impossible gusts, then ascended once again and flew off into the night, until its awful whirring din could be heard no more.

Dama thought of Lang. The Bird-King had appeared this morning in the form of a kite and now, it seemed, the spirit of war was here again in the guise of something inconceivable to a young orang like him.

Trying to remain calm, Dama climbed over to an orchid bowl halfway up the trunk, and hid behind it. Although he barely dared to look, he periodically swung his head around, back towards the clearing.

For a long time, nothing happened. Then, when the moon had made its way to the other horizon, some very odd pops sounded, and the land-orangs who'd come out of the Bird-King's belly burst from the eastern tree-line and onto the clearing.

The pops grew in intensity, as flashes of light blazed from the ends of the metal sticks these newcomers brandished. Dama felt intuitively that the tools were violent things; the tree cutters were scared of them: they froze where they were, with their hands held high in the air.

One ground-man came forward. 'Think you could outsmart us, did you, foreigners?' He snapped his fingers together, and two of his companions stepped up to wrap a length of fabric around the eyes of the tree cutters, before shoving sticks into their backs to make them walk.

Dama couldn't understand the tongue of course, but to his ears the voices that followed sounded like they were spoken in fear and anger respectively.

'We have permission to farm here! We're not insurgents!'

'Shut your mouth, invader! You – tighten his blindfold!'

'Please! If you're going to kill me, at least let me send a message to my family first!'

'Did you let my brother send a message before you butchered him? Well, if it's good enough for us Dayaks, it's good enough for you, Madura dogs.'

Just then another bare-chest came sprinting out from the cover of the trees. He sprang into the air, both feet in front of him, and sent a newcomer tumbling with a powerful kick, and the pair fell to the ground in what Dama knew right away was a fight. It didn't last long, however: soon, the bare-chested individual was hoisted up onto his feet by several others.

'Nice try, foreigner! But it's over. This invasion of our land has to stop somewhere, or us natives will be ruined. For too long have you terrorised the peace-loving Dayaks of Kalimantan. Now you die like the pig you are.'

Almost too afraid to keep watching, Dama looked on as the furious individual held out his hands and took the bare-chest by his throat. It appeared to Dama that the fingers of the attacker then began to tighten.

The eyes of the captured man bulged, then rolled back into his head. His tongue came out and flickered between both edges of his wide-open mouth. Dama, who by now had fully broken his cover in order to better see, knew he ought to be more cautious. Yet he was mesmerised by what he was witnessing. Was it some kind of game?

If it was, it ended in a way that wasn't at all exciting: soon, the man simply dropped to the forest bed, and the others were led away. And, as if nothing had happened here at all, everything went suddenly quiet again.

With dusk warming the east, Dama went to ground. When he was sure no others were nearby, he crawled over to the land-orang they'd left behind.

Bringing his face above him, Dama looked into the blank eyes. At first, he thought the creature was sleeping, but the closer Dama went, the more his doubts grew. Life was necessary in order for sleep to happen, and none was here now. Curiously, it was as though the thing had *never* been alive. It was just a husk: a jagged, broken jackfruit shell that housed no fruit.

Dama felt his lips curl into a mirthless smile. A light had blazed once inside this ground-man, and now another of their kind, using nothing but his hands, had put it out. What an astonishing power!

He looked down at his own hand, just visible in dawn's soft light, and tracked the fingers. Between the palm and the nails were the three grooves of the knuckles. It was *exactly* like the land-orang's hand!

No tree-man had ever spoken to him of this incredible ability – and there was a simple reason why.

Not a single one of them knew what Dama himself now did:

That death itself resided in their own fingers.

1

THE BASIN

On the rim of a vast bowl of rainforest, a young orang named Bili peered out over the vista of his home.

Of all spots, this section of ridge was his favourite. Long ago, perhaps ten monsoons or more when he was still a baby, lightning toppled trees up here and left behind a wide scar. New growth had been quick to spring up again – the forest wouldn't have it any other way – but even after all this time, the ironwoods were still mere saplings, and the magnificent views remained unbroken.

Hidden beneath the palm fronds that lay beside his feet was the thing he'd been working on all afternoon. His friends had been off playing, but were now making their way back onto the ridge, hooting so impatiently for a first glimpse that Bili's hand was beginning to tremble with nerves. But he'd put in too much effort to be rushed by this rowdy mob, so he took a deep, calming breath, and placed his arms over the fronds to keep the mysterious creation concealed until he was ready to reveal it.

Noticing Akan wasn't among them, Bili's shoulders

sagged. 'Where's my brother? He said he'd be coming back with you.'

Rafi squeaked half a reply, then went coy. 'He went off to find—'

'What?'

The orangs eyed one another with bashful glances. 'Not *what*,' said Rafi. 'We think he went to look for your bapa. All the aunties are saying he left.'

Bili gave a dismissive swish of his hand. There was little point worrying about *that*. For as long as he and Akan had known their father, he'd come and gone as he'd seen fit – sometimes whole monsoons passed without so much as a sighting of that wide-cheeked tree-man.

With a cheeky grin, Rafi sprang toward the fronds, aiming to sneak a peak at what was waiting beneath. Bili bounced off his bottom at once to chase him away, but the moment he left the area unattended, the others were quick to rush across, resulting in a mass tumble that spilled onto the very edge of the covered work. Bili let out a cross shriek, but just as his temper was about to overcome him, his brother appeared from out of the canopy.

The boys leapt away, jumping in excited circles. 'Akan's here! Did you find him? Did you find your bapa?'

'Of course he didn't,' huffed Bili. 'He wasn't even looking for him, were you, brother?'

Akan smiled shyly.

'I knew it, Akan! I watch your eyes every time we come up here. You're always looking beyond the basin. You did it, didn't you? You went down the outer slope.'

Akan threw down the bunch of figs he'd carried up, bringing the others piling in, and a few moments of feasting served to settle everybody down. Although Bili didn't much feel like eating, he nestled in tight to his brother while he snacked away happily and spat stones onto the dusty ground.

'Aren't you having one?'

'Not now,' sighed Bili. 'I want to get this out of the way first.'

Akan's eyes opened wide and he rubbed his brother tenderly on his shoulder. 'You make it sound like one of the chores our mothers make us do!'

With a shrug, Bili ambled over to the palm fronds, peeling them back with care so as not to disturb what lay underneath. So unceremonious was this unveiling that it was witnessed only by Akan, who went alone to stand beside what had been placed there.

Bili, overwhelmed with shyness, shrank away. But it did little to soothe his worry, which only deepened when the others hurriedly crowded around Akan in a tight semi-circle.

All fell silent. Bili, vulnerable like he always was at such a time, braved a single look back at his friends as they studied it. At least nobody was reaching down and flinging bits away this time. But each silent second seemed longer than the last, and as time went on without any reaction at all, Bili began to wish he were one of the termites disappearing into a hole in the rock beneath his feet.

They hated it. He knew it. They detested what he'd done.

When he could stand their silence no more, he turned around to face up to his shame. 'I tried my best,' he said. 'But it's awful, isn't it?'

Akan's brow was scored with a deep frown, his two fingers hooked over his bottom lip as he stood in silence.

'You're disappointed, aren't you? That's it. You don't think it's as good as the last one, the seven-tier waterfall. But that one was different, you see, because—'

Akan stretched out his arm and lay his hand on Bili's shoulder. 'Relax, brother,' he said, appearing suddenly embarrassed. 'The truth is, it just looks like a bunch of forest litter to us. We don't know what we're supposed to be seeing.'

Bili winced. It was a relief to know the others didn't simply despise it, yet their inability to really *see* his picture told him he'd done a bad job capturing the likeness of the subject. Had he merely *imagined* it was finished?

The orangs scooted closer as Bili came in to check what lay in front of them all. His eyes carefully scrutinised the wide ring of twigs that he'd flattened just slightly into an oval. On the inside of the oval, leaves were sloping to meet a central point, and on the outside, they fell more gently away.

For a brief instant, Bili looked up at the vista, then brought his gaze back down to the ground.

Yes! It was exactly as it was meant to be!

He held out his hand and traced the circle. 'Look,' he said. 'Follow my finger.'

The eyes of the other juveniles moved slowly from right to left as Bili's long index finger went around the oval.

'Now,' he said, this time sweeping his finger around the horizon, 'look up.'

The others obeyed, and peered out through the gap in the trees at the perfectly round ring of rocks crowning the forested escarpments of the interior.

Akan was the first to notice how the landscape matched the picture. 'It's – oh! I see now!'

The boys, however, remained blind to it, so this time Akan directed them, firstly by going around the small circle on the ground, then around the vast one on whose southern end they themselves were standing. And, one by one, the others finally made the connection.

'Bili's done it again!' shrieked Rafi. 'How do you do that? How do you know how to make not-real things look like real things?'

Bili looked at his feet. 'Don't know. I just do.'

He was delighted with his friends' reactions, yet none mattered to Bili more than his brother's; Akan, however, wasn't whooping and jumping like the others. Instead, he continued to stare down at the picture, breaking his gaze only to look up through the gap in the trees.

'Well?' said Bili. 'Now that you get it, do you think it's as good as the seven-tier waterfall?'

Akan reached out his long arms and wrapped them gently around his brother's neck, and for a few quiet moments they remained nestled in an embrace. 'It's even better,' he answered. 'The more I look at it, the more I can see. It's like you've brought the whole landscape right here onto this tiny patch of rock.'

'I call it: "*The Basin*".'

Akan's finger hovered above one section of the picture where a twig lay on a sharp angle – it was clear to Bili that he didn't dare touch it for fear of disturbing the way it was all arranged – and his eyes smiled. 'You even put in that toppled tree. And the waterfall on the west slope is right here, too! Bili, I think you're the cleverest orang I know. I bet you can't wait to make one like this for Aunt Effie.'

Bili smiled widely. But just then, a shrill wail sounded in the clouds – '*Cheeeee!*' – and every boy froze.

Above, a kite was soaring, its white head bright against the golden brown of its body and wings. And at the sight of it, the youngsters sped off the ridge and into the trees, desperate to be back at their mothers' sides.

At the slope's bottom, they found the forest darkened by rainclouds. An almighty rumbling began to rock the sky, followed immediately after by a downpour, and the orangs took shelter beneath some larger palms, relieved that the rains had come at last. But the flashes and grumbles went as soon as they came. Sadly, this was just another shower.

The boys continued on their way, but Akan had

stayed back in his cosy nook. When Bili noticed, he dropped behind from the others and went to him. 'Since when were you bothered by a bit of rain?'

'I'm not bothered by it at all. There's something I want to look at. But there's no point while the earth's wet.'

A flush of melancholy unsettled Bili, and he held his brother's hand. 'Is it true?' he asked. 'About bapa. Has he left?'

'It looks like it. But who knows with him?'

Bili sighed. 'You're going to go soon too, aren't you?'

Akan's head twisted around to face him. 'Why do you say that?'

'Come on, Akan. You know you are. This place isn't enough for you anymore.'

'I love it here!' said Akan. 'But who wants to be stuck in one place their whole life?'

'You're talking about our home, brother. There's nowhere more beautiful than the basin.'

'How do you know?'

'I... Well... I don't *know*. But I'm sure of it. How can there be?'

Akan glanced over to the western sky and rose off his bottom. 'It's cleared up over there. Think I'll go check it out.'

'Suit yourself,' said Bili, bouncing off into the dense swathe of forest. 'I'll see you back at the home range.'

With the shower now nearing its end, the air was pleasingly cooler. Bili went across to shelter from the last of it beneath a wide frond, and sat entranced by the atmosphere. Just moments ago, when the forest trembled with the force of the deluge, nothing in nature could compete with its deafening din. Gibbons could be hooing as they flung themselves through the canopy and he wouldn't have known about it; even the cackling of a hornbill as it stooped to pluck a fig would be lost in a roar as ferocious as that. But now it had stopped, and the sense of peace was almost overpowering.

He listened to the drips of rain as they spilled from the tip of a leaf and splashed into a waterlogged ditch. The sound – round and full – was a satisfying one.

Glop, it went.

Glop.

Glop.

So regular was the splashing – it was as steady as the beating of his heart – that between each drip Bili was able to sneak in a second sound by tapping a stick against a buttress root.

Glop.

Tik.

Glop.

Tik.

Glop.

Tik.

Bili's lips curved into a smile. He could take this even further, couldn't he?

Throwing a long arm out behind himself into the tree's towering roots, he retrieved a fallen leaf. This, he pushed back and forth against the forest bed, producing a faint rustle that differed just slightly according to the direction.

Without breaking the timing, he introduced the new sounds.

Glop.

Tik.

Swish, swosh.

Glop.

Tik.

Swish, swosh.

At this, Bili toppled to the side with laughter, and slapped his palms against the floor. It was just too funny to keep up any longer. When it next rained, he'd show his mother and brother his neat new trick. Hopefully, it wouldn't be so long this time – it had been four whole days since the last drop fell.

Lifting himself off the ground, Bili climbed a young bamboo palm, swaying it from side to side until he'd reached enough power to spring over onto a mangowood's limb. By now the canopy had grown steamy from the rapidly heating air, but he made steady progress through the upper boughs, which he tackled with a combination of swinging and balanced running.

Stopping for a snack just once on his way back to the home range, he was ready to crash the moment he saw last night's nest. But it was nowhere near bedtime yet, and since a used bed was never as comfortable as a new one – and since his mother wasn't in it – he went to the ground instead.

The wide eyes of the younger children followed him as he traipsed by. One held up a half-chewed sweet fern for him to take, which he popped into his mouth with a soft air kiss of thanks. Then he saw, spreadeagled on the limb of a teak tree, his mother.

'Hey!' he called. 'Mama!'

Effie, not hearing him, turned over to face the other way.

'Mama!' he yelled again. 'Guess what I did, mama? I talked with the rain!'

He wrapped his arms partway around the wide trunk, and began to lift himself to her. 'It was dripping, mama, and I noticed it was like a heartbeat, and I tapped my stick to go with it then brushed a leaf to—mama?'

Effie was rolling off the limb, catching hold of a branch which swung her in a wide arc across to a pole of bamboo.

'Hey!' said Bili as he tried to catch her up, 'I was telling you about the rain. Mama?'

This time, his call contained anguish. She was making him feel as though she were deliberately ignoring him, which was preposterous. Not once in his twelve monsoons had she done such a thing.

Effie was about to leap for the apex of a long-dead

softwood, so Bili anticipated her move and made a sharp turn to the left. Hurling himself off the teak's limb, he landed on the first of the three branches hanging between them, which bounced him, as planned, onto the second. This one dipped a little further than he'd hoped, but with a huge stretch he was just able to grip the third, and was brought up onto the softwood right as his mother was arriving.

'Silly mama went deaf!' he said, offering out both arms for the hug he'd been craving all day.

But something very unusual happened then. Rather than hook her arms around his torso to pull him in close, Effie simply held up her palm and blocked him from getting any closer. He craned his head around her hand – she'd quit this ridiculous game the instant she saw the sadness in his eyes – but it made no difference; she had turned, quite purposefully he felt, to face away.

This wasn't just some new game she was playing.

'Mama. I just wanted to tell you about—'

'No, Bili.'

'But the rain, mama. It—'

'No, Bili!'

Effie let her outstretched arm drop to her side, but this time Bili made no attempt to go closer, and went instead to the forest bed while the sun dropped and the light of day faded.

His heart aching with sorrow, Bili brooded in his thoughts. It might be that his dear mother was just out of sorts this evening, that something else was happening in her life that he lacked the maturity to understand. But if that were the case, all she had to do was say so.

He got up at last, to try once again to get his hug. But right as he did, Bili heard a ferocious bark in the midtrees above.

It was that most terrifying of warnings – an adult male's long call.

'Whaak! Whoo-aak! Hoo Hoo!'

The infants scattered haphazardly, and Bili jumped behind the nearest bush. It had been some time since the long call had been heard around here, but it always had the desired effect: it told less dominant orangs to make themselves scarce.

It sounded again. 'Whaak! Whoo-aak! Hoo Hoo!' Bili craned his neck around the plant to see who the male was, certain now that this cry was not the signature call of his father.

On a bough, standing upright with his chest out in front of him, was Iki. Along with Bili's own father, Iki was one of the largest males in the whole basin, and like Bili's father, he wasn't often seen in this home range.

Unable to remember what Iki looked like, Bili braved a peep at the visitor. Was this huge tree-man always so ugly? One of Iki's eyes was milky with blindness from a vicious scrap, and a frayed scar marked his side where he'd once come off a branch and had been ripped by the barbs of a rattan plant.

Bili pushed further out to see more clearly, but as he was about to place his foot down on the ground, he noticed a giant millipede passing beneath. So startled was he by the sight of it that he stumbled out from his cover – and instantly attracted Iki's one good eye.

The visiting orang leapt straight down to the forest floor. Bili cowered low, and covered his head in his hands while Iki slapped the ground with his palms, sending blunt echoes tripping up the trees.

Above, his mother called. 'No, Iki!'

But the huge male went nearer to Bili – close enough that his breath tickled the hair at the edge of the youngster's lean face – and slapped the ground a second time; refraining from clobbering Bili, however, Iki, with a few giant swings, ascended back into the treetops.

Bili's heart raced as he looked up at his mother. Sitting as she was, slightly to the side, he could see the faint outline of a bump in her stomach. One of her hands was making its way to it; he watched as her fingers curved over the roundness, as though she were attempting to shield it from the outside world.

And suddenly, Bili understood. His mother, the protector who'd watched over him for all his days, was now protecting the new life growing inside her. And as such, she had no more time for him.

2

PITCHER PLANT

ALTHOUGH HIS MOTHER didn't know it, three monsoons had passed since Akan first wandered solo.

His explorations of the basin began when he'd awoken one morning with a hunger only one thing would satisfy. But delicious tarap fruit didn't grow near their home range, so he'd left Ivie's side for the morning, travelling across the low trees until he sighted one. With great excitement, he plunged his fingers through the spines of its golden orb and pulled the husk apart – and as Akan feasted on the creamy pods of flesh, he thought it the most satisfying meal he'd ever tasted. You could have what you wanted, it seemed, if you were willing to look for it.

Of the regions he'd not yet managed to survey, there was one which proved particularly tantalising for Akan, and it was to this area of limestone hills that he was now headed. This morning, right before he'd gone up to the ridge to see Bili's new picture, he'd noted a single line of black smoke over there, and was desperate to investigate. But knowing Bili would be crestfallen if he failed to show up, he'd put it off until now.

As Akan advanced steadily to the west, he smiled at the memory of his brother's latest creation. *"The Basin"*,

Bili had called it. How very clever he was. Were there more tree-men out there, beyond the basin's exterior slopes, with the same wondrous talent as Bili? It seemed impossible.

Taking care to avoid the rattans' thorns as he swung from limb to limb, Akan thought how lucky he was to have a brother like Bili. Most orangs grew up without ever seeing such a thing as a picture that captured the likeness of the real world. And Bili had other talents, too. He noticed things. He had a unique patience for simply sitting quietly and watching, and he liked to help others observe those tiny details. It was likely Bili would always find a way to feel content – and that was just as well, because soon his sensitive heart was going to be broken, as he learned his beloved brother was indeed leaving the basin.

Journeying on until he came to the river, Akan rested a while among the buttress roots, cooled by the breeze that blew off the water. Then, so fleetingly he doubted himself, he caught a whiff of the smoke he'd been seeking.

He proceeded along the banks in a crawl. There was little chance of a forest cat trying its luck at this hour, but vipers lurked on riverside trails like this, so he watched his every step.

Around a meander, the smell of smoke suddenly grew strong, and Akan gave a whoop of delight. He used the twisted knots of a dangling vine to haul himself higher, and, gliding from one tree to another, went to where the air was foul. Pops and crackles began sounding in his ears, and then he found himself looking right at it.

Fire!

Entranced, Akan watched the red flames as they flicked like pythons' tongues out from the foliage. Bili's pictures certainly were beautiful, but not even they could match this leaping, flickering light. Inside the basin, or beyond, surely nothing existed as beguiling as this stuff.

As the weird substance made its way across the heap of fallen leaves, Akan began to wonder just how far it might travel, and pieces of a conversation drifted into his memory.

Long ago, the mothers had talked of flame. They were discussing favourite play spots as children, when Aunt Effie had given a sad smile. 'There was this island,' she said, hoisting baby Bili up to her breast, 'where two rivers met. My friends knew how to use bamboo stalks as stilts, and they'd walk across to it, but I couldn't master the trick. But a few times, when there was drought, it was low enough to wade. I loved that island. It made you feel like you had the whole forest to yourself.'

The brow of the other females furrowed. '*Two* rivers? But there's only one in the basin.'

'I grew up on the outside,' replied Aunt Effie, taking hold of Ivie's hand. It was obvious that the memory was still painful for her, even after so many monsoons had passed. 'But then land-orangs came to my home with tools and cut away the edge of our forest.'

Akan recalled how Bili had looked up from Aunt Effie's breast, his tiny eyes ripe with worry. 'Did the ground-men cut down your home?'

'Not exactly,' replied Aunt Effie. 'They took only jungly foliage, but this they lit up, and when the wind suddenly changed, their flame was blown into the old growth. It moved all the way through the rainforest, eating up nearly everything in its path. Since only the giant lowland trees were left, there wasn't nearly enough canopy cover, so we had no choice but to move on.'

A ripple of sorrow went through the mothers, but one of them appeared confused. 'How did the flame eat up the rainforest, Effie? Why didn't the rains stop it?'

'Because there was drought.'

Together, Bili and Akan asked: 'What's that?'

'Drought is when the forest dries out, boys. Rain of the heaviest kind can fall, but if none comes for eight days, we'll have drought. And it's even worse if the soil swamps go up,' she continued – but by then the two half-brothers had grown bored, and took off to play.

With his eyes presently fixed on the flame, Akan watched the dancing spires of light. It was time to head back to his mother, yet he wasn't done here yet. This stuff was just mesmerising! How could something be there in one instant, and gone in the next? Would clever Bili be able to make sense of it?

Shielding his nostrils with a supple leaf, he inched closer and closer to the light. It was like the sun were right here on the forest floor! He then reached out his hand, and though his inner voice told him not to, he let the edge of a crackling tongue gently brush against the tip of his finger.

He gave a pained 'Oo!', sending a bright yellow flycatcher flapping onto a nearby branch.

And as he stuck his finger in his mouth to cool the burn, he vowed never to let fire touch him again.

Poking his head through the treetops, shielding his eyes as he looked up at the sun, Akan told himself off.

It got darker faster here on the basin's western slope, and soon the sub-canopy would be lightless. By letting himself get so distracted by the flame, he'd run out of time to visit the limestone hills nearby, where he'd really wanted to go. There were rumoured to be caves in those cliffs, but exploring them would now have to wait until another day.

Racing off east, Akan swung at the full length of his arms, quickly covering a great distance. But soon the character of the forest began to change, and he came to jungly heathland where the soil was sandy and uncovered by canopy.

With trees less tall, and vines less secure, he was

forced to slow, making it easier to spot snacks, and when he saw a bean tree, he stopped. Choosing a pod that had split where its elongated seam had coiled around on itself, he plucked out the bitter beans one by one, and was quietly munching away when he noticed, down on the ground, a pitcher plant.

He moved in close to study this plant of prey. Dangling from a tendril, it was as odd as every other. The anatomy of the thing was just fascinating: beneath a hood shaped just like a leaf was a plump bowl filled with liquid, and around the top of the bowl was a rolled lip. Akan swiped across the rim, taking care to avoid the insect bumbling around the perimeter, then licked his fingertip, buoyed by the sweetness of the nectar.

The edge of Akan's mouth rose into a smile. The shiny beetle wasn't able to resist this treat. But the foolish creature had no idea it had been baited by the pitcher plant. The beetle thought it could get for free what other creatures had to work for – but nothing came without a cost, and the price of this particular snack was death.

Akan had seen it happen time and time again. Usually it was ants, though sometimes small spiders and crabs, occasionally a minuscule frog, and once a jungle shrew. The hapless beings enjoyed a few moments of pleasure, but their feet soon slipped on the waxy lip, and they were sent tumbling into the bowl, where they first drowned, then were digested by the fluid. There was no more perfect trap in the forest, as far as Akan was concerned, and he stopped each time he came across a cluster of pitchers to watch things tumble to their doom.

This beetle, however, was firm-footed. Busying its mouth parts with the nectar, it went over to the far side of the lip without so much as a stumble, then turned and made its way back. The plant's many delicate hairs – all of which faced down into the bowl – did nothing to cheat this bold guest.

Akan gave a huff of disappointment as the beetle's

shell began to open. It had outsmarted the plant, and was about to unfurl its wings and make off, satisfied with itself.

That wouldn't do at all.

He brought up his hand. Creating tension between his forefinger and the end of his thumb, he released a powerful flick into the body of the beetle, sending it into the bowl, where it bounced off the back side and landed in the pool with a faint plop – to hoots of laughter from the young orang.

After journeying without pause back through the trees, Akan reached the nests of the home range right as the sun was creeping below the ridge; he'd timed his excursion perfectly. But he noticed at once that a strange atmosphere was lingering around tonight's nesting area. Something had happened while he'd been off venturing.

Above him, he felt his mother's glowering gaze, and as his eyes caught hers, his head drooped.

'Why do you smell like that, Akan? You've been near flame!'

He gave a cool shrug. What did it matter?

'You're not to go anywhere near that stuff! Ever!' yelled Ivie, turning to the juveniles who sat beside their mothers. 'That goes for you all.'

'But mama,' said Akan. 'You said it yourself. We'll be adults soon. Our business then is no concern of yours.'

'You think a mother stops fretting for her child when they no longer share a nest? You're mistaken, Akan. I'll worry about you every day. Even more so, if you decide to start a family of your own some place where flame has an easy path to your beds.'

Akan scanned around, but saw no sign of his brother, which was odd, since Aunt Effie was right among the other females, snacking on berries.

'Where's Bili?'

Ivie turned to Akan. Though her expression was still

displeased, there was something else there, too. She appeared almost ashamed.

'What is it, mama? What happened here?'

'It's just the way of nature, Akan,' said Ivie, grabbing his hand and placing it on her belly.

Fitting perfectly beneath the arc of Akan's palm was a small bump. He looked up at his mother, wide-eyed.

'You know what this means, don't you, son? It means a change is coming.'

An explosion of pain fired through Akan's heart. It was like a rope of lightning above rain clouds: searing and violent.

Yet, like lightning, it was also fleeting. He'd accepted many monsoons ago that the bond with his own dear mother would break. There was sorrow – then as now – to think of all that would be lost. But the promise of independence, of journeying through the trees to new places and seeing new things, seemed compensation enough.

Besides, he'd seen this day coming: Iki, with his prominent cheek pads, had been lingering in these parts a while now.

Akan brushed his fingers across his mother's face, so delicately that barely any contact was made. He'd seen this happen many times: every monsoon, some miserable youngster would show up in the forest, lost and heartsick for his mother's withdrawn care. For a few days, the lonesome orang would linger, trying in vain to win back her favour, before finally accepting that the life they cherished had reached its end.

Akan was willing to accept the way of nature, but Bili had remained wilfully resistant, refusing to accept it would ever be his turn. Almost certain to be skulking in the nearby ferns, Akan rose to find him, eventually locating his brother at the foot of an ironwood, where he was absentmindedly waving a stick back and forth.

Since Bili's face was beset with gloominess, Akan

decided to avoid the topic of their mothers. 'I'm tired,' he said. 'Why don't you tell me a story.'

'Don't want to.'

'Come on. Tell me about Lang. That was his call we heard up on the ridge today, wasn't it?'

At the mention of the spirit of war, Bili's eyes rose from off his feet, and he let his stick drop to his side.

'That's it,' said Akan. 'Tell me about the Bird-King.'

Bili sighed, and looked away at the fireflies emerging from the bushes, glowing brightly as they hovered among the saplings. Akan was ready to give up, but to his surprise, his brother then began a story.

'Once, a strange fog settled on the forest. It looked just like the white mist that sits upon the canopy each morning, but it was different in one way: it brought an uneasy feeling to all who lived there. The tree-men stayed in their treetop nests; the long-tailed macaques quarrelled with the pig-tailed macaques; the fat-nosed monkeys of the mangroves got even more dizzy on the unripe fruits they ate all day.

'The air become heavy with the threat of violence, so the Bird-King glided down from the skies in the form of a kite. But as it wasn't the time for creatures to fight one another, Lang gave no shriek. Instead, he beat his majestic wings with such incredible strength that the white clouds of vapour began to break apart into ribbons, and soon the forest dwellers became peaceful again, and everything in the trees, and above the trees, and below them, was happy. Except the leeches, of course. Leeches aren't ever happy.'

'Oh, Bili!' snickered Akan. 'You just don't like them, that's all.'

'You mean you *do*? Ugh! I'd rather fall from the top of an ironwood and land on the thorniest rattan than have even one of those horrid things on me. All they want to do is drink the life right out of you!'

Akan smiled, as questions overflowed in his mind

about his brother's peculiar account of the Bird King. But just as he was about to ask the first of these, Aunt Effie went passing through the mid-trees above, and Bili, with startling abruptness, snatched up the stick and shot away after her.

Scrambling after Bili as quickly as he could, Akan tried to stop what followed from happening. But he got up the trunk just after his brother began lashing out at Aunt Effie, and could do nothing but watch as his brother struck her on the back with his branch.

'Bili!' hooted Akan, remaining tight to the trunk. 'What's the matter with you?'

Aunt Effie gave a squeal, more from shock than pain, and held her mouth open to let her son see her teeth. When Bili swung his stick a second time, his mother caught it in her hand and wrenched it out from his grip. Then, with a suddenness Akan had never before observed in his aunt, she leapt towards Bili, and pushed him with such force that he stumbled back on the bough.

Horror consumed Akan as he watched Bili tip off the side. Thankfully, though, he threw out his arms on the way to the ground, catching hold of some cascading branches which swung him up to the top of a palm. Bili reached under the fanning fronds and ripped away a banana, and promptly threw it, with all his strength, at Aunt Effie.

Missing by quite a distance, Bili went to ground again and began crying out. 'Where's my bapa? He won't be happy to know you don't love me anymore!'

Aunt Effie, glowering with anger, made her way closer to her son. 'Your father,' she snarled, 'has left the basin. Not for one of his wanders. He's gone. For good.'

Akan did well to get to Bili before Aunt Effie did. He gripped hold of his brother's wrist and yanked him away. Bili, however, had gone deliberately heavy, rooting himself to the dry soil.

'Are you crazy?!' Akan shrieked. 'If she gets you, you're going to know about it!'

Bili slapped his palms against the ground. 'I'm not going anywhere!'

'Well I'm not going to be anywhere near this,' shrieked Akan as he bounced away. He'd tried to help, but Bili had made his choice.

But his brother came to his senses just in time. With Aunt Effie lunging at him, Bili dodged her grasping hands and sped up the nearest tree, and together the brothers swung off from the nesting patch without once looking back.

3

CAVE OF SECRETS

WITH THE WHEEZING of the cicadas came the whooping of gibbons.

As dawn exploded noisily to life all around him, Bili instinctively reached out for his mother's hand – then winced to remember she wasn't in the nest.

He rolled onto his front and pushed himself up from off his knees. Through the dim light, he peered across to the neighbouring tree, where Akan had also spent his first night alone. But he wasn't in it now; extending his neck to see over his nest's scruffy ledge, Bili saw no sign of his brother's bright pelt on the forest bed, either.

Fleeing their mothers as they'd done last evening, while their emotions were so amplified, could easily have ended with a careless tumble from off a bough. Yet, as it was, the pair had journeyed westward through the gloaming of twilight without so much as a misstep. Since it was a bad time for travel – the darkness gave opportunistic clouded leopards an advantage – they stuck to the canopy the whole way, and it suited Bili fine that Akan wouldn't be drawn on where they were going: all that mattered was that they got far, far away from mama, who'd injured his heart so very callously.

Eventually, they'd come to a hilly area unknown to

Bili. Skylined against the moonlit night were limestone cliffs crowned with islands of spiky forest, making it obvious that Akan had chosen this place in order to explore the caves. But by the time their journey had ended, the pair of them were far too exhausted to fuss, and spoke to one another only very briefly to discuss Bili's nest.

Akan had been annoyed with him. 'For somebody as clever as you,' he'd grumbled, 'that's a very poor effort. You haven't even woven the branches.'

Bili looked at his brother with a shrug. The truth was, he *could* make a nest – it was just that, without mama there to skilfully shape the branches into a pocket upon the fork of the tree, he was entirely too miserable to want to.

When Bili's nest had taken on a basic shape, he climbed inside, immediately forcing shut his eyes. But the night had passed wretchedly, and with morning finally dawned, he felt even more tired than he did before he'd fallen asleep.

Extracting himself now from out of the mess of fractured branches, Bili descended into the lower canopy to a heat that was ferocious, hopeful that today the rains would arrive to slake the thirst of the forest and all its inhabitants. Eyeing the wall of limestone towering into to the sky, he reckoned the caves in these cliffs would offer a cool retreat from midday's fury. Akan, no doubt, was desperate to begin exploring them.

At the tree nearest the cliff, Bili shimmied down the trunk, and was met with a vapour of decay that was as obnoxious as it was overpowering. What could be making such an awful stink? It was vaguely familiar; it had a decrepit character, like one of the giant ground flowers his mother once showed him, whose innards shone bright like the sun, but whose stench was anything but pretty.

He called out for his brother, but when no reply came,

Bili went closer to the limestone. Its face was a bright white, yet the bottom of the cliff was darkened where time and weather had eroded it. A high archway – the cave's entrance – loomed ominously on Bili's right side; the mere thought of going in put chill bumps up his arms. Caves were where shadows dwelt, and shadows hid nasty things that could cause harm to a couple of young orangs like them. And there were leeches in them too, probably.

The lingering smell grew even stronger, confirming in Bili's mind this was a thing gone to rot. His stomach went watery; not even a giant ground flower in full bloom made a stink like this.

From out of the cavernous entrance came the squeaking of swiftlets. For such tiny voices, the reverberations were enormous, hinting at the vastness of the cave. He tentatively called his brother's name again, but its echo was lost to infinity.

The air temperature dropped. Standing now in the entrance itself, Bili swallowed hard. By now the odour had grown noxious enough to warrant pinching his nose in his fingers. Though he didn't wish to take one step further, the feeling of loneliness weighed too heavily, so he took a few hesitant strides forward, where he saw, on his right side, a heap of bright shaggy hair.

Akan was laying down.

Bili's heart began to beat so hard he could hear the whooshing of blood in his ears. 'I don't want to play now, brother! Stop messing around!'

But Akan gave no response.

Panic dried Bili's mouth and tightened his chest. His innards grew fluttery with a feeling like nothing he'd felt before – then, when a voice from behind said his name, he sent a scream of fright down into the bowels of the cavern.

'What's the matter with you?' shrieked Akan, dumping a cluster of figs onto the cave's floor. 'I just went to get some breakfast for us, and now I find you exploring the caves without me? Well, thanks. You could have— Urgh! What's that smell?'

Akan fell silent. His eye found the pile of hair up ahead, the exact same red-brown as his own. 'Is that what I think it is?'

'It's an orang,' said Bili, only now getting his breath back from the shock of the fright.

The body belonged to a male tree-man. Though the cool cave had helped to slow the decomposition, flies buzzed enthusiastically around it.

The dead orang lay on his back with his legs splayed open and his arms flat out by his sides. There was an absence of blood on the body, and the ground surrounding him was clean.

'Perhaps his face got injured,' suggested Bili, thankful that the head was facing away.

Akan shrugged his shoulders. 'Care to find out? Go nudge his head to face us.'

'No way!' said Bili. 'Let's just walk around the other side.'

After just two steps, the brothers froze. Just beyond the body, a second orang lay. Also an adult, he too was dead.

Oddly, no injuries were anywhere to be seen; the brothers searched, but the two dead orangs gave away no clues as to their fates.

How strange it was though, to observe fellow forest-men whose life had ended. In death, Bili surmised, the two males were just objects. Recently, something was in them that distinguished them from pieces of wood rotting in the soil. But in the absence of whatever that thing was, rotting logs was all they now were.

With a hand covering his nose, Bili went to the first body. He could hardly stand to open his eyes fully, but suspecting some small detail might clue them in to what had happened here, he wanted to be thorough.

Ignoring the flies, Bili scanned over every inch of the orang's body. Starting at the soles of the feet, he surveyed the legs and groin, then tracked along the leathery trunk and down each arm. The hands warranted especial attention, but as the palms were face up, this meant having to actually *touch* the body.

He did what he had to do. Pinching the flesh of the palm, Bili rolled each hand at the wrist, but saw nothing on the backs that interested him very much. The nails, however, offered a hint. Though it was hard to see for sure, it appeared that blood was crusted at the fingertips.

'Maybe it was old age.'

Bili looked across to his brother, who was at the other body. 'Old age? Look at them, Akan. They're barely any older than bapa.'

'But adult males don't die for no reason, Bili. It's not possible. I wonder if they took something from the forest they oughtn't have. Sourberry is in season.'

'They'd have to be pretty dumb to eat poison like that. Unless they ate it deliberately?'

Akan had moved a few paces deeper into the cave. 'Know what I think?' he called back. 'I think they fought each other to the death.'

Bili moved in to resume his close inspection, lingering over the chest and neck area. With the light just a degree stronger now that the sun had climbed above the horizon, some marks on the throat were visible that hadn't been before. Although they were difficult to distinguish against the dark skin, small, crescent-shaped impressions – four on the left, and three on the right – were located on the throat.

Bili gave a grunt. 'What do these look like to you?'

Leaning over the body, Akan studied the area Bili was pointing to. 'I don't know. But they're on that body, too. The same number, and in just the same place.'

Bili came away from the body and swept his eyes over what could be seen of the cave floor. A curved object, like a caterpillar at rest, was laying on the ground. Furry, and orange in colour, Bili felt his heart quicken as he approached it.

'Akan,' he called back. 'Check his hands.'

'What?'

'That one. His hands. Check them.'

Akan obliged. 'What am I looking for?'

'Count up the fingers.'

'There's five on each, Bili. Why? How many has your one got?'

'Same.'

'Then, why are you asking, brother?'

'If these orangs have still got all their fingers,' said Bili, holding aloft the thing he'd found, 'then whose is this one?'

Most afternoons, Akan liked to go off somewhere by himself. It didn't much matter where, so long as it was to a place other orangs kept away from.

This afternoon, however, Akan wished for company, and none was to be found, since Bili was napping in a mangowood, exhausted after his terrible night. Akan had tried to rest, too, but the discovery in the cave meant his eyes wouldn't stay down very long. So he simply hung around, snacking on the occasional giant ant when one was foolish enough to approach him.

By now, the heat of the day was stifling, unleashing a deafening din from the cicadas. There couldn't have been a single creature in the basin who didn't welcome yesterday's shower, yet it had vanished as quickly as it had come, and the leaves of every tree were as blistered as they'd been before. Even the birds were suffering; flowerpeckers and spiderhunters, usually so energetic, remained now on their perches.

As he waited for Bili to rise, Akan found himself

thinking about bapa. Again and again, he heard in his mind the words his mother said last evening. 'Your father's left the basin. *For good this time.*'

Why did she that? Everybody knew Dama wandered far, yet he was always glimpsed again in some corner of the basin sooner or later. What had happened now to make him decide to leave permanently? Perhaps it wasn't his decision at all. Perhaps it was all down to that brute, Iki.

Rustling sounded. Bili, at last, had woken up. Akan felt a hand on his shoulder, then his brother came in to hug.

'Sleep?'

'Not really,' said Bili.

'Let me guess. The dead orangs?'

'Yes. But, well, mostly I was thinking about bapa.'

Akan huffed with mild amusement. 'Me too.'

'Iki did this,' announced Bili.

Akan pulled out of their clinch in order to see his brother's eyes, and gave a nod.

'He chased bapa away,' Bili continued. 'But he got himself all charged up. I think maybe Iki was overcome with violence.'

Akan stepped away to where a toppled palm had made a bridge across to a shelf on the face of the cliff. 'Maybe you're right. But that's not our problem.'

'It is, though.'

'How?' asked Akan.

'It's bad for the whole basin if Iki has become crazed. The balance of things will be upset. If bapa knew what that brute had done, he'd come back for sure. We've got to find him and tell him.'

'What? No, Bili.'

'Yes, brother. With Dama back in the forest, bullies like Iki wouldn't do such terrible things as he did in the cave.'

Akan turned away. Every time he'd considered his

imminent journey to independence, the excitement was spoiled by a sense of guilt: his actions were going to impact very negatively on his brother. That familiar pain was within him now, too, but what Bili was proposing here could make things easier. This might be a chance to depart from Bili in a way that let his brother have a say in it.

He shrugged his shoulders, as though it mattered little. 'You mean, you want to *leave* the basin to bring him back?'

Bili's eyes grew heavy with sorrow. 'I don't *want* to, no,' he said. 'But yes. That's what I'm saying.'

'Alright, then,' said Akan. 'We can do it on one condition.'

A long sigh escaped Bili. It was obvious he knew what Akan was about to say. 'What?'

'We can go and find Dama together. I don't know how you think we'll possibly be able to entice him back here, but we'll try. But after we go over the basin's ridge, that's it for me. I'm gone.'

'Don't.'

'Bili! I've got to. You know that, don't you?'

'Yes.'

'Well, then you understand.'

'Still, though. Don't. Stay here.'

'No.'

Bili began to cry. Akan held out his arm and brushed his brother's face. Like his own, it was still flat with immaturity, yet Akan found it hard to imagine that Bili's cheeks would ever grow round with wide pads.

'Come on,' Akan said, squeezing his brother around the shoulders. 'We can't do this until we've returned to the home range to report what we found. If Iki really is as dangerous as we think, we need to warn our mothers first.'

When the brothers arrived back at the nesting area, their friends hopped off the branches in a buzz of excitement, and soon Bili and Akan were surrounded.

'Where've you been?' hollered Rafi. 'Did you nest all by yourselves? Weren't you lonely?'

Bili gave them a sad smile. If they only knew just *how* lonely.

Holding hands with Akan, Bili glanced up into the high trees in search of mama and Aunt Ivie. After yesterday, the thought of approaching either of the females filled him with dread, but he knew it must done, so he led Akan up the ironwood, where they sat a while on a wide limb and waited for the thrill of their appearance to settle.

All the way here from the limestone hills, Bili had thought about how best to impart their warning. Should they mention the dead males in the cave? It was so completely implausible that Iki would have killed those orangs that their mothers may accuse them of telling untruths – an accusation that Bili, with his frequent accounts of things that never happened, was used to.

The two females, notified of their sons's return, soon came swinging through the mid-trees, and Bili braced himself. There was no choice in the matter: unless he described what they'd found, their mothers wouldn't know the seriousness of the threat.

Effie and Ivie sat, and turned to watch the boys. Bili's eyes moistened at the sight of his mother, but he did his best to remain composed. He drew a breath. But just before he could tell them the news, a roar sounded.

An adult male with round cheek pads stood on a bough above them, his throat sac fully inflated as he issued his long call.

It was Iki, and he'd been awaiting their return.

Dropping down with speed and agility, the large male landed between the brothers. They squealed, but Iki was here to make a point. The adult threw out a hand and clawed Bili across the face, then, with his other hand, he grabbed hold of a clump of Akan's hair and dragged him into his wide body, hoisting him around to the side and slamming him into Bili.

Both boys were now flat on the ground. 'What's this I hear about you attacking Effie?' Iki barked, squeezing his fingers into a fist. He then proceeded to thump each of the brothers on their faces, and held open his mouth to reveal a pair of long, sharp fangs.

Now pinned to the ground beneath Iki's wide bottom, Bili was glad to see Akan had rolled away. But the jaw of the adult above his face was so terrifying he couldn't stand to look at him, and he scrunched his eyes shut in the hope this would all be over soon.

'Get off him!' screamed Akan, and Bili opened his eyes just in time to see his brother leap onto Iki's back.

A grapple ensued between Akan and Iki, allowing Bili to wriggle free from underneath the adult. He lunged into the melee of swinging limbs and hoisted his brother away, right before Iki's teeth connected with Akan's shoulder.

The brothers stood panting and wide-eyed before the furious Iki, anticipating his next attack. Both of them were bleeding – Bili more so than Akan – though neither had yet been dealt a blow fierce enough to cause any real damage. Iki's throat sac inflated once again, amplifying his call so viciously that the birds scattered from the canopy with cheeps of outrage.

Just then, Effie's voice drifted down from above. 'Iki! You've made your point!'

Bili looked up to see his mother. Her eyes were sad, but they were not the eyes that had loved him for so long.

Iki gave a grunt. 'Consider this your final warning. If I catch you near my females again, I'll see to it that the pair of you get the kind of beating I gave your father before I chased him off.'

4

SMILES MADE OF PEBBLES

ON THE SEVENTH tier of the waterfall, at the very crest of the basin's western rim, Akan allowed himself a look back.

Some day, after they'd found their father and presented their case to him, Bili would stand here again. But for Akan, this was it: every minute of his life had been lived inside the boundary of the basin, and this would be the last time he ever looked upon the magnificent forested slopes of its interior.

The water that ran down the rock flowed in a mere trickle. As he sat and caught his breath, Akan dangled his feet into the shallow pool and imagined the roar of the torrent during monsoon, a river cascading down each of the falls. Squinting his eyes, he looked at the gorge at the basin's foot, and wondered if the river's height had ever been so low. The shy rains, once again, had kept away.

Splashing his face, he let the cool water run down his cheeks, which stung where Iki's nails had clawed him. But the pool's offering quickly soothed the burn, and slaked a thirst that had deepened with each new ledge he'd reached.

'Bili. Come wash the blood off.'

No reply came.

'Bili? Bili!'

Akan turned to see his brother playing with a bearcat. This boy really did have to be the least practical orang in the entire basin! He'd do anything before taking care of his basic needs.

Last night was a perfect example. After they fled the raging Iki, the pair had swung hand over hand until they couldn't manage one more branch. They'd only made it half the distance to the waterfalls, but the failing light of day forced them to stop for the night.

Bili, however, hadn't much felt like making a nest, and whined as he got on with the job. When he announced he'd finished and climbed into his haphazard effort, Akan couldn't believe his eyes. As an orang who noted the many different ways tree-men put their sleeping spots together, he quickly concluded that his brother's was the worst he'd ever seen.

'You know that thing could break apart in the night, don't you?'

'It won't,' said Bili.

Akan grunted with annoyance. 'Well, if you're happy sleeping on the earth like a land-orang, with the scorpions and snakes and biting ants, then I'm happy for you.'

It was actually one of their father's nests that had given Akan his appreciation of how they could be built. Many monsoons ago they'd encountered it, quite by chance, and in spite of his mother's protests, Akan had rushed up to study it.

While Effie and Ivie always entwined two fractured branches around each other, the nest he discovered that day had been woven using three. The difference in sturdiness was obvious at once: Akan had bounced up and down in it until the very tree swayed, earning himself a painful backhand from his unimpressed mother.

He smiled at the memory of it. Did their bapa still

make them this way, or had he found some even cleverer method after all this time? But his mirth abruptly ceased when he saw his brother now running the bearcat's long fluffy tail through his fingers.

Bili had made no attempt at all to feed himself upon rising this morning, and had simply waited until Akan brought him figs. He was lazier than a mangrove monkey! There always seemed to be time for his whimsy, though. Perhaps Bili thought such encounters with other creatures were all the nourishment he needed to survive in the rainforest?

His patience now depleted, Akan hooted across to him.

Bili blew a raspberry in return. 'You startled him, Akan! Didn't you see that he was just about to climb onto my lap?'

'Never mind that bearcat. You need to come and wash. The blood is attracting flies to your face. Do you want to get an infection?'

Bili didn't move, so Akan tried another tactic.

'The leeches will come, too.'

At that, Bili scampered over. He threw out his arms for a hug, which Akan obliged, briefly, before rolling his brother onto his belly so that his head flopped over the edge of the rocks.

'So refreshing!' Bili hooted after holding his face in the pool for a second. Then he turned back to face the vast panorama. 'You know,' he said, 'I think our basin looks even prettier from up here than it does from the clearing. When I get back, I'm going to come up here a lot. Shame it's such a steep climb, though.'

They quietly took in the beauty of the canopy until Bili's arms came out at the sides in an exasperated shrug. 'How are we possibly going to convince bapa to come back?'

Akan let out a yawn. The heat of midday was

approaching, and he was ready to nap through the worst of it. But Bili's eyes were fixed on him. 'I think,' Akan said, hoisting himself up from the smooth surface of the rock and shimmying across to the treetops standing level with the plateau, 'that you're worrying about the wrong problem.'

'What does that mean?'

'We'll be lucky if we can even *find* him out there,' he yawned, as he lay face-down on a bough and let his arms and legs dangle.

Drifting off at once, when Akan next opened his eyes, the shadows had grown long. He stretched his back, and crawled along his sleeping branch, then, with one big leap, he made it onto the plateau, relieved to see the shallow pools hadn't all evaporated.

Where Bili had sat, there now lay an assortment of stones. Observing their peculiar arrangement, Akan knew right away it was another of his brother's pictures. He smiled, and hurried closer for a look, excited by the challenge of figuring out what it might mean. But Akan found this one impossible to read.

Positioned on the rock, in a row, were three circles, the central one larger than the two either side of it. Inside each circle, near the top, Bili had placed a pair of pebbles, and at the bottom, a crescent-shaped line like an upside-down rainbow.

Akan hooked his fingers over his lower lip as he studied it. Was it meant to be fruit? The circles were rambutans, perhaps. But where were the stalks which fixed those spiky little fruits to the trees? Bili must have forgotten to add them.

Since the pebbles inside the circles were such a poor representation of a rambutan's spines, Akan reached down and plucked them away. He then, very tentatively, attempted to create the stalks by laying the pebbles in a line from off the circles' tops. But as he sat there looking at the new arrangement, he realised he couldn't remember too well what a rambutan even looked like, and at once began to regret what he'd done.

He scanned over his shoulders for signs of his brother, but Bili was still off somewhere by himself. What had this silly picture looked like when he found it? There were two pebbles in the top half of the circles, that much he remembered for sure. But were they side by side, or on top of each other? Were they spaced apart, or did they sit together? He let two stones drop, leaving them where they'd fallen at random, then focussed on the bottom.

This section was even more confusing. There was something like a rainbow, wasn't there? But how did you make pebbles look like a rainbow? Akan's eyes rolled as he heard the echo of the thought in his mind. What a ridiculous question! With the remaining stones, he proceeded to build up a crescent shape in the lower portion of the circles until there now sat three arches, like little ant mounds.

'What are you doing?'

Akan jumped to hear his brother's voice. 'Nothing. You forgot to put the stalks on the rambutans. I thought I'd help.'

'What rambutans? Those aren't fruit. They're us.'

With a sharp tilt of his head, Akan resumed his assessment of the picture. 'What do you mean, Bili? How can it be us?'

'The circles are our faces.'

Akan's brow grew creased, and his cheeks flushed with a mild tingle of anger. Why couldn't he see what his brother had made? Was he really so inferior? 'But how, Bili? For one thing, we're a pair. But you've put three circles down.'

'Yes, Akan. You and me are the small ones. And in the middle is bapa.'

Bili went to his picture and pointed his finger into the heart of it. 'And we're—'. He fell quiet for a moment. 'That's not how I left it. Have you moved the stones?'

'I told you, Bili,' said Akan, covering his face with his hands, 'I thought they were rambutans, and that you'd forgotten the stems.'

'So you *broke* the picture apart? How could you do that?'

'I didn't mean to break it, Bili. I thought I was helping.'

'Well, it would help if you left things alone that aren't your business. If you want to make a picture of rambutans, that's up to you. But I wanted to make a picture of what our faces will look like when we find bapa. And now you've taken away our smiles and turned them upside down. Look what you've done to me! See how I look now!'

Akan, growing nauseous with shame and embarrassment, peeped through his fingers. 'You look sad.'

'Not just sad. Dead! You've made me look dead, you silly orang!'

Bringing his hands away from his face, Akan had grown tired of this nonsense already. They were just wasting time. 'I'm sorry,' he said. 'But it's not important. We need to get moving now, brother.'

'Not important?' hooted Bili. 'You don't see what this is all about, do you?'

Akan rose off his bottom and turned to the endless expanse of rainforest stretching out into the haze of the western horizon. 'Of course I do. It's play.'

Bili's face grew serious. 'It isn't play. *This* is how we're going to bring bapa back,' he said, as he put the smiles back the way he'd done them before.

'What do you mean?'

'We can use my pictures, brother. We'll remind bapa what he's missing. Then, when he finally comes back, he can take care of that bully Iki.'

Akan was getting impatient, calling back as he descended the basin's exterior slope, but Bili, heartsick and lonely, just couldn't find the will to step off the ridge.

'Come on, will you? I'm not making your nest again tonight!'

In some ways, the pair of them were just so different. It confounded Bili. His brother didn't seem at all saddened to be leaving his home, whereas for Bili, the bowl of rainforest behind him was everything.

Perhaps Akan was right, and the beauty waiting beyond this high ring of rocks matched the beauty they enclosed. Maybe there *were* other basins where the morning mist hung in such a way that the entire landscape filled with clean white clouds. Where a creature could know his whereabouts simply by the direction the shade fell. It may even be the case that red-beaked kingfishers were common out there, and he'd be able to watch every day as their feathers of lilac and orange and blue shone so delicately when a ray of light kissed them.

One thing he certainly would not find beyond the ridge, however, was mama. And she was the most beautiful thing of all.

Akan gave another yell, this one more angry. All day, he'd been clear that he wanted to be off the exterior slope by the time the sun fell. But with the moon's radiance growing stronger in the sky above them, that seemed increasingly unlikely. 'You can sort your own meal out tonight, too!'

But it wasn't easy for Bili to tear his gaze away from his home. How strange it was to observe that in the basin it was *already* bedtime! The entire swathe of forest on the western escarpment was hidden beneath shadow, yet on the outer slope, the forest was still bathed in light!

He smiled as he realised something very exciting: it stayed lighter later outside the basin because the sun's journey to the horizon was no longer obstructed by the basin's ridge – which meant he'd be able to actually *see* the sun meet the edge of the world!

Energised by this revelation, Bili placed a foot and a hand onto a treetop branch, and let himself swing off the plateau. And that was that – for the first time in his life, he had left his home.

As he raced to catch up with Akan, Bili's mother lingered in his thoughts. Remembering her treatment of him caused physical pain, like a rattan's spikes piercing his flesh. The more he dwelt on it all, however, the more he realised he'd given her no choice. Mama had asked him to spend more time away, as Aunt Ivie had asked Akan. But while that was easy for his brother, who saw in their basin something lacking, Bili felt that everything he needed was right at mama's side.

By now, the sun was the deep red of a pitcher plant's bowl, and the sky was ablaze with colour. Yet the sense of awe was not powerful enough to replace Bili's tense mood, and as he travelled, he observed how his neck and shoulders were growing increasingly stiff.

What was Akan thinking, destroying his picture like that? He'd worked hard at it throughout the afternoon, and was just about to finish, yet Akan had come along and, like it were nothing more than some debris scattered on the rocks, had shunted it this way and that with his clumsy hands.

Bili huffed. To entice their bapa back, he was going to have to get better at making pictures, but how was he supposed to do that if Akan always spoiled his practice?

The weight of it all suddenly felt very heavy. Unless they could find some way to show Dama what he'd left behind, they were likely to lose their wide-cheeked father forever. And then, Iki's dominance was assured.

Just then, a call sounded, barely audible over the long line of chirruping bats that had flown up into the air from some hidden cave. 'Bili!'

'Alright!'

He knew he needed to get ready for bed, but the truth was the setting sun – it was now actually touching the horizon! – was simply too magnificent to even hope to turn away from.

Besides, Akan was always so helpful, and was bound to get a nest ready for the dear brother he cherished so much.

✦

Roused by the gibbons, Akan awoke in a stupor.

For so long, he'd looked forward to his first night beyond the basin, but it had passed more fitfully than any in his life.

Peculiar noises sounded all through the dark hours. It may have been the case that these clicks and swishes and scratches occurred just as frequently as they ever did when he'd shared a nest with his mother, but for some reason, they'd never bothered him before.

Now, though, he interpreted each one as a sign of imminent danger. Perhaps a python had found its way along the bough? Or maybe an orb-weaver with its eight striped legs of black and yellow was wanting to sink its fangs into him while he slept? The thought had been enough to drive Akan out of his own nest and into his brother's, and they'd remained in a tight huddle together until they all but passed out from exhaustion.

Yawning, Akan left Bili and climbed out from the hastily constructed nest. Once down, he gave a whoop of delight to discover a blanket of nuts on the forest floor. He sat and feasted, observing from impressions in the soil that a boar had recently been by.

Already, the cicadas had come to life, their ceaseless groan a sign of the heat. How many days was it now since proper rainfall? Akan made a spiritless attempt to count the mornings, then gave up. Too many, it was enough to say.

In places, the slope on which he stood was steep enough to make a tumble likely, so Akan went up to the mid-trees in the hope of finding figs. As he investigated the area, a screech sounded from the sky, and a bolt of cold shot down his spine. But looking up, he saw only a kestrel. Thankfully, this wasn't Lang, the Bird-King, about whom their mothers often spoke.

The mighty spirit of war, they said, only gave one of his terrifying screams when a time of violence was coming.

Remembering this, the hairs on Akan's forearms suddenly stood on end.

A few mornings ago, after Bili had shown his picture to the boys up on the clearing, the kite had flown above them and wailed. Then, the next day, two orangs showed up dead in the cave.

It was obvious, then: Iki had heard the Bird-King's call, and it had lit up some awful instinct within him.

'Akan!'

Distracted by his brother's call, he looked across to the shambles of a nest. But that wasn't where Bili was calling from.

'Akan! Come see this!'

Well, at least Bili was up. 'Not now, brother,' he called back. 'I want to travel down from the slope before the sun gets any higher.'

'Come! I think you'll be interested.'

'Bili, we don't have time for your pictures now.'

'I haven't made a picture. Come see.'

Akan hoisted himself up a strangler vine and onto a branch. He swung across on another vine until he was in Bili's tree, and craned his neck up to see his brother sitting on a limb.

Even from here, Akan could see that, beside Bili, was a nest. And with its branches entwined in a three-way braid, he knew at once their chances of finding Dama had just greatly improved.

5

TRACKING THE EXILE

A DAWN and a dusk followed a dawn and dusk. Now starting their third full day outside the basin, the brothers were on the trail of what they felt sure was their father.

Akan used three clues to get a sense of Dama's movements. Firstly, there were the nests. The ones he'd seen in the past were in mangowood trees, and always where the trunk forked three ways. It was likely other orangs had just the same preference as their bapa, so the pair they'd already found may not have been Dama's at all. However, the presence of nearby poo – clue number two – gave them vital information: the seeds inside were those of the jackfruit which, according to Effie and Ivie, was always bapa's favourite.

As they advanced ever further from the basin, the boys sought out jackfruit trees, and kept a close eye on the ground for droppings. Whenever they located a pile, they established its freshness: if the seeds hadn't yet germinated, the owner had been by too recently for it to be Dama. But where spindly green stalks stood at a fingernail's height from out of the poo, the timing matched with their father's journey, and they altered their course accordingly.

The final clue was their bapa's scent. As they

navigated the forest, the brothers sniffed for traces of Dama on trees. It wasn't especially effective – their noses were the weakest of their senses – yet it was clear that a large male had been roaming in this area. That was the one positive thing about the continued absence of any rains: it allowed scent to linger.

Advancing this morning on a south-west course, Akan was distracted by the wide columns of sunlight that streamed in through the treetops on their right side. What was causing that? It was as though the canopy itself were punctured at multiple points.

'I'll go investigate,' said Bili, though it was obvious to Akan his brother had an ulterior motive; really, he only wished to get high up so he could sneak a glimpse back towards the high ridge of the basin.

From the treetops, Bili gave a surprised squeak. 'The rainforest looks very strange from up here!'

'What do you mean?'

'It's like it has an *edge*.'

Akan remembered their own river, which flowed through the basin from the foot of the seven tier waterfall. From a high enough vantage point, that snaking waterway appeared as a gap in the trees. That was probably all this was, too. 'Don't worry,' he called up. 'It just means we're coming to a river.'

'No,' Bili yelled. 'It's not a river. The forest just *ends*. There's nothing beyond it but open space.'

Akan hurried up the trunk to join his brother. Bili was right: at the end of an undulating skin of deep green canopy, the trees simply stopped. Only hazy fields stood in the gap where the forest ought to be, with nothing more than a single strip of trees in the middle of the clearing carrying on to the horizon.

Noticing Bili straining to see back east, Akan hooked his arm around his brother's shoulder. 'You still want to go back, don't you?'

Bili gave a sigh. 'Yes. But I want to bring him back,

too. Imagine what Iki's ugly face will look like if we get back to the slopes with bapa by our side. But do you really think we're on his trail? We might be chasing the wrong male.'

'There's a chance we are, Bili. But I think we should keep looking for jackfruit trees and poo piles. With a bit of luck, we'll come across the next nest.'

'What about *that* though?' asked Bili.

Akan peered out again to where the forest ended and the fields began. The whole region seemed to have grown even hazier already. '*That* could be our bit of good luck, Bili. The narrow strip north of the fields is a corridor.'

Bili's face contorted with confusion, and Akan, pleased to discover his brother wasn't always the clever one, offered clarity. 'Remember that time you waded out too deep into the river?'

'I thought I was done for.'

'You would have been. But that strip of terrain in the middle saved you.'

'I was lucky,' said Bili. 'That little island took me all the way back to the forest floor.'

'Well, those trees there, in the middle of the clearing, is just like that island. If we're really on bapa's trail, we have the same two options as him.'

'Take the island, or risk the water.'

'Exactly. Go through the trees, or venture out onto the clearings.'

Bili gave a faint smile. 'That's no option at all. We'll go along the corridor. But I want to stop soon, brother. I have a new picture in mind. I need to have a practice to see how difficult it's going to be to put together.'

'Alright,' said Akan, leaping into the neighbouring tree. 'We can stop on the way to the corridor. And I promise I won't touch this one.'

Making steady progress as they swung on through the sub-canopy, they journeyed until they came to the forest's edge. But it wasn't Bili's need to practice his picture that drew the brothers to a halt.

It was the smell.

Smoke now filled the air.

Akan grew animated. How exciting it was! Soon, he might be able to glimpse that special kind of leaping, searing brightness again!

Hastily, but with maximum care, he pushed out towards the tree line. In the clearing below him, a group of strange creatures stood around, and, astonishingly, they'd learned to wield that most transfixing of forces:

Flame.

❧

The land-orangs were fascinating.

Only once before, when they appeared in the basin hauling tools on their backs, had Bili seen them.

Though he and Akan were only babies then, he remembered well how their arrival caused excitement among the infants, and how mama's face darkened with worry the moment she knew they'd come. It was something she seldom spoke of, but he knew how her own childhood had been made arduous by their kind.

As mysteriously as they'd appeared, those land-orangs vanished again, and no trace of them was ever seen again in the basin. They were as harmless as a visiting troupe of grey leaf monkeys: certainly nothing that should have caused mama so much worry. Yet her face remained pained a long time after.

Seeing them again now that he was on the very cusp of maturity, Bili couldn't take his eyes off the ground-men as they worked in the clearing. How like orangs they were! The way they clutched their wooden sticks in their fingers as they brushed leaves onto the burning piles was just how Bili had himself held the branch when it last rained, as he'd beat a rhythm upon the buttress roots.

The ground creatures' arms were gangly, though fell short of the actual ground, and while their stalky legs lacked the agility of a tree-man, they were nevertheless set upon a pair of flat feet. Their faces were similar, too, if a bit flatter, and mostly hairless. The only other real difference was that none of their males had cheek pads – which suggested to Bili either these ones weren't yet fully grown, or that their behaviour was different. After all, adult orangs didn't share space with other males.

One aspect of their appearance that was almost uncannily alike was the eyes. The land-orangs looked around with the same searching gaze as every forest-man Bili knew. At once probing and intense, their emotions were visible within them.

Bili peered around. On the branch beside him, his brother was watching closely. But he seemed far more taken with the industry of the creatures than he was the creatures themselves. Akan hadn't stopped going on about the odd substance he'd found, and now that Bili saw it with his own eyes, it wasn't hard to understand why: flame was like nothing he'd ever before encountered.

Just what the ground-men were doing with it was unclear, though. They'd felled trees to make the clearing, with many of them now chopped into smaller logs that were piled near their machines. They'd left a handful as trunks, however, and had positioned these in a kind of square around the sides of the burning field. Akan might have his own ideas as to why they were doing this, but to Bili it seemed as though they might be trying to contain the flame, to prevent it from moving into a section of the forest where they didn't wish for it to be.

For a time, Bili remained rooted to the spot, watching the red line of flame as it washed along the field like a very strange wave. It was indeed beautiful, but its special quality was spoiled by the smoke it made; the moment the first cloud of that horrid stuff wafted into Bili's face, his throat constricted and he began coughing, and within seconds, the entire space around him was filled with a dirty fog. It became impossible to even see his brother now, and the air had become so thin that not one of the laboured breaths he took seemed to relieve him.

Unable to stand any more, Bili rose from his perch to creep blindly along the bough, leaping off its end. Three wide swings ensured some distance was put between himself and the land-orangs, and though the air he found was still clouded with thick haze, it was just about clear enough here to allow a clean lungful.

'So, that's the stuff you wanted to show me?' he asked Akan, when he joined him on the forest floor a short time later. 'You didn't warn me it was so smelly.'

'It is smelly,' agreed his brother. 'But it's so pretty! Did you see the way it flickers and twists? It reminds me of the Bird-King. Beautiful and dangerous.'

Bili rubbed his needling eyes with the backs of his hands. Although they streamed with tears, he saw the strange expression on his brother's face – one that was unlike any Bili could ever recall seeing.

While the sides of Akan's mouth curved up into a smile, there was a pained sorrow to him too, as though he were harbouring some kind of torment he didn't wish to share. It might just be that Akan's own eyes were blazing where the smoke had irritated them, but Bili was sure something was there that he wished to keep concealed.

He called over to him. 'What are you looking so pleased about?'

'You're not the only one with something to offer, Bili.'

'Come on, will you? We need to find a pool to wash our eyes. What are you going on about?'

'You think the only way bapa will come back is if he likes something *you've* made. Well, I can make things too, you know.'

'Great!' hooted Bili. 'Maybe we can make it together?'

Akan gave a grunt. 'I don't think so. All you have to

offer is pictures, but you can't do anything with those things.'

'That's not true!' protested Bili. 'You can look at them and enjoy them as often as you want.'

'But what's the point if you can't even touch them? All I did was move a few of your pebbles and the thing was ruined. Well, what I have to offer is something useful, Bili. And I really think bapa is going to love it.'

＊

The corridor of trees led back to open forest, and no sooner did the brothers enter the dense jumble of ironwoods than they heard water cascading.

Side by side, the pair went to the sandy soil of a waterfall's pool, and washed the smoke from out of their eyes. Bili was so excited to gather materials for his next picture that he took off at once, but Akan, laying flat on an exposed bough, took a while to let his hair dry.

He ought to have felt refreshed. But as he set off from the waterfall to traverse the canopy, dark thoughts began to trouble him.

Why did everyone love Bili more than him? Ever since they were babies, it was his brother the other boys wanted to play with. *'Bili does the best tumbles!' 'Bili's raspberries are the loudest!'*

It was always Bili the mothers cooed over, too, anytime he learned some new trick – even though it was Akan himself who first worked out how to catapult himself from a young tree, and who first mastered cracking apart a coconut husk by driving the crown into the edge of a rock. Even their bapa, on the few chance occasions they'd met him, showed a preference for Bili.

It was a stain on Akan's very spirit, the memory of the day when Dama first descended from out of the misty treetops. At once, the females had gone into a state of alertness – and Dama himself seemed every bit as surprised as them to be suddenly faced with a creche of youngsters and their mothers.

The large male with the wide cheek pads had a reputation for getting cross quickly, but it was with calmness that he approached the group of babies. Though it took some time for him to single out his own offspring, what followed was the most intense experience of either of the brothers' young lives. Looking first into Akan's infant eyes, Dama appeared to be searching for something. Akan was stunned by the sight of the dark, moon-shaped face glaring down at him, but held his father's stare. He perceived something in that forest-man that he'd never felt in any other, as though Dama possessed a kind of capability beyond what was natural for one of their kind. On and on that moment went, until, when Akan was sure his bapa had found what he was looking for, Dama broke the stare and moved across to his other child.

Their bapa maintained eye contact with Bili for a similar duration. But, at the end of that engagement, he gave a deliberate nod – then promptly departed.

How was Akan ever supposed to make peace with that? Why had Bili, alone, got a nod? There existed something within Bili that wasn't in him, and whatever that thing was, it was of special value to their father.

Well, bapa hadn't seen what Akan could do yet. But he would soon, and then he'd know that he too possessed the same valuable essence as his brother. Dama would come to see them, at last, as they equals they were.

Having now arrived at a grove of banana palms, Akan felt the intensity of the sun sapping his energy. Where were the rains? He reached out and plucked a handful of wilting leaves, which were so brittle they went to powder in his fingertips. There was unlikely to be a single thing, below the canopy or above it, that didn't ache for a whole day's downpour.

Languidly, he went to the top of the tallest ironwood

to read the landscape, seeing in the distance a hill. On top of the mound, barely visible through the hazy sky, was something that resembling tall rocks; it was hard to say for sure, since whatever it was appeared to be standing in separate pieces, like individual trees. The sight of it was sure to excite Bili, though, who'd be reminded of the circular ridge enclosing the slopes of his beloved home.

The heat in the mid-trees was slightly less fierce, but it was on lazy arms that Akan swung, and, around halfway towards the odd hill, he stopped to pluck a few berries away. And that was when he noticed, in the middle of a hardwood whose trunk forked three ways, a nest.

What good luck! It was just the right profile for one of Dama's, yet had required no effort at all to find. Akan went to sniff at the carefully arranged branches, and picked up at once the strong odour of an adult male.

He'd bring Bili to see this later, when he was done with his picture. For now, though, Akan was more interested in the mysterious stone spires standing erect on the hilltop.

The rock formations were so very strange! Comparable only to those odd fingers of stone found inside certain caves, these were vastly taller – all the juveniles in the home range stood upon each other's shoulders couldn't hope to reach the top of one of these. But what the spires boasted in height, they lacked in hardiness: whole slabs of the stuff looked set to drop away at any moment, with mounds of shale sat at their feet evidencing earlier rockfalls.

Actually climbing one was very obviously a bad idea. Yet Akan couldn't help wondering just how many more of these strange structures may be waiting beyond the brow of the hill. So, on careful strides, he wound through the brittle towers, to eventually be met with a whole valley of the things.

Though he'd never in his life imagined such a sight, it

was exactly the kind of thing Akan had yearned to leave the basin to find.

There was still plenty of daylight left, yet there seemed little wisdom in exploring this forest of rock now. Besides, Akan's curiosity was growing all the time. Just what was Bili making back there on the waterfall's beach?

Back in the canopy, he'd just started on the route back to the water when his eye was attracted to a flash of red-brown from the mid-trees. He halted, and watched carefully. There was no mistaking what was moving down there. He'd stumbled upon a female orang.

Should he approach? He certainly wanted to. Bili was good company, most of the time, but a chat with another of his kind was appealing. Hooking his fingers over his lower lip, Akan pondered the best thing to do. But just then a long, intimidating call – one that was familiar to all who resided in the basin – struck up nearby.

'Whoo-ook! Whooo! Whoo-ook! Whaaw!' it went.

It was, unmistakably, Dama.

And it was very clear he did not wish to share this territory with any other orangs.

Leaves rustled violently nearby as the adult male approached, and this was the only signal Akan needed – he took off back towards the waterfall as quickly as he could, in no doubt at all that *he* was the one now being pursued.

6

THE NINE-FINGERED TREE-MAN

AFTER SCAVENGING on the forest floor among plant life old and new, Bili was making his way back through the forest giants to the waterfall's pool. He knew he'd never make a perfect picture, but the work in progress on the sandy beach had already taken shape to his satisfaction – and this last item was going to elevate the whole thing.

Following him everywhere he went was the dirty scent of smoke, which clung to his hair like moss on a rock. How utterly horrid those burning fields had been! Day after day, he'd been longing for the rains to come, but around here the only thing that fell from the sky were speckles of hot ash.

Thankfully, the haze had begun to melt away as soon as the ground-men brought their peculiar business to an end, leaving Bili free to survey the shaded earth in comfort. But even while he'd foraged, each residual wisp that blew over reminded him just how much his throat had burned earlier. Yes, flame was beautiful. But, for Bili, it did not compensate for the mess it made.

Arriving now back at the pool, Bili plucked the bright blue fungus out of the palm of his closed fist. Holding it delicately between his thumb and forefinger, he set it down onto his picture in what he thought was just the right spot, and stood back. A smile lifted his lips: this would make any orang take notice.

But it wasn't *any* forest-man he needed to impress.

They'd only ever met their father a few times, and Dama had revealed so little of himself that neither Bili or Akan could say for sure whether bapa even cared for such things as pictures. In fact, Bili couldn't say with any confidence a single thing that might be true of Dama, save for how wronged he'd been by the brutish Iki.

As Bili looked upon his latest creation, his self-doubt swelled. But he *had* to go on with it; he just knew, the way he knew that smoke followed flame, that his own strange talent was somehow important.

His arrangement lay scattered in a heap of seeds and ferns, dirt and leaves, bark, pebbles and branches. It was a bigger version of the landscape he'd presented to Akan and the boys on the ridge, but whereas that one had depicted a simple circle with sloping sides, the picture coming to life here was far more sophisticated – primarily because it used an additional dimension.

The realisation had hit him with suddenness and force: *pictures didn't have to be flat.* Before, Bili was able to work only with length and width. His previous creation stretched out from left to right, and from top to bottom. Now, though, he'd figured a way to bring height into it as well, such that shapes *stood up* from off the sand to enter the space of the sky.

The effect was as he'd hoped it would be. Although it was bewildering to begin with, it soon settled on the eye into a pleasing, miniature world: the entire world of their home. All that was needed was the sparkling river, which he'd hoped the blue mushroom might capture.

He tore the fungus along its length, and lay out both strands in a line, and at once the river was there before his very eyes. So pleased was he, Bili let out a breathy 'ahh!' With a few final touches, this was going to be even better than he'd hoped it would be. If there was only a way they could pick it up and take it with them when they went back to the basin!

No. Not when *they* went. Akan had made his condition clear: Bili would be returning alone.

Refusing to let sorrow ruin this exciting moment, Bili reached down. The ridge section was still a little messy where some pebbles were balancing delicately on a pile of dirt, so he moved in closer to tidy them. But just as he began, he heard his brother calling urgently from behind him.

He turned his head to the side. From out of the trees, Akan appeared, panting. 'Let's go!'

'Go? But my picture's not quite ready!'

'That doesn't matter – we need to move right now!'

'What? But I'm not done. Come and see what I've made, brother. This is my best practice yet. I—'

'I don't care about your picture, Bili! We need to hurry!'

'What's the rush, Akan? Let's just—'

'Come on, will you? We're in danger. We've got to head north this instant.'

'Alright. Just give me a chance to—'

'No, Bili! Now!'

'Just this little b—'

In his frustration, Akan picked up the nearest thing to him – which happened to be a flat piece of rock – and flung it up into the air. Before Bili could even finish making his plea, the object landed right in the middle of his work, and the whole miniature basin collapsed in on itself.

Barely a heartbeat passed before Bili lunged at his brother, and the pair fell into a heap on the sand. A frenzy of scratching and kicking and punching followed, and Bili didn't care one bit if either he or his brother got seriously hurt. The only thing that mattered was that Akan pay for that malicious, envious outburst.

But Akan, who always was stronger than him,

managed to roll himself on top, a glint of true fury lighting up his eyes as he brought his head down to deliver a bite into Bili's face.

The blow, however, was interrupted by a voice sounding directly behind them.

'Whoo-ook!' it went.

'Whooo! Whoo-ook! Whaaw!'

It was Dama's long call.

And it was loaded with violent intent.

❦

Dama cast his wide shadow upon the brothers as they grappled on the sandy edge of the waterfall's pool.

Akan suddenly felt rather silly carrying on this ridiculous brawl with Bili. The only imperative now – for the pair of them – was to evade a territorial male with a reputation as fearsome as the teeth now on full display.

He released Bili and crouched low. With crushing anxiety in his chest, Akan braved the briefest of glances at Dama's eyes, and waited for the huge orang to make his move. He then scanned for an escape route: the fallen log on his right side could be cleared with a single leap, getting him to safety before his father could reach him.

Bili's vocalisations alternated between fear squeaks and annoyed grumbles. Akan had seen his brother angry many times throughout their childhoods, and physical scuffles were common, but never had Bili been quite so incensed. Akan bitterly regretted hurling the rock into the heart of his picture, especially given that their father was actually towering above it right now.

The seconds rolled on, and still the awful tension persisted. Though some of Akan's worry had calmed – if Dama meant to attack, it was likely he'd have done so already – his inability to predict what the adult might do next made him unwilling to stand from his crouch.

Bili, however, had already turned back around. From

the noises, Akan could tell that his brother was rebuilding the collapsed parts of the damaged work. Dama, clearly intrigued to know what Bili was up to, hoisted one leg in front of the other and began to move forward, causing matted strands of shaggy hair to shake where they dangled off his arms and torso. Akan leapt away without delay up onto the escape log, but Bili stayed exactly where he was, either oblivious to the approaching danger or else unfazed by it.

On the sand, Dama dropped down onto his backside beside Bili and fixed his gaze on the intricate arrangement of materials.

'We want you to come back, bapa,' said Bili.

Dama, however, simply watched the youngster at work.

'Iki has stolen our mothers. And we know what else that brute did. We saw the bodies in the cave.'

Tentatively, Akan began to edge down the log. Bili wasn't scared at all; did that mean he shouldn't be either? Still too cautious to stand close to the adult, however, he watched his brother from the edge of the picture.

'Our mothers said you left for good,' continued Bili. 'But the basin needs you. Why don't you come back there with us, bapa?'

What was happening here? Akan simply couldn't understand his brother's lack of fear. What did he know about their father that he himself did not? All males – whether or not they were your father – were risky to be around. But ones with cheek-pads as wide as Dama's could be some of the most aggressive creatures in the entire forest. How could Bili possibly have known he was in no danger?

Bili craned his head low as he looked over his work. 'I made something for you, bapa. I thought it would remind you of how beautiful the basin is. But Akan threw a stone into it just before you arrived and now it's ruined.'

Dama moved his gaze slowly to where Akan was sitting. For one heart-stopping moment, Akan felt his father's eyes burn into him – and then they returned to the picture.

Still, Bili went on delicately placing pebbles here and leaves there, smoothing things down beneath his palms where he felt they should be smooth, and pinching up peaks in the soil with his thumb and forefinger where he felt there should be peaks. All the while, Dama watched in silence.

'It was almost perfect before, bapa. You would have known exactly what it was. But now it's just a big mess and I can't get it right again.'

It certainly was a mess. Akan had no idea just what it was supposed to represent. Bili's other pictures sort of made sense after a few moments looking at them, but even before the rock was thrown, he doubted that thing could be worth anybody's time.

Where some soil made a little hill from off the sandy ground, Bili attempted to position a few pebbles, but these kept rolling back down the slope, causing him to give whimpers of frustration. But then, just when Akan feared that Bili might lash out and cause their father to react, Dama brought one hand out and picked up a bright strand of blue fungus that lay outside the bottom of the picture. This, he placed delicately in a very specific spot, and Bili's mouth curved into a very faint smile.

Dama's own face remained perfectly neutral, however.

'You can see it, can't you, bapa? It's our basin.'

Their *basin*? How was this jumble of junk their basin? Akan fiddled with his lower lip while he desperately tried to see what the other two could see.

Dama brought his other hand up and reached for a twig, which he placed at a precise angle on the left side of the picture. A moment of stillness followed, then their father gave a single nod, turned, and disappeared back into the trees.

Now, though, Bili wasn't smiling, and Akan knew why:

The hand that had placed the twig down was missing its middle finger.

☙

The hostile mood between the brothers lingered on into dusk.

Akan had already made his nest and was coming, as usual, to help. But tonight Bili didn't want any assistance, and emphatically informed him so with a single bark.

If only making a nest was as fun as making a picture or thinking up some account of an incident that had never happened. Bili knew a good nest when he saw one, and understood well enough the principles of putting one together, but when it came time to do it for himself he just couldn't be bothered to spend the energy on it. Nevertheless, it was something that was necessary for a young orang cut loose in the wilds, and if time *had* to be devoted to the task, then he may as well make a better job of it than he had before.

Remembering his mother's method, Bili fractured branches back on themselves before shaping them into a pocket. Ordinarily, he'd grab any old piece of tree to accomplish this, but the past few nights he'd had some jagged twigs digging into him and didn't much fancy that again, so the ones he'd chosen now were smoother, their wider leaves allowing the pocket to be better sealed.

When he was done, Bili felt the tension in his shoulders relax. It could never rival the thrill of creating a beautiful thing from out of nothing, but he saw now how a bit more care towards mundane tasks could yield better results. As he leant back to close his eyes, he reckoned he could do an even better job tomorrow evening.

The clicking of bats struck up, and an owly-eyed slow loris issued an anguished squeal below as it hurried through the saplings. Bili was tempted to have a look to see if a clouded leopard or a civet cat was giving chase down there, but before he could shift his weight to lift himself up, his brother's face popped up over the edge of the pocket.

'What do you want?' Bili huffed.

'This is a good nest, brother. I told you you could do it.'

'What do you want?'

'I'm sorry about your picture. I only threw the stone because it was urgent.'

'That's not true. You threw it because you don't like it that I can do something you can't.'

'I didn't! Really I didn't! Bapa didn't know it was me he was chasing, and he wouldn't have known it was you, either. If he'd got us, he would have hurt us. I was trying to protect you.'

Bili gave a grunt. 'That picture was really good, Akan. Not perfect, but really, really good. If bapa saw it as it was before you ruined it, he'd have felt it in his heart the way I do. Instead, he hated it.'

'He didn't hate it.'

'He hated it! He didn't have a single thing to say about it because it was just a pile of rubbish on some sand. You saw his face. He barely even acknowledged it before he took off.'

'But you smiled when he placed the fungus down. Whatever it was you'd made, he saw it, Bili.'

'He didn't.'

'Well, you can say that. But you know he did.'

'What do you want, Akan? I'm tired.'

'Are we going to speak about his hand?'

Bili shifted in the nest, a wave of skin bumps breaking out across his neck. He shunted himself to one side begrudgingly, allowing a space for his brother, who promptly jumped in and wrapped his arms around Bili in a cuddle.

'It was him who did it.'

'I know,' said Bili.

'He must have lost his finger fighting the orangs in the cave.'

'What do you think it was about, anyway?'

Akan gave a sigh. 'Same as it always is. Territory. Females. Like Iki and you and me. The two dead tree-men in the cave could just have been us.'

'No.'

Akan broke away from the embrace. 'What?'

'Did you ever hear of a fight to the death?'

'There was that incident with Feki. He tumbled out of the canopy after fighting Mula.'

'But my mama said he died because of the fall, though, not because Mula actually killed him.'

'Then, no, Bili. I haven't heard of such a thing.'

Bili's shoulders grew tense again. '*Two* tree-men, Akan.'

'We don't actually *know* bapa did it, though.'

Bili's eyes widened. 'Remember the marks we found in their necks? They were made by hands missing one of their fingers. They were bapa's hands.'

The glow of dusk faded into night, and a pale crescent of moon shone above the treetops. Akan climbed back out of the nest to head to his own, and when he looked briefly back, Bili noticed how his brother's eyes had lit up with an odd kind of exhilaration. 'I wonder where he learned to do a thing like that?' Akan said, bouncing away.

Below, the fireflies had come out, hovering in their purposeless way. Bili sat up to watch them awhile, and as he did, an acrid scent disturbed his nostrils.

But this time, it was not the scent of his own fur. Somewhere nearby, a new patch of green was turning to orange.

7

FIREFLY AT THE PINNACLES

AFTER A BREAKFAST OF FIGS, Bili followed Akan to a dense swathe of forest.

They went via the hill, which was every bit as strange as his brother had described it. Looking up at the tall spires of rock that stood from the plateau like quills on a porcupine, Bili struggled to make sense of this peculiar landscape. Were they once trees, gone somehow to stone through a very unusual kind of decay? They seemed ancient, these structures, of a time before orangs swung on the boughs, if ever such a time there was.

Fearing rockfalls, the pair avoided the spires as best they could, walking instead across the level path at the plateau's edge. With less shale underfoot, the going was easier this way, but, with a steep ledge dropping away to their left, not more safe. The price of a single stumble here was, almost certainly, death.

They reached forest again just in time to hear another of their father's long calls ringing out in the treetops. Bili looked at Akan, whose worry, he knew, mirrored his own. They were going to have to be very careful how they attempted to lure Dama again.

At the foot of the first of the ironwoods, the pair halted. Although it gave Dama time to lay claim to an ever greater area, they were glad of the rest, suffering as they were in the heat of yet another rainless day.

While they waited, Bili went over to the clifftop's edge and braved a glance down to the open tract of grassland. This clearing stretched on all the way to a river, and dotted upon it were dwellings fashioned by the hands of ground-men. As Bili suspected, Akan, laying next to him, was entranced with the small fire burning beside one of the huts.

Some of the land-orangs were sitting around the flame, eating. They were too far away for their voices to be heard, but when a hoot rolled up the limestone of the cliff, Bili thought how like laughter it sounded. Turning to Akan, he noted that mischievous look in his brother's eye once again; evidently, he was concocting some plan, and was rather pleased with himself about it.

When Dama's long calls finally abated, the brothers moved off into the greenery of old growth, limiting the noise they made by traversing the high boughs, on their feet where it was possible. Then, when hunger announced itself in their bellies, they wandered down to ground to sit in the shade of banana palms.

While Akan feasted on the fruit, Bili ate the fallen banana blossom, peeling away its purple petals one at a time to savour their sweet, flaky texture, noting how the petals would make excellent materials for the next picture he made. But the thought of it made his shoulders droop. Would there even be another picture?

His last effort had failed to impress. Throughout the morning, he hadn't managed to think up any alternative that might do the job of enticing Dama back. If the rains ever came, he could show his father the funny way he beat the branch against a buttress root in time with the falling drops. Perhaps that might work instead?

Out of the corner of his eye, Bili then caught a flash of brown-orange passing beyond the towering hardwood.

Alarmed, he grasped his brother by the wrist, and pointed over to it with his face.

'orang,' said Akan, who seemed unfazed. 'Female.'

Bili grew skittish. This could mean trouble.

Akan cast a glance back the way they'd just come. 'So long as we keep away, we'll be alright. Let her move off. She's going to bapa's call.'

Nervously, Bili popped the last bit of the flower's stem into his mouth, then felt his brother's hand upon his shoulder. He twisted his neck to see a naughty smile. 'You know,' Akan said, 'this might be a good time for you to go practice your picture again somewhere.'

Bili gave a squeak. 'Why? Where are you going?'

Bouncing away, Akan was now backtracking. 'I have some business of my own,' he hooted happily.

🦟

Back at the high plateau on which the stone spires sat, Akan stared down at the ground-men's grassy clearing, wondering whether he might have to descend the rockface itself, like some deeply strange gecko.

Hoping to find a better option, he wandered, and was rewarded for his efforts when he eventually sighted a direct route down. Beside a level patch of grass which crowned a rocky outcrop overhanging the cliff was a pathway tree. Its uppermost branches stood at the exact height of the clifftop, providing a perfect way to the open tracts.

Now knuckle-walking on the ground's soft grass, Akan went and plucked away a bunch of rambutans from out of the shrubby undergrowth. These, he carried over to where the land-orangs were sitting.

A female sighted him first. 'Hello! Where have you come from?'

She took a few cautious steps closer to where he sat,

and tilted her head gently on its side. Her face opened up into a wide smile.

'You're hot, aren't you? I am too. Want a drink?'

The female turned and marched away for a moment, returning with a bigger group and a dish filled with water. She set this in front of Akan, but since flame was way more interesting than water, he rose from the dry earth and went to the other end of the table, where a circle of rocks enclosed a few low tongues of the pretty red substance.

While he prized the translucent fruit from out of the rambutans' casings and worked the flesh off the stone with his tongue, Akan listened to the land-orangs chatting.

'It's this drought, I bet. Brought this young'un down from the trees.'

'He's been up there in the Pinnacles. Rough terrain for an orang-utan.'

'What are their numbers like around here, Professor Krause?'

'Fairly low on this side of the corridor. Better further south, though. This one will just be passing through.'

A low voice called from nearby. 'Cave team! Boats are ready for you!'

Akan jumped slightly when half of the party abruptly banded together and began to move off. 'Have fun with the amphibian survey today!' one of them called back to the remaining half.

The female was now holding out a banana for Akan, but as he was happy enough with his rambutans, he refused it.

'I bet mum's worrying about him.'

'I wouldn't have thought so,' said the female. 'He's just about at the age of independence. We've observed younger adolescents than this ranging solo. Then again, we've seen older ones too who still travel with their mothers.'

'Bit like us. My brother lives at home, and he's thirty-eight.'

The carefree mood of the group made Akan feel settled, but the moment another man arrived, he grew wary.

The newcomer was bristling with tense energy. 'We've got a problem. Our Dayak guides have just found out the porters are from Madura.'

'So?' said the man nearest Akan.

'So, there's tension between the Dayaks and the Madurese all across Borneo right now. Let's just say there's a bit of a history between the two groups. We could do without this for our expedition – we're going to have to handle things delicately.'

The low voice called out again. 'Amphibian team! Boat's ready for you!' and with that the last of the land-orangs stood and moved away. On her way past, the female crouched beside Akan and gave the hair on his back a few gentle strokes. The touch of one of their kind was not unpleasant, but neither was it one he wished to experience again.

A loud, juddering rattle sounded from the direction of the river, and a thin puff of blue and foul-smelling smoke drifted over the clearing. When all was quiet again, Akan went closer to the flame, now just a flicker within the ring of rocks. How sad it was to think it would be gone any moment. But where would it be when he could no longer see it? A thing didn't simply vanish. It was just another of the many fascinating aspects of this beguiling stuff.

Around the corner, he found a row of adjoined wooden dwellings, sheltered along their front side by an overhanging section. The scent of land-orangs lingered strongly here, pungent and sweet and occasionally sour.

Akan entered the first of the huts. Pieces of fabric – the ground-men's coverings – were draped over horizontal beams. While most were damp, a single one was dry, and Akan plucked this away and carried it out with him to where the little fire was flickering.

The ground-men who burned the fields had fed the flame with leaves and branches; ever since he'd seen them do it, Akan wondered if *anything* could turn into the beautiful stuff. He held his pilfered piece of fabric above it, and watched with amazement as its edge lit up, then slapped the ground with mirthful hoots before going off to explore the rest of the ground-men's mysterious world.

⚜

Bili scoured for materials for most of the morning, but as the sun rose higher, so did his desperation.

The problem was the landscape. This enigmatic expanse of towers yielded precious little foliage. There simply wasn't any chance of assembling something good enough to appeal to their bapa. Unless…

He reached down to pick up a chunk of shale. Wielded the right way, this stuff could be useful. His lips spread into a full smile as he realised what he needed might just have been beneath his feet all along, among these very stone trees.

With a new type of picture now visible in his mind's eye, Bili began rummaging through the thin slivers of shedded rock. A pile began to grow next to him: pieces most suited to the work he wished to produce. Then, just as he was ready to start transporting them across to the plateau, a gentle hooing sounded in the trees behind him.

He halted. With shards of shale in either hand, he crouched low and twisted his neck around to the mid-trees nearby. The lone female who'd passed earlier was coming by again. Akan, quite sensibly, had suggested they keep well away. But that was before Bili had a use for this journeying individual.

Hurriedly, he skirted the edge of the plateau. 'Hello,'

he called out, when he reached the trees. 'My name's Bili. What's your name?'

The female twisted her body away, haughtily.

'That call you've been following is coming from Dama. I'm Dama's son.'

She swivelled her head, ever so slightly, back his way.

'There's something I need to show him. But it's not safe for me to enter his territory. He's really going to like it though, and it would make me so happy if he could just look at it for a moment.'

'What is it?' said the female, intrigued now.

'What's your name?'

'Dena.'

'It's a picture, Dena.'

'A picture?'

'Well, not quite a picture. You see, I learned a way to make a new dimension. Now it doesn't have to just be flat on the ground. It can have a shape, too, like real things.'

'I don't know what you're talking about, you strange little orang,' said Dena. 'What is it you want from me?'

'Through these spires, the plateau falls away into a sheer cliff. There's a nice clear patch there – could you lead my bapa to it? He'll follow you for sure.'

'When?'

Bili considered this. Assuming he was even able to do it at all, he needed enough time to create the vision that had popped into his head. The longer he took, however, the greater the risk became that Dama would leave the area completely.

'Sundown. Lead him to the cliff edge at sundown. Will you do that for me, Dena? I only need a moment of his time.'

'We'll see,' sniffed the female, and swung away.

Bili spent the rest of the afternoon transferring his chosen fragments across the uncomfortable terrain to the cliff edge. Then, when he was sure he had everything he needed, he set to work.

The idea was to recreate the image he'd attempted back on the basin's ridge, the one his brother had spoiled when he mistook its three circles for rambutans. Using its basic composition as the foundation for today's effort – bapa in the middle, with each brother either side of him – Bili understood that all he had to do now was somehow turn the circles into spheres.

He began with Dama. The flat fragments were long and narrow, and mercifully light, and arranging them was easy enough to start with. But while building a circular wall caused him no trouble at all, his attempt to widen the wall out into the sphere's bottom ended in a collapsed mound every time. The shale shards just wouldn't balance! If his brother were here it might be easier; at least then one could be held steady while Bili piled the next sliver on top. But Akan was nowhere to be found, and was unlikely to want to help anyway, since he was set on organising his own thing now.

On and on Bili went, alternating between excitement and dismay as first the wall rose higher, then came tumbling back down again. All the while, the sun arced ever further to the west, drawing the hour of Dena's visit closer. And, of course, the central head was only one of three: capturing himself and Akan on either side of his father was going to need days at a minimum.

With a heavy heart, Bili gave up the dream of depicting his family in three dimensions. But there was no time to dwell on the failure; if he didn't put something together soon, there'd be nothing for his father to see beyond a pile of rubble.

Two dimensions would have to do.

Shards that had proven so difficult to stack into a sphere were, as it turned out, the perfect material with which to make three flat faces. So adeptly did Bili brandish the slivers of rock, he'd completed the basic composition before the sun had begun its descent. He busied himself now with the finer details: his father's wide cheek pads; Akan's narrow eyes; his own ears which, he'd always felt, were pointier than those of most other young orangs.

When he was putting on the finishing touches, a mechanical puttering sounded from the river below. Bili looked down to see a boat arriving from around the corner. It pulled up beside a wooden structure, and was joined, moments later, by a second, then a third.

Squinting his eyes, Bili could see a crowd of land-orangs assembling on the grass. Though they were far away, it was apparent they were quarrelsome. A couple seemed to be shoving one other.

Then something else caught his eye down there. Making its way towards the large pathway tree linking the clearing to the cliff's top was a sole point of light.

Was it a firefly? It had the same yellowish glow. Yet it was too big, and was apparently encased too, somehow. With the evening light dim, it wasn't possible to say whether the light were moving by itself, or whether a ground-man was carrying it in his hand. Perhaps Akan would understand the scene better.

So busy had Bili been throughout the afternoon readying his picture, he hadn't given much thought to his brother's whereabouts. All day, Akan had been off somewhere, up to something he evidently wished to be kept secret. But why did he feel the need to conceal his activities? Bili had been nothing but open about his own plans to entice their father back to the basin – not once had he tried to hide his pictures. In fact, he'd sought Akan's input, since all that mattered was that the effort was good enough. Yet his brother obviously felt he had something so special to show that it would somehow be tarnished if Bili saw it, too. Well, whatever it was he'd come up with, he'd better hurry up – Dena was on her way here now!

Bili turned around to face the approaching footsteps. A second set became audible behind her, too.

Dena had pulled it off. Bapa was following her.

He glanced anxiously down at his work. Would it suffice? It was time to find out.

Bili braced himself. What he was about to do was very, very risky. It didn't matter that he was Dama's son: territory trumped family when it came to an adult male seeking a new mate.

From behind the nearest tower, Dena emerged. Ignoring Bili completely, she sat among the shrubby bushes, coolly picking away a few handfuls of berries.

A voice called out from the spires, given resonance by the inflated throat sack of a territorial male.

'Whoo-ook! Whooo! Whoo-ook! Whaaw!'

Bili swallowed hard to see the rich, orange-red hair of his father, which seemed to light up the stone spire as he passed in front of it.

Casually, Dena rose, and moved closer to the youngster. Bili wanted to shoo her away, lest his father think she was more interested in his son. But she went by as though he wasn't even there.

'Whoo-ook!' called Dama.

Bili felt his chest tighten as bapa looked in his direction. Surely he wouldn't regard this as an encroachment? After all, it was Dama who'd wandered out of his forest territory.

Complex emotion blazed in the large male's eyes as he looked upon Bili. But then Dama noticed the carefully arranged shards of rock on the ground, and, on all fours, he began to advance.

Feeling extremely grateful to the selfless female, Bili gave her a nod of appreciation, and she vanished into the stone spines. Dama, meanwhile, sat himself in front of the picture. His brow furrowed in concentration as he carefully examined it.

Bili opened his mouth to explain to his father just

what he was looking at, but before he could speak, an oversized firefly emerged from the top of the pathway tree.

Father and son, equally startled by its sudden appearance, quickly span to face it. But this was no firefly.

Flame had made its way to them through Akan; in his hand was a glass box housing an individual point of fire, which leapt and pranced and gave light to the darkening sky all around it. It was a tool from the world of the land-orangs.

'Bapa!' Akan called out. 'You must go back to the basin and tell all the orangs there how you sired the smartest sons. Look how clever we are, bapa! Bili, with his pictures, and Akan, who holds the beauty of flame in his very hand.'

Bili's eyes widened at such a sight. It was his brother he'd seen moving across the clearing just now! Akan had taken this tool from the ground-men below, and had climbed with it up the tree!

Akan stared at his father with a smile on his lips, but Bili watched as this twisted into crestfallen disappointment; Dama had simply turned his back, and was now looking again at the picture on the ground.

'It's you, bapa,' said Bili. 'You and your sons. Look how happy we are in the basin. We need you to go back there, bapa.'

For the briefest of instants, a kind of satisfaction settled on Dama's face. For the first time, Bili saw something in his father that looked like peace. Some terrible darkness seemed to follow this mighty creature wherever he went, yet now, fleetingly, he appeared lightened.

'Look, bapa!' shouted Akan, who'd moved now over to the berry-laden shrubs. 'Look what I've learned to do!'

Bili turned in time to see his brother drag his flame across the leaves; eight mornings since it had last rained, the coarse, dry foliage lit up instantly with a bright wave of light.

But their father simply stayed as he was, leering at the three picture heads arranged on the ground.

Fearful of how quickly the flame was spreDamang, Bili edged away. But more alarming was how upset his brother appeared to be getting. Akan had arrived too late to know Dena was nearby, and was therefore oblivious to the domineering energy coursing that would be coursing through their bapa's veins.

Compelled to warn his brother not to do anything to anger the adult, Bili tried to meet Akan's eye, but the moment he did, his brother flung the box towards them.

Bili bounced away to the side, narrowly avoiding being struck, and the thing landed directly beside their father with an explosive and foul-smelling burst. The land-orangs' curious box poured flame as it rolled along the ground, and when it eventually cascaded over the edge of the cliff, it landed on the clearing far below with an almighty crash.

The three picture heads were now entirely engulfed, and the shrubs blazed with tongues of fire. Yet nothing burned hotter than Dama's rage.

Jumping away from the flaming circles with a lightness that defied his bulk, Dama reached out to grab a chunk of the shale, which he swiftly threw at Akan.

Akan was rooted to the spot in terror. Reflected in his eyes was the inferno that now blocked the way into the stone spires and kept all three of them trapped on the cliff's edge. In his terrified state, he made no attempt to parry the fragment of burning rock, which struck him forcefully on the side of his head.

Like a jackfruit fallen from the branch, Akan hit the ground with a dull thud. At once, Bili sprang forward to give him aid – but their bapa got to him first.

Dama slammed his palms down onto Akan's face. He bit his neck and heaved him to and fro with immense force. During one particularly mighty tug, he lost grip of the young orang's arm and Akan came away; with blood streaming down his face, he struggled up onto his feet, searching for a route to safety, but finding the shrubs to his left engulfed, and the pathway tree to his left lit up in an inferno.

Reaching out his long arms, Dama then gripped Akan by the shoulders.

'Bapa!' Bili called out. 'Please don't hurt him!'

But the enraged adult was out of control in his fury, and threw Akan onto the ground, before assuming a very peculiar pose.

It was as though Dama were carrying something very heavy in front of himself – yet nothing at all sat between his hands. With his nine fingers set into converging points, he began to approach the throat of the dazed Akan.

'No!' barked Bili, who understood now that his father meant to clasp his hands around Akan's neck, to squeeze the life out of him as he had the two tree-men in the cave.

'Cover your throat!' Bili called out.

Akan, in no doubt just why his brother had issued so precise a command, flipped onto his front, but Dama took hold of the back of his neck. Akan brought his own fingers up to meet his father's, such that his head was now encircled completely with hands, and the voice that spilled from him as he tried to protest the violence came out in a strained kind of gurgle.

A thump sounded behind Bili: a sapling had toppled to the ground where flame had eaten through the bottom of it. With no time to even consider the wisdom of his actions, Bili lifted this branch and thrust its burning leaves into his father's side. Dama gave a roar of pain, and stumbled back onto the stone faces. Though the rock pieces were no longer aflame, it was evident from Dama's squeal that they were still scorching. Clutching his foot, he fell onto his side.

Bili's hands were blistered from the heat of the branch, but he ignored the pain and leapt across to his brother. The clearing at the foot of the ledge was lit up with an eerie orange glow – ground-men were down there in a state of apparent panic – and small but numerous pockets of fire ran down the height of the pathway tree.

Hoisting Akan onto his feet, Bili had to shout to be heard; crackles and snaps – the voice of the forest crying out in anguish – exploded in the intensity of the furnace. 'We need to get down!'

'How?'

'Stick to the trunk!'

But before the injured orang could even consider it, Dama rushed up behind the two of them and shunted Akan with full force, sending him flailing over the side of the cliff, and all Bili could do was watch as his brother crashed through the flaming boughs before landing with a sickening thump on the earth far below.

✦

One day, near the beginning of their forth monsoon, Bili and Akan were travelling through the forest with their mothers. They were on their way to a fruiting durian tree, whose prickly, malodorous treats were ripe for the picking.

As they advanced through the canopy, they came to a stream. One of the many tributaries of the basin's only river, this particular spot was shallow and calm and known for the small fish that nibbled the dirt and grime from the underside of your feet. At Aunt Ivie's insistence, they made their way down for a refreshing dip in it; Akan, however, had other ideas.

Keeping his plan to himself, he remained up on the limb of the fig tree, pushing himself along it until he was directly over the water. Bili knew exactly what his brother meant to do. Over the preceding days, Akan had been learning a particular kind of drop. With his hands gripped firmly on the limb he sat on, he'd let himself tumble off backwards. Somersaulting over in the space between his arms, he'd then wait until his body got to its lowest point, before falling the rest of the way to the ground and landing on his feet. The first attempt was made above soft soil, so that when Akan misjudged the distance and hit his head on the limb, the fall caused no harm, and with that single mistake out of the way, he'd perfected the move.

Ready to debut it in front of the others, Akan waited until all eyes were on him before he turned away from them. With a rocking motion, he let himself fall back; his hands took his weight comfortably as he fell to his arms' length, then he lifted his knees to undertake the roll.

But something went wrong. Right as he tucked, he lost his grip, and, when he was completely upside down, he plummeted out of the sky, landing on his head in the water with a loud splash.

Bili burst into tears instantly at the sight of it, though whether it was the fall itself or the horrified reaction of his mother that so upset him was impossible to say.

For a few terrible moments, Akan lay on his back in the stream, his eyes screwed tight as though the force of the fall had knocked the life out of him. But then they flickered open, and he stared up into the bright blue sky, and promptly gave a hoot of laughter. The females laughed too, but the shock of it prevented Bili from seeing the funny side; the belief his brother had died was enough to spoil many of the days that followed.

That time, Akan was lucky.

Now, there'd been no stream to break his fall.

At the bottom of the tree, crumpled upon the grass, Akan was laying perfectly still. Dama had fled through the burning foliage the moment he'd pushed Akan, leaving Bili alone on the plateau, with only the encroaching flames for company.

Finding a way down was now a matter of life or death. Reaching out for some branches, Bili moved into the blackened canopy of the pathway tree. Isolated fires still raged in it, but as these tended to be out on limbs, he carefully descended down as central a route as could be found.

He eventually reached the halfway point, where thick white smoke was billowing into the dusk. The shorter trees and bushes directly beneath him were all aflame, ensuring that the rest of the way simply couldn't be negotiated without at least some exposure to the flame itself. But since moving *closer* to such a lethal force went against every instinct in Bili's body, he had to ignore the fearful voice in his mind, and proceeded through the searing heat as quickly as he could.

On the lower half of the pathway tree's trunk, Bili paused to catch a breath and rub the worst of the debris from out of his eyes. As his vision came gradually back to him, he baulked to see a pair of land-orangs – a tall female and a short male – moving at speed towards Akan.

Nearby, faintly audible over the multitude of exploding twigs and leaves, was the mechanical roar of the boats: the rest of the ground-men were readying to move along the river once again. But this pair remained where they were, on their knees at Akan's side, as they rolled his limp body onto a sheet of fabric.

'What about the others, Jane?' said the male, whose frantic eyes darted around the clusters of raging vegetation. 'The sanctuary can accommodate dozens of orang-utans.'

'The fire's spreDamang across the whole HQ!' yelled the female. 'You heard what Jonathan said on the rDamao. More have broken out upriver, too. This is the big one, Mark – the whole of Borneo is about to go up!'

The male worked frantically at Akan's side. 'Come on!' he cried. 'If we're not on the boat in the next couple of minutes, we'll be trapped!'

As they hoisted Akan's body off the floor, Bili heard a feeble groan spill from his brother's mouth, and a ripple of relief washed down his spine. The fall was sure to have damaged him – not to mention the force of the rock flung at his head by Dama – but he'd survived it, and that was more than Bili could have hoped for.

The pair of land-orangs turned back for the row of wooden dwellings. 'What about our equipment?' said the male. 'We'll never finish the surveys without our equipment!'

'Surveys? This expedition is over, Mark. The porters have loaded everything they could get their hands on. Let's just hope the university has good insurance.'

With that, the two land-orangs sped away, Akan's enwrapped body swinging where the male held the fabric bundle in his hands.

Bili followed them with his eyes, but already the smoke was blinding him. He shuffled out on a limb to try and see better where they were taking his brother, but, feeling the heat rDamaating up from the inferno below, he scooted quickly back.

Within a moment, the spot he'd occupied was engulfed. Squeaking with terror, Bili moved to another bough, above flames that were licking upward. With no other limb to leap to, all he could do was hold on while the destructive red waves climbed the trunk and advanced towards him.

Then the bough fell, and the next thing he knew he was on the ground. The leaves of the limb had cushioned his landing, but he was stunned nevertheless, and stumbled out into the clearing.

He looked up to see the clifftop's plateau now aglow with a bright and flickering light. Every tree cluster on the clearing was engulfed, too, and the wooden roofs of the ground-men's dwellings were beginning to catch.

With a limp, Bili waddled along after the land-orangs. He reached the bank of the river in time to see a cloud of blue smoke belch out of the back of the last of their boats, and then, as though they'd never been there at all, the ground-men were gone.

They had taken his brother.

8

SWINGING ALONE

TWICE THE MOON had fattened in the weeks since the
ground-men took Akan, and in his loneliness, Bili felt he
was going half mad.

Always, he got a sense that somebody was behind
him, stalking him through the boughs with the silence of
a shadow. But he soon supposed it was just a symptom of
the unbearable isolation from his own kind, and that he'd
better start getting used to it. After all, a tree-man was
solitary by nature.

Pondering an adult's state of mind was never
something Bili had done in the past, yet now he was out
in the wilds by himself, he wondered if he might be
getting a glimpse of what awaited him once a few more
monsoons had come around. Without company, his
thoughts were going to dim like the light at dusk until, in
the darkness, nothing would remain in his mind but
instinct: forage; mate; rest. No chatter with a sibling. No
questions to probe the truths of the forest.

And certainly no pictures to devise.

His nightly creations were just about all that linked
Bili to his former life in the basin. Each evening, when the
sky came aglow with pinks and purples, he went to
ground to gather what he could, working fast to capture

the likeness of some flower or insect or fruit before heDamang up to a nest built with care. But without any audience, he had to imagine what might be said of his pictures, and he saw his brother, with a finger hooked over his lower lip, labouring to make sense of one but always getting there in the end.

As Bili sat slumped now in the fork of a mangowood, sheltering from the fierce heat, he ached for Akan. That dreadful day played over and over in his mind; even when he closed his eyes to rest, he relived it all: the burning trees; the ruins of the ground-men's dwellings collapsing in flames onto the grass; his descent down the pathway tree as fire consumed it fully; his frantic scramble to the river on which poor Akan was being carried away on a boat.

The clearing had been so foggy that day with the choking fumes of burned foliage, but he'd managed to find his way onto the pebble beach, and had gone straight into the water, hopeful he might be able to chase after his brother. But the river was deep, and the current strong, and he knew if he surrendered to it, he would drown for sure. So, with the flames creeping ever closer, he could do nothing but wait in the shallows for a pole of bamboo to drift by, and when it finally did, he jammed it into the bed of the river, before climbing to the top of it and vaulting himself across to the adjacent bank.

The hazy air waiting on the other side had been just clean enough that he could breathe without fear of a smoky powder clinging to his nostrils and throat. But on each horizon, in walls of grey-white smoke that billowed up into the sky, many more blazes awaited.

And that was when he'd realised that the fire of the land-orang grasslands was not an isolated incident:

Amid so severe a drought, the whole rainforest was catching.

Bili shuddered to remember the feeling of panic that day. But that was unhelpful to dwell upon now, so he hoisted himself up out of the mangowood's fork, then shimmied down to the underbrush to pick fallen nuts off the sloping forest bed.

As he sat there chewing, trying his best not to ponder how wretchedly alone he was, he suddenly felt vibrations in the soil. Something was moving on the other side of the rise. And it was *heavy*.

Quietly, he rose from the ground. He limited his time in the canopy during these haze-choked days – even the mid-trees were a challenge – but it was risky to approach a large animal any other way than from above, so he climbed the steep buttress roots of an ironwood and advanced with caution to the peak of the hill.

On the other side of the rise, at its foot, a female forest elephant was stripping leaves. It was obvious she was in a worried state, and as she stepped forward to strip the leaves off a branch, Bili saw why: she had a calf with her.

Since a glimpse of these gentle giants was rare, Bili forgot about his journey and dropped down to the hidden side of the rise's ridge, where he saw, advancing sideways across the soil below, the infant's bottom half. A flurry of questions began swirling in Bili's mind: what were its ears like? Were they floppy and wing-like, as its mother's were? What about its horns? Were they banana-shaped? And the trunk! Could it wield it with the same dexterity as an adult?

When the mother made a stride forward, Bili was suddenly afforded a view of the infant's adorable face, and he let out an involuntary hoot of laughter. At once, the mother stepped backward to shield her child and her wide head turned his way. The hill protected Bili against a charge, but if she saw another creature sneaking by so close, she might be tempted to sound an alarm, and any kind of chaos could follow.

But Bili stayed concealed and, eventually, the adult elephant stepped forward again. A ripping sound signalled she'd resumed feeding: he'd gotten away with it. But he wasn't done looking at the infant just yet.

Further along the ridge was a tree whose flared base appeared just tall enough to hide a young orang. With the stealth of a clouded leopard, Bili inched across to it. Then, when he was sure he hadn't been discovered, he braved another glance.

With its little trunk, the infant was nudging a stick-bug on the forest floor, and when it took to the sky in panic, the startled calf gave a cry and bolted beneath his mother's leathery underside, and, once again, Bili's view was blocked.

He crept around to the other side of the tree. Underfoot, the ground was uneven; to balance himself, Bili brought his foot up and rested it on the wood of the trunk. Since the infant was over the shock now, it emerged from out of the shade of the female, and Bili shifted his weight in order to track its next movements. But as he did so, his foot, which had actually been propped up by a rotten section of bark, crashed through into a hollow – where a nest of leeches was waiting.

As quickly as he could, Bili pulled his foot out, observing, with total horror, that his entire lower leg was now covered by the wriggling parasites, with many of them already feasting on his blood.

He screamed with fright, immediately eliciting a deafening blast from the female, who ran off into the dense hills with her child in tow, bringing to an end Bili's time with the forest elephants.

He patted down his leg with urgency, pulling away the attached leeches, which left round spots of blood where their mouths had attached to his skin. Every fibre of him groaned with revulsion, and he had to try hard not to simply drop to the ground and begin crying.

Instead, his shoulders slumped as he lamented the precious little calf. Still, he'd got to see it, at least.

And that made today one of the good days.

Meetings with the rarer residents of the forest were victories of a kind, and ever since circumstances had forced him to swing by himself, Bili made sure to feel thankful whenever one occurred.

There'd been an encounter, weeks ago now, with a pangolin, who'd done so much to bring a little peace to a mind addled with angst. Pangolins were relatively common, but since this particular creature was the first animal to acknowledge Bili in the days after fleeing the burning clearing, it gave him comfort to know he wasn't entirely alone. As the scaly fellow licked up ants with its long tongue, it had not only tolerated Bili, but actively engaged with him. But no sooner had they begun to play than a thick plume of smoke drifted across to where they sat, and the pangolin rolled itself into a tight ball, and couldn't be persuaded to come out again.

It was seven more dawns until he saw the tarsier. Nearing the end of a day made taxing for the constant rain of ash, Bili had just gone into the trees to make his nest when he caught, out of the corner of his eye, a tuft of hair at the end of a long tail. Following it up the sapling, Bili saw the little beast clinging on, and he locked eyes with the massive circles of the creature's own for a while until the burning haze forced an early twilight, at which time the tarsier vanished with a single, impressive leap.

Next came the rhinoceros, but the encroaching line of flame saw to it that he couldn't get near enough – which was especially disappointing. But then, as today, he told himself that a glimpse was better than nothing, and when he went to sleep that night, he held onto the image of that squat, powerful animal, keeping it alive in his mind until he drifted off into oblivion.

Half a moon had gone by until the next encounter. Staying as close as he could to the river, Bili came to a brackish tributary hosting a mangrove forest, and there a troupe of fat-nosed monkeys were lounging in the trees, their round bellies gurgling as they digested bitter young leaves. Starved of any company for so long, Bili knew he was risking antagonising the animals, but they tolerated him, either because they failed to view him as a threat, or because their feast had left them listless. He climbed up and sat beside some females and their young, and though there was nothing for him to eat, he was happy enough just to be with them, and he adopted their sluggish way throughout the heat of the afternoon until, at the command of a male, they all sprang off the tree and were suddenly gone.

And that was it until today, when the elephants brought just an ember of cheer to a heart frozen with loneliness.

Spots on his leg were still trickling blood where he'd plucked off the leeches, and as he dangled now from a bough and cleaned them up with a wetted finger, Bili suddenly heard a snapping of branches on his left side.

A tingle of excitement washed through him: the elephants were coming by again!

As slowly as he possibly could, he hoisted himself onto the bough and shuffled along to the trunk. The hazy air affected how sound travelled, and when some more twigs ripped, he wasn't sure in which direction to look, so he lay flat on his belly, and strained to see the movement in the bushes. Then a hoot of greeting sounded, and Bili realised the traveller was actually above him.

He looked up to see one of his own kind, and his eyes filled with tears. He'd wondered if he'd ever meet another tree-person again.

The orang dropped down to him and introduced herself as Diah. Stirred by pity, she reached out and began to groom the hair on Bili's head.

'Why are you alone?' she asked. 'Shouldn't you be with your mother?'

Bili tried his best not to let Diah see his tears, but they streamed as he replied to her questions. 'My mother has a new child growing now, so I left the basin with my brother.'

Diah's face contorted. 'What is the basin?'

'The basin is where we grew up. A whole bowl of forest sat inside a ring of high rocky ridges. Haven't you been there? You really must go. It's the most beautiful place you could ever imagine.'

'I'd like to,' said Diah. 'Where is it?' But Bili realised with a deflated droop that he really didn't know.

'And where's your brother now?'

'He fell. Some land-orangs picked him up and took him onto the river.'

'Did he die?'

'I don't think so. But he was badly hurt.'

'Oh,' said Diah, her lips lifting into a warm smile. 'Well, they've either made a pet of him or taken him to the sanctuary.'

'What's the sanctuary?'

'It's a place for orphans and the injured and for creatures who've lost their home. Land-orangs go around the forest in search of them. Then, when they've made them all better, they usually let them out again.'

'And that's where my brother is?'

'Maybe. There's going to be a lot of animals heDamang there with these fires.'

Bili looked sadly at his hands, still blistered from where he'd jabbed the flaming branch into his father's side. The wound on the right one was open again where he'd swung out on a rough length of vine.

He let out a forlorn hoot. 'I don't like fire.'

'Nobody likes it, boy.'

'When's it going to stop?'

'Hard to say. Even if we get some rain, it won't put out the peatlands. Once that boggy soil catches, it will burn for moons. Say,' said Diah, lifting Bili's chin with her finger, 'what are you looking so guilty about?'

Bili averted her eye. 'I think my brother caused all this. He got angry at my picture.'

Diah hooted with laughter. 'Silly thing! Your brother? This is the work of land-orangs, boy. They burn their fields. They think they can control flame. But no creature can control the wind. As soon as the breeze blows, it lifts the fire right out of their clearings and into the forests. And if the trees are dry from too little rain,' she added, sweeping her arm across the horizon, 'this happens.'

'But how will I find the sanctuary? Is it far?'

'It is far, yes. But it's on the river. If you follow the slope of the hill westwards, sooner or later you'll come to the busy territories of the ground-men. Be warned, though. With these fires, sticking to the river is going to be difficult.'

Diah then began to descend. 'Take my advice: fire spreads faster than you can imagine. Don't let yourself become encircled by it. I'm going to find breakfast now, so I'll wish you good luck, boy.'

'Wait!' called Bili. 'How do you know about the sanctuary, anyway?'

'Because I was one of its orphans. My mother was killed when ground-men burned our forest.'

And with that, Diah swung away.

⁃

Today was a *very* good day.

Making his way now through the scrubby underbrush of a heath forest, Bili was filled with hope that he might again encounter Diah or the elephant and her calf. He chuckled to recollect his earlier scream; if he should ever be so lucky to see forest elephants again, he'd take extra special care where he rested his clumsy feet. The last thing he needed was another mosquito cloud like the one hovering around the bloody blotches the leeches had left.

The sandy soil of the heath grove was adorned with whole swathes of pitcher plants looking to bait a meal, and led Bili back into the deep green of old forest. He suspected the day was nearing its end – it was impossible to know with skies so permanently corrupted with burning haze – meaning soon it would be time to nest.

He entered into the trees, but was taken aback to learn this wasn't forest at all: it was merely an island. Ahead of him, just a single ironwood's height away, was another edge. Advancing forwards on a single swing, a particular scent came wafting through the sub-canopy, bringing Bili to a sudden halt. Worry dipped his brow. Had the fires found him?

Carefully, but with urgency, he swung on low boughs until he reached the outer skin of trees, and his heart quickened at the sight of a land-orang village standing in the clearing beyond. Had he come already to the sanctuary Diah had spoken of?

Keeping himself concealed from the eyes of the ground people as they went about their business, Bili observed their world from out of the canopy. Some cultivated tracts were spread over dusty plains, dotted between the few wooden structures. Muddy patches were located here and there, where buffalo chewed grass. Distantly, several female land-orangs were tending to fruit and vegetable crops, while, on a field in the centre of the village, children were chasing a ball in a game that looked to Bili to be rather fun. The males were clustered around a contained form of flame, over which flesh was cooking.

This wasn't the place Diah had described, though. It was too small, and was barely any distance upriver.

It was, however, large enough to stand as an obstacle on his route along the waterway. He mulled going around the village, but as he hung in the treetops he saw that the other direction was marked by a line of thick smoke. Moving closer to an inferno was not an option – as such, he knew the only way to get into the next section of rainforest was *through* this village.

It was possible the land-orangs wouldn't mind him. But could the same be said of their dogs, whose barks were heavy with menace even now, when there appeared to be nothing to bark about?

He shuffled along the wide limb, and went as deep as he could into the cluster to eye a nest for the night. If the activity of the land-orangs grew quiet in the dark hours, he could maybe chance it then, but for now it would do to get some rest and leave them in peace to finish their day.

A hollowness in his belly, however, drove Bili lower for a quick snack of leaves, and as he reached the mid-trees his eye was drawn to something moving in the nook of the buttress routes.

A sole ground-man was down there. A little one. It was an infant, and he was making a strange sniffing noise. What was he doing? And why wasn't he with the others in the clearing they'd cut for themselves?

After a time, it became apparent to Bili that the infant was crying. Water lines washed tracks through his dirty face, and he let out sad whimpers between each of his sniffs.

Slowly, Bili dropped onto the crest of the buttress route. Then, when he was right above the child, he dangled upside down until his face was level with the child's own, and the little land-orang first jumped with shock, then burst into laughter.

'Orang-utan!' said the child. 'Are you Oli's friend?'

Bili came to ground and sat beside the boy, who held out an arm. But before Bili could take hold of it, the child quickly withdrew it again, seemingly questioning the wisdom of the act.

'Anisah took my bird carving,' the child sniffed. 'She

said I'm not allowed to have it, because Nasri gave it to me, and he's a Dayak, not a Muslim. But really she just wants it for herself.'

Bili studied the dark eyes of the child. They were so like his own!

'Nasri says my carving is the Dayak god of war. I really wish Anisah would give it back. It's my favourite toy. I told papa, but he said I have to share nicely, but I don't want to share because it was given just for me.'

Suddenly, the eyes of the boy opened wide with fear as a yell lifted up out of the clearing. It was filled with unmistakable anguish.

'Yahya is coming! Those Dayak thugs have found us!'

In unison, Bili and the boy craned their necks towards the edge of the trees. Little lights, like fireflies, were travelling across the tract and making their way to the dwellings.

But Bili knew enough already about the kind of fireflies that could be held in a hand to understand that something very bad was about to happen.

9

COMING TO

AKAN'S EYES opened to a rushing of green and blue, then flickered shut again.

A dull, constant sound, like a cicada made of machinery, hummed in the space around him, punctured by the voices of creatures not of the forest, which rose and fell in accordance with his consciousness.

Something cool was draped over his body, somewhere; with only a vague sense of himself, he felt as a thing in a dream: formless, fleeting, remote.

After that, black. Time flowed not like the current in a river but in a series of jumps. He emerged from each bout of oblivion to a dull jumble of emotions. He was confused and frightened, but sad, too. There was shame, and regret and – most pronounced of all – anger.

But then it all dimmed completely, and when his eyes opened once again Akan knew he'd been gone a long while this time.

The muscles in his face came back to life with a soft tingle. He scrunched an eye against his cheekbone, pulling up the edge of a mouth that was as blistered as the canopy's leaves, then pumped his brows several times. To his breath he supplied voice, producing a raspy and feeble groan.

It then occurred to him to look around. He didn't have to stare right ahead at the drab stone blocks surrounding him – he could actually sweep his eyes from side to side.

'He's waking up.'

Land-orangs were beside him. Their brown skin stood in high contrast against the white fabric that covered their bodies.

'Hi there,' said the female.

'Glad you could join us,' added the male, placing his hands delicately on his head, soothing him.

Exactly what they wanted was a mystery, but in his sedate state it was of no concern. The female brought her hand onto the back of his own and hooked her thumb beneath his palm. As she lifted it up, Akan watched as the red hair of his arm hung down in front of him; he had no sense that this long limb belonged to him. Down and up. Down and up. Then, on the third repetition, his arm became imbued with his own will, and he resisted her control.

'Good! You've got it. Now, let's see if you can manage solid food.'

Akan felt the mango in his mouth that the male held for him. He pushed his tongue around the fruit's side, feeling its curve, but he didn't know what to do next. The female gently lifted his lower jaw higher for him, severing the fruit in half. Chew. He was supposed to chew.

With a slow, unenthusiastic motion, Akan began to eat, and as the sweetness brought life to the soft parts of his mouth and throat, so did it awaken a sharper sense of his being here in this moment.

Just where was *here,* though? There were four walls around him, their grey blocks spaced apart by thin and perfectly straight white lines. Above was a roof made from stripped branches, from which a blade was hanging that whirred as it rotated and produced a pleasant breeze across his body. In the middle of the blocks was a tall rectangle of wood, closing off the outside world from his view. Through its cloudy glass, he could see that greenery was beyond this structure, and a sudden longing to be among it overwhelmed him.

What was he doing here? He searched his memory, but couldn't find anything to help him figure it out. In fact, he couldn't find much of anything at all, and his heart began to race with panic as he considered he didn't know who he was.

But the heavy bursts of air that blew out from his nostrils began to calm as he remembered the vast slopes of a bowl filled with mighty ironwoods. As he chewed the rest of the mango – and happily accepted the offering of more – he let that image linger in his mind's eye. A ring of high rocky peaks encircled the forested inner sides, and a river ran right into the heart of it.

Yes!

That was the basin!

That was his home.

He remembered endless shades of green in a forest canopy. And bright dapples of light on the ground far below. There were vines that hung from the air, twisting and turning as though in a battle with themselves, and vast fronds that fanned out where younger trees had managed to compete with the old growth of the rainforest.

And creatures: there were creatures of every size, shape and colour that expressed themselves through every conceivable sound. Flying things that cheeped; swinging things that barked; slithering things that hissed; bouncing things that croaked. There were silent inhabitants, too – at least, silent to the ears of an orang; beneath every single leaf was a crawler; inside each and every flower a hoverer.

Yet that magnificent world stood empty in his mind of creatures like him. Furrowing with concentration, he tried – and failed – to determine with whom he shared that place.

Although Akan's stomach was filling, a feeling of emptiness was invDamang the rest of him. He was like one of those palm trees: hollow on the inside. There *must* be another like him. His head slumped back in despair, rolling around to rest in the valley of his shoulder. And as it did, he saw again the red-brown of his bright hair, and he suddenly remembered her.

He wasn't alone! He had a mother! Ivie, was her name. She wrapped him in her arms when he was small, and cuffed him when his play became too boisterous. The trace of a smile spread on his lips as he recounted the time she blew air against his nose. She'd bring her face closer, imitating a kiss, but just before her lips met his own she'd send a puff of air right into his eyes, and he'd roll away, hooting with laughter and slapping his hands against the dry earth of the forest floor.

They used to nest together. He'd hold onto her underside as she climbed the tree. Hanging upside down, she grabbed this way and that at branches, which she fashioned adeptly into a shallow pocket, and together they'd lay throughout the night, beneath the pale light of the moon, her softly expanding and contracting with her breaths, and him so excited to think of the fun awaiting them after the coming of the dawn.

That was how it was, then. There were just the two of them.

So where was she now? Had she brought him here to see this pair of land-orangs who washed the right side of his head and dressed it in cloth? She was waiting on the other side of that wooden rectangle, perhaps.

His eyes began to droop once again as he felt the lure of oblivion. And he was on the very cusp of crossing over into it when, from outside the structure, a shrill shriek sounded, and he remembered with terror that, along with his mother and him, a bird dwelt in the basin, too.

A mighty kite, he was, with feathers the same colour as his own hair, and a head of brightest white.

Lang. That was his name. He was the Bird-King.

He was the spirit of war.

＊

As time passed, the ground-men gave Akan less of their attention. They'd push open the wooden rectangle and enter, but it was only ever to give him banana and mango – never to reunite him with his mother.

He was pleased when the land-orangs ceased stabbing his leg with their sharp point. It was a sensation he hated – but in the absence of it, it seemed as though his whole body began to hurt. First, there was a dull throb that rDamaated from his upper leg where it had been wrapped in a hard casing. This screamed with pain whenever he put weight on it, so he remained as he was, horizontal on the soft shelf. His ribs ached, too – though, again, if he limited his movement, it didn't cause him too much trouble.

Less easy to ignore, however, was the pain at the side of his head. It was strong enough at times to make him feel sick. There was even a day when it made the very act of opening his eyes unbearable, so he'd lay back, blind to the coming and going of the land-orangs as they got on with their business. But the morning after it wasn't quite so severe, and he'd managed to keep his eyes open all day, and in the days that followed, he found he could tolerate it just a little bit more.

Akan wondered constantly why the side of his face hurt so much and why the ground-men dressed his head in cloth every day. One morning, they brought in with them a piece of reflective glass, and placed it in his hand. He held it in front of himself while the female land-orang unfurled the white fabric from around his head.

After he saw himself, he no longer wondered where

his pain came from. To the side of his eye, just above the temple, was a wound. Though it was freshly healed-over, it had left behind an angry red scar that spread like a web from a central point right up his forehead and down to his ear. He lifted a finger; it stung to brush the scar, but he continued to paw at it, again and again until the male leaned closer and pulled his hand away.

'In a few weeks,' the man said to him, 'there'll be no sign of a broken leg or fractured ribs. But *that* you're going to have forever.'

The web-like scar on his head wasn't the only way Akan had changed. Along his left side, whole clumps of his hair were missing. The exposed areas prickled uncomfortably, especially in the middle of the day when it was hottest, and the skin was fibrous and coarse like the bark of a coconut palm.

But as it had come, so did the pain eventually subside, and one day they took him through the tall rectangle of wood.

He'd spent so long wondering what was on the other side of the walls, and now he could see for himself that he was in a forest. Only, it wasn't a forest, since it was somehow *contained* within something else. Like the neat stone blocks of the structure, some boundary existed around this place.

Alone in a little yard, Akan grabbed at the net surrounding him. Although he couldn't get out, he took comfort to know nothing else could get in, and he spent long periods in his wheeled chair looking through the gaps at more nets, in which other creatures lived. The sky thronged with their voices: whistles and squawks and yelps and roars joined bleating, cheeping, chittering and chirping. Very occasionally, Lang shrieked.

One hot morning, when the hazy air was filled with an unpleasant stench of burning, the land-orangs took the hard casing off his leg, and lifted him out of his chair. Sitting on actual soil was a delight, but they wouldn't allow him to revel in the sensation long, for they quickly had him up on his feet.

They held him in his armpits while he took his first strides. His legs were tired – and the left one was sore – and he couldn't get to the netting without taking a break at first, but the longer the land-orangs spent with him, the better he could stay up, and eventually he didn't rely on their support anymore.

When that time came, he longed to climb. In his enclosed yard, the only chance to do this was if he pulled himself onto the ledge that sat at the foot of the glass, but it was unsatisfying. Still, he needn't have been frustrated: as soon as the ground-men found him on top of the wooden rectangle, they smiled at one another.

'You're ready to go into the main enclosure with the others,' they said, and they took his hands in their own, and led him out along a pathway to where a group of orangs just like him were waiting.

⁓

Throughout that first afternoon, the others kept back from Akan.

This was a huge relief. Since he didn't really understand his own nature, it stood to reason that he didn't understand theirs either. It may be the case that they were an aggressive species, and with his injuries only just healed he wasn't sure whether he would be nimble or quick enough to make an escape.

At the thought of breaking out, Akan surveyed the space with his eyes. This yard was bigger than the other one, but he was still enclosed; if the other orangs had a quarrel with him, there would be no choice but to confront them.

Only when the sun began to lower, with the horizon flushing with colour, did Akan stop worrying about being ambushed. The land-orangs had come by with fruit and leaves, causing the enclosure's residents to gather near the netted front side. Driven by his hunger, Akan approached too, and the other forest-men didn't seem bothered at all when he snatched away a bunch of bananas. So, rather than scuttle off to eat them in peace, he lingered with them.

When all the food was gone, a couple of the younger ones came across to check him out. 'What happened to your head?'

Akan shrugged. 'Don't know.'

'Why?'

'I can't remember things. One day I woke up and I was here.'

The youngsters gave squeals of laughter.

'What is this place, anyway?' asked Akan.

'Park.'

'No it's not,' protested the littler of the pair.

His companion gave his head a playful slap. 'What is it, then?'

'It's a zoo.'

Akan hooked his fingers over his lip in confusion.

Then a third – deeper – voice began grumbling from the lifeless tree in the enclosure's centre. 'It's a sanctuary.'

Akan looked around. Hanging from the tree's one bough was a large black circle, and in it, an adult male was swinging. His moon-shaped face pads indicated he was older than the others.

'Many different creatures are brought here,' continued the large male. 'Some, they let out again. But most of us live out our lives in these enclosures.'

Akan moved closer to the young pair and muttered softly. 'Who's that?'

'Mali. He's been here longest.'

The pair introduced themselves as Ari and Riz, but before Akan had the chance to ask them any more questions, they hastily moved off inside a wooden dwelling at the enclosure's edge.

Akan peered around. Most of the other orangs were in the tree in the corner, a sorry old mangowood that was in the last phase of its life. They hung from branches in silence; with the horizon now yellowing, he knew he ought to get off the ground, too. Instinct told him it was unwise to join Mali in his tree, so he went to the others, and in the mangowood's bare and exposed top, he longed for some branches to pull into a nest.

When it was almost dark, Mali swung down from the central tree and made his way into the same hut Ari and Riz had vanished into earlier. Seeing the adult do this, the other orangs in the far corner came down too, and followed him inside. What was in there? Why didn't they wish to stay in the open?

Overcome with curiosity, Akan shuffled back down the trunk and onto the bare ground. Walking on his knuckles, he went over to the edge, noticing that the wooden hut was marked with a single circular hole. Nervously, he stuck his head through.

Inside the dwelling, all the tree-men were resting on piles of grass and twigs. Several unclaimed piles stood by themselves, awaiting, he supposed, the others. Was he meant to go in there, too?

After so long confined behind the stone blocks of the walls, Akan relished the chance to sleep in a tree – even one without a single leaf growing on it – so he turned his back on the hut. He gingerly walked around the perimeter, checking the net to confirm his suspicion that there was indeed no way through to the other side. Then he went back to where the land-orangs had set down food earlier, and rummaged among the skins and stalks. What was he supposed to do now? He wanted more to eat, yet there was nothing to be had.

From nearby, a sudden commotion struck up. This was the song of the gibbons, and since it reminded him of home, his heart filled with sadness and yearning. Why hadn't his mother come yet?

By now it was so dark that he cast no shadow, and as he was still too energetic to lay on the bough for sleep, Akan went to the central tree to investigate the black circle. He shuffled along the limb, and performed a backward roll off it, catching himself when his arms were fully extended. He smiled. It was good to know he could do something like that.

He pulled himself back up, and stood on the bough, ready to perform his trick again, but this time into the circle itself. But before he could get the chance, Mali kicked him off the branch.

He hadn't even heard him coming, which was too bad, because now the adult male was angrily lashing out at his face and head, scratching and biting and digging his elbows into Akan's already-sore sides.

So vicious was the attack, that if a land-orang hadn't shown up at that very moment with tools and a small wheeled bucket, Mali would almost certainly have killed him.

10

EMBERS OF VIOLENCE

ROOTED to the forest floor by terror, on the edge of the ground-men's village, chill bumps stood up on Bili's arms.

The same voice that had called out so fearfully before yowled now a second time – 'Yahya is here! Run!' – and at once, the female villagers screeched shrilly, and the children began to wail.

Bili watched the little land-orang beside him, who crept, on careful, purposeful strides, deeper into the hardwoods. It seemed to Bili that his infant companion was looking for just the right tree; when he found it, the boy pressed his body tightly into it.

Taking hold of a woody vine, Bili hoisted himself up onto a limb. Sitting with his feet dangling down, he watched blankly as the strange scene unfolded in the open tracts.

A new set of land-orangs appeared at the dwellings, wearing strips of yellow fabric around their foreheads. In their hands, they clutched all manner of tools. Some were sharp. Some were hard. Some flickered at the end with tongues of orange flame, like oversized fireflies.

A man with a hairless head and menacing eyes called out. 'Bring me the head of the village!'

There commenced a scramble among the folk of the clearing. Into the huts they vanished until, a short while later, a man emerged and went and stood before the arrivals. The lines scored in his face, coupled with his slight build, told Bili this was an elderly individual.

'What is it?' said the old male. 'Why have you come here, Yahya?'

'Our boss was stabbed this morning in a restaurant. What do you know about it?'

'That's a question for the police, friend.'

'Don't take us for fools. Everybody knows you Madura dogs paid off the police already. Now, where's Budi?' His voice suddenly rose, and he barked into the hot evening air. 'Budi, you scoundrel! Come out! Let's do this the easy way, huh?'

'Listen to me, Yahya,' said the elderly male. 'With God as my witness, Budi is not with us.'

There followed a volley of shouting from the mouths of the yellow fabrics, its fierceness enough to make Bili's blood run cold as he went down to sit beside the boy on the forest floor.

'Show yourself, scoundrel!' went the voice of the smooth-headed man. 'Come on out, or we'll burn you out!'

The tension fascinated Bili. It was as though a sickness had spread around the village folk, a kind of bug so virulent and powerful it could be held in the palm of his hands. Seconds beat on with an unbearable weight as the ground people eyed one another with worry.

Even the child seemed to be infected by it. He shuffled nearer, squeezing into Bili and resting his little head in the crook of the orang's shoulder, and in that moment, Bili questioned the wisdom of allowing this closeness.

Certain creatures were just so very unpredictable. Gibbons, for instance. Sometimes, all an orang like him had to do was look at one of those long-limbed fellows, and it would flee with unmatchable swiftness off into the canopy. But then, at other times, gibbons allowed him to sit with them in the treetops, and through those brief interactions, Bili came to know the tender way they regarded one another, their preference of leaf – and, above all else, their absolute love for the forest.

But the ground-men were mysterious on a whole other level. The floor dwellers saw in the forest something more like a tool than a home. So content were they in their lives outside the trees that they sought no friends beneath the canopies and, as such, remained almost entirely unknown to its residents. And that made it impossible to trust them.

With caution, Bili extended his arm around the land-orang's neck and cupped his hairless hand in his own. He studied the curved creases that divided each of the boy's little fingers into three segments, then the dirty crescents of the nails at their tips. Given a wisp of red fur, this hand would be almost indistinguishable from his own.

Perhaps their respective kinds weren't all that different. Maybe the ground-men liked pictures, too, and made-up accounts of things that had never happened. Perhaps the boy drummed along with the dripping of rain sometimes, back in the days when rains fell. Sitting so closely to the child, Bili became attuned to the rate at which the infant's heart was beating, observing how closely it matched his own. He smiled: any moment, they were going to synchronise.

But the matching of their heartbeats never occurred, for a terrible, ear-splitting pop rattled through the air then, and the boy's heart suddenly began to race.

Now, the fireflies were no longer elegant points of light: as they hovered along the roofs of the dwellings, they suddenly swelled into wide waves of bright red fury and the sky, once again, began to fill up with the choking stench of burning.

A panicked voice called out. 'Rahimi! Rahimi! Where are you?'

Without delay, the child sprang to his feet and ran out from the trees.

Bili darted up to the highest branches, leaping to the edge to see, where gaps in the smoke allowed it, the extent of the mayhem that followed the brandishing of the glowing sticks. Each of the dwellings was now engulfed, as were the cultivated fields, across which other yellow-fabric men were running. But the panicked village folk didn't seem as concerned about the crops as they did the wooden structures themselves: in what looked to Bili to be a very dangerous endeavour, they were going inside these, pulling out onto the dry soil their tools and other treasures.

The newcomers with their yellow fabric were making it difficult for them, however. Some were swinging crescent-shaped blades of metal this way and that, driving the villagers out of the clearing and over to the trees on the other side.

'Please, Yahya!' the villagers cried. 'The government granted us this land! We have every right to be here!'

'You sacrificed that right when Budi killed our boss! Now we will take back what is rightfully ours!'

What happened next happened suddenly. Some of the villagers turned back to face the tool-wielding arrivals, and the yellow fabric men lashed out with their fists and feet to pummel the faces and stomachs of the males. Many of the females, meanwhile, rushed back to the flaming dwellings, desperately trying to get inside before all that remained was ash.

A flash of flame fired from the end of a metal tube, which emerged with a dreadful bang. Bili watched as one female came running over to scoop away the little land-orang; by now the rest of her companions had vanished into the forest on the other side of the clearing. As the female hurried off after them with the little boy bouncing in her arms, something seemed to attract her eye, and she suddenly halted. 'No, Luqman!' she yelled. 'Leave it, son! None of it matters!'

The male she was addressing was young, and had a face just like the child's. But a grimace of anger betrayed the strength of his feeling, and he fought back against the yellow fabrics with a chaotic swinging of arms and legs, until a swift crack around the head sent him toppling onto the ground, where three other males were quick to leap onto his back.

The bald-headed man took the fallen youngster by the hair.

'Go for it, Yahya!' yelled his friends.

He hoisted back the young man's head. Then he took out a pointy tool, whose shiny surface reflected the inferno of the dwellings, and pressed into the throat of the immobilised male as he lay flat upon the dusty clearing.

'No!' screamed the female.

'Brother!' wailed the little boy.

'Tell Budi we're coming for him!' yelled the man with the smooth head, and he swiped the tool from one side to the other, sending blood flowing to the ground. While the young land-orang thrashed his legs and beat his free fist against the soil, the bald-headed male continued to rock the blade this way and that until there was no more flailing.

A cheer went up among the yellow fabrics. Then Bili noticed an unusual phenomenon, something he'd never before encountered in the world of the ground dwellers:

The young man's head and body stood apart from one another.

The cruel-eyed individual called out into the trees. 'We're coming for you!'

Another cheer.

'We're taking back what is ours!'

Another.

'You slash and burn our fields! We slash and burn

you! And we won't stop until every last one of you is back in Madura and our land is returned to us!'

Bili wrapped his arms around his own head, hoping it might suffice as a substitute for a hug; he longed for his mother, and his brother. Through a gap in the crook of his elbow, he watched as the rest of the villagers retreated into the forest, leaving just a few of their companions laying in the dirt. Like the younger adult, their heads stood apart from their bodies, too.

The newcomers wasted no time spreDamang across the clearing. In the buffalo patches, they sliced the throats of the animals, and somehow brought an abrupt end to the yapping of the tethered dogs. Whichever crops were not yet aflame, they swiftly set alight. Then the full group reassembled in the central field which just a short time ago had hosted children gleefully playing.

There was a sense of glee now, too. But it was of a complex nature, and Bili couldn't understand it. The yellow fabrics jumped up and down, pumping their fists high in the air. 'Dayak land for Dayaks!' they called out, musically. 'Down with the Madurese!'

†

Sleep eluded Bili as the dark hours wore on.

By now, he was used to being awake at night; at various times between dusk and dawn, his brain would activate, eager to know if Akan was back and nesting nearby. In the early days of his solitude, such interruptions had been terrible for Bili's energy levels, but now he barely noticed it.

As he passively endured the passing of this night, Bili kept perfectly still on a high bough, noting everything that rustled, waiting for the first opportunity to move on. At one point, a twig snapped beneath the force of something heavy – or so he thought; when he turned to look, nothing was there. It was just the madness of loneliness stalking him once again.

His sole concern was getting to the river. Diah had been clear: to stand any chance of finding Akan, he had to find the sanctuary – and that meant hugging as close to its banks as possible. But the only way to the water was across this clearing, and that remained blocked by the yellow fabric land-orangs who'd replaced the original inhabitants.

With the dreadful mayhem now over, the newcomers were in raucous good cheer; at this rate, it was likely they'd carry on until the sun came up. They lay around slaking a thirst which seemingly couldn't be quenched; it seemed to Bili that the more they drank, the more insensible they grew. They sang slurred words, and though some of them did eventually curl up to sleep beside the smouldering embers of the burned-down dwellings, there were always more who wished to talk, or sing, or quarrel.

Finally, things did calm. The chattering voices grew silent, leaving only a single one who sang drearily to himself, and though the situation was far from ideal, it was enough to convince Bili to head to ground. So, on light feet, he crept through the trees, passing beyond the spot where he and the boy had sat together, then entered at last into the open.

He came to the first of the villagers, whose eyes were fixed open as though he were looking very intensely up at the stars. Bili waited for any sign of movement from the fallen male, but since none came, he crept further onward.

At the halfway point between the two forested sections, Bili froze. Something to his right was shuffling along the dusty clearing. Faintly silhouetted against the embers of the burned dwellings was a land-orang, who'd risen from his slumber and was staggering toward a coconut palm. Bili's heart thumped in his chest while he watched the lone male prop himself against the trunk. A splashing of liquid sounded, then, to Bili's immense relief, the man dropped back onto the ground beside his snoring companions.

Up ahead was another body. Again, Bili held back, anxious that the individual may sit up at any moment. But he needn't have worried, since the twisted angles of the broken individual made it unlikely he'd ever get up again.

Step by careful step, he narrowed the gap to his target: the field at the edge of the clearing. His confidence began to grow: the land-orangs, now a real distance from him, were no longer a threat.

Waiting for him at the field, however, was a new problem. The smouldering crops were wider than they'd appeared from afar, and stretched from the burned dwellings right to the edge of the river itself. A squeak of frustration spilled from Bili's lips. The entrance to the forest stood just a short distance away, yet while the blackened vegetation belched smoke, he risked burning his feet reaching it.

He was going to have to get creative.

With extreme caution, he approached the rubble of the villager's huts, finding, upon a pile of rubbish, a bunch of palm fronds. An idea began to take shape in his mind – but before he could act upon it, a voice yelled out from the darkness.

'Who's that sneaking around over there?'

Bili gripped several of the fronds and lifted them off the heap, causing a pile of spindly bamboo poles to suddenly slip. With a clatter, they rolled beneath his feet, prompting an outpouring of angry yells.

'Wake up, Yahya! It's that pig, Budi! He thinks he can ambush us!'

'Stop him!'

A smashing of glass sounded. The land-orangs were throwing missiles. With no time to shield himself from the exploding shards, Bili lumbered as quickly as his legs would carry him back to the smouldering crops.

He threw one of the palm fronds down flat, and walked out on the bridge he'd made, which barely protected him from the heat of the burned earth. At the end of the leafy stalk, he lay down the next frond and hopped across, repeating the process a third and fourth time.

'That's it! You pair had better run, whoever you are!' yelled the bald-headed man. 'If I catch either of you here again, I'll cut off your miserable heads, too!'

Finally, Bili made it across to the trees. Coursing with excited energy, he went at once up the nearest trunk. Footsteps were close beneath him – one of them must have followed – but he wasn't worried now: in forest, no ground-man would ever catch him.

On his long arms, Bili swung further and further away from that terrible place. Was all their territory like that? Land-orangs seemed entirely unable to share the same space. The clearing *was* small, but there was more than enough ground for them all to share. So why had one group been so insistent on driving away the other?

He remembered what Diah had said about the 'sanctuary', about how it could be found in a busy place. Even greater numbers of land-orangs would dwell there – which would mean even worse strife among its residents. A lump formed in Bili's throat as he imagined poor Akan caught up in the middle of their violent affairs. But that supposed his brother had even survived the fall.

A flicker of light up ahead caught his eye, and Bili settled on a limb for a moment. He was back in an unbroken expanse of real forest now, where such light wasn't usual. Whatever its source, it would need to be approached with great care.

Remaining high, Bili altered his course, leaving the river on his left side. As he neared the light, his apprehension grew: had the wildfires made it this far so soon? He sniffed the air. Although a smokiness was present in the treetops, it was far too faint to be of any real concern.

He went lower. Now just above the ground, he pivoted his body from sapling to palm, taking care to release each stem of foliage carefully in order to minimise noise.

Land-orangs were here. It was the folk who'd left the village. Sheltering beneath a stretched out sheet of fabric, they sat around a low flame. Although they were being quiet, every now and then a tormented wail disturbed the peace of the deep forest.

The little boy, his eyes heavy with worry, was seated beside his mother, clutching hold of her the way Akan used to clench Aunt Ivie. Bili watched him awhile, until another sight drew his eye away. A small creature, with red-brown hair just like his own, was tethered to the items the people had hauled with them.

Bili was nervous about being on the ground in the absence of sunlight, but crouched low in the underbrush and moved as slowly as he could across to the bundle of possessions, where the tether was fastened to a spike in the ground. He gave the rope around it three firm tugs – and then something surprising happened: a very young orang appeared.

Bili gave a hushed squeak. 'Who are you?'

But the infant said nothing.

'What's your name?'

'Oli.'

'How old are you?'

'Three monsoons.'

'Why are you journeying with the land-orangs?'

Blankly, the infant stared.

'Where's your mother?'

'No mama.'

A voice, calm but anguished, came from the other side of the mound. 'Be quiet, pet!'

Bili, happy just to see another of his own kind once again, continued his interrogation. 'Where are you going?'

'Home burned. We go forest now.'

Studying the thin piece of rope around Oli's neck, Bili felt he could free him. But when he brought his hands closer to the little creatures neck, he let out a hoot of fright, prompting a second outburst from the land-orangs.

'Hush, pet! Rahimi, go play with him. We can't have him drawing attention to us.'

A rustling sounded from the pile of possessions. The young land-orang had come. He and Bili smiled at one another.

Oli leapt into the arms of the boy, whose sad mouth upturned just slightly. When Bili reached out his own hand and took hold of the boy's as he'd done earlier, the little land-orang's smile rose even higher. And in that moment, Bili knew how he could help this lost and frightened group.

He heard Diah in his memory. 'It's a place for orphans and the injured and for creatures who've lost their home.'

Brushing his fingertip gently down the tracks where the boy's tears had streamed, Bili pursed his lips and spoke softly to the infant tree-man.

'You must come with me to where I'm going,' he said. 'You must come with me to the sanctuary.'

11

MELTING MISTS

TO BE BACK behind the stone blocks of those four walls again was, for Akan, a very special kind of suffering.

Over the solitary dawns that followed Mali's attack, the fire of Akan's spirit died down to a mere cinder. A single point of light within a suffocating darkness, not even a star in the night sky was as cold or as dim.

It might be that he'd known worse misery in his life – he still couldn't remember most of it – but his second stint inside this hut was even worse than the first. He'd been privileged with ignorance, then. The days had passed that much faster, as he busied his mind with dreams of what lay beyond the walls. One day, he'd told himself, he'd be back among the splendour of the forest, sheltering in its dense greenness as monsoon rains cooled the air and soothed his soul. It didn't matter how long it took, he'd reasoned, because a time was coming when he would be free to climb into the canopy once more, to snack on berries, to clamber from dawn until twilight as his heart desired.

There was hope, then.

But now, there was a bully called Mali, and a stupid black circle swinging from a tree without life. *That* was the sum total of what he had to look forward to.

On the tenth dawn, the land-orangs took him back to the netted enclosure, and two days after that, his ribs stopped hurting.

This morning, they were bringing Mali back, too. Ari and Riz and the rest of the juveniles were making the most of swinging in the circle while they still could, but Akan remained in the corner, making his mango last by rolling it around in his mouth rather than simply chewing it up and swallowing it.

His interactions with the other orangs had helped Akan to fill in some of the blanks in his memory. He remembered now certain incidents in his childhood, like the time he learned to use a pole to pivot himself across an inlet of their river. His friends had hooted and leapt in circles at the sight of him misjudging the distance and landing in the water with an almighty splash, and after they pulled him out they made him take another shot at it, knowing that he wouldn't make the same mistake again. And he didn't: he was known among the infants of his generation as the best vaulter of them all.

Yet there remained many murky spots in his mind, like patches of pure white morning mist adorning the canopy. He told himself it wasn't a problem, that if a thing was worth remembering, it would come back to him.

What Akan couldn't accept, however, was the blankness surrounding how he came to be here in the first place. Throwing away the mango's stone, he brushed his fingertips against his face, feeling the spidery scar. It had something to do with this, he was sure. And then there were the scaly spots down his side where no hair grew. He'd been injured, that much was obvious. But how? Was he careless on the forest bed, allowing some beast to get at him? Perhaps he'd done the very same thing that had landed him back in the hut: nosed around in the territory of an older and bigger rival.

To have so significant a part of his history remain out

of reach was agonising. There was a place, or an event, or an individual that held special importance in the story of his life so far. Yet whenever he looked for it, he found nothing but a resonance. It was like trying to grab flowing water.

In his frustration, Akan became aware of the tension in his body. His heart quickened, and his fingers clenched into fists, and he found himself grinding his teeth against one another as he futilely surveyed a mental landscape dotted with banks of fog.

With no more mangoes to snack on, Akan stayed in the bare tree throughout the morning. Then, when the sun climbed up into the highest part of the sky, the moment he'd been dreDamang arrived: the land-orangs brought Mali back.

Ari and Riz scurried down from the black circle as though their lives depended on it, which they quite possibly did. Mali, however, bore no grudge – at least, not one that was immediately perceptible. Instead of lashing out and shouting about it, the adult contented himself with an amble around the perimeter of the enclosure.

Eventually, Mali came to the far corner, where Akan was cowering. Ready to leap at the first hint of an attack, Akan's thighs were loaded with springy energy. But Mali showed no sign of aggression; in fact, he now seemed curious about him, and sat a while on the other side of the trunk, eventually moving right up to investigate the wide scar on his head.

Akan let Mali carry on. But he was surprised by just how much ill-feeling was coursing through him: a taught, tingly force that was as potent in his belly as any hunger. Oddly, he felt this same curious energy in his face, too. As long as Mali sat near him, Akan's cheeks prickled; at one point, his nerves registered it as something close to physical pain, as though he were being somehow squeezed, or crushed – and rather than put up with it any longer, he went to play with the younger orangs near the enclosure's front side.

'Mali is sorry for hurting you,' said Ari, absentmindedly shaking Akan's arm where he held it at the wrist. 'You can see it in his eyes.'

Akan bristled, but said nothing back. He turned to face Mali again, and as the adult's eyes flickered to meet his own, a curious thing happened: from out of nowhere, an account appeared in his mind. But it wasn't of his history – it was of an incident he knew had never happened. And he felt a sudden compulsion to share it. 'Want me to tell you how I got this scar on my face?'

'Yes!' squeaked the others. 'Please tell us!'

'Alright. I will. I was struck by lightning.'

His friends' eyes opened wide with shock. 'Lightning? But how?'

'There was a storm. The rain was falling so heavily that whole boughs were falling down from the canopy. My mama was sheltering on this one limb, but the tree was too old, and the limb cracked and she tumbled onto the wet ground, and I knew she was going to get hurt any second so I swung down to protect her. Then a huge rope of lightning came whipping out from the sky, but I jumped in front of it to stop it lashing against mama, and it hit me right here.' He lifted his finger and pointed to his temple.

'So that's how you got scarred on your side too?' said Riz. 'The lightning burned you?'

Akan gave a nod, and was about to add even more details to this false account, when he noticed the ground in front of Riz.

The young tree-man had made a rough circle out of pebbles.

A name suddenly popped into Akan's head.

And that name was Bili.

The afternoon rolled by languorously. Distant thunder rattled the haze-choked skies, but once again, no rain came to slake a land in desperate need of nourishment.

On the other side of the enclosure's net, land-orangs were sweeping leaves from the walkway. Typically, the ground-men who came here were seen once and never again. Whether they were adults or children, they looked through at the orangs with smiles on their faces. It seemed to Akan that they derived a certain pleasure from their fleeting glimpses, though what was so amusing about tree-men in an environment devoid of trees was not quite clear.

Some of the land-orangs, however, were here everyday – like the ones currently sweeping away leaves outside the net. They brought food and water, and wheeled out the poo. They replaced the nests in the wooden hut with new ones, and occasionally they came into the enclosure to sit awhile beside select individuals. Yesterday, they'd sat with Akan. Noticing him alone in the corner of the net, they'd gone over to him, and one of them did something astonishing with a brightly coloured ball: she pressed it into her fist, but when she opened her fingers, it was gone! As if that wasn't amazing enough, she then opened her other fist and, to Akan's complete bafflement, the ball sprang out!

Most days, the regulars contented themselves with their tasks in a carefree manner. Today, though, it was obvious in the lines scoring their faces that something was bothering them. Normally so placid, the chatter that passed between them as they brushed away the leaves was loaded with angst.

'But what are they being accused of exactly?'

'Parading their wealth, apparently.'

'Wealth? Are you kidding? The people from Madura I know don't have two coins to rub together.'

'Yes, but it's not only that. My dad and uncles say the

Madurese are getting more benefits than Dayaks these days. He says we shouldn't put up with it anymore.'

The shorter land-orang frowned and looked at her feet. 'Su-su is from Madura originally, isn't she?'

'Half the staff here are. Mr Tan only pays so low because they're willing to work for it.' She took in a breath of air, deeply. 'You have to admit, people from Madura *are* pretty rude.'

'Su-su speaks her mind, yes. But it's culture. That's just their way.'

'I guess. They don't do themselves any favours though.'

On and on the pair went like this, until Akan ceased to even notice them anymore. Besides, their business was not more significant to him than his own was.

Like the brightly coloured ball conjured out of the air, Bili had burst into Akan's consciousness from nowhere. How utterly mysterious that, in just one moment, his brother should be there in his memory, his entire history now known to him.

As though it were happening in front of his very eyes, Akan could see them together playing, learning, growing. There they were, hopping through the canopy, stealing windfallen durian fruits, imitating the barks of hornbills as best they could while they fell out of the trees laughing.

Yet, it wasn't *all* there. They'd lived a happy life, always so close to each other. But where was he now?

Searching his memories, Bili existed in Akan's mind no later than around the time they found two dead orangs in a cave. He could picture his brother, holding something aloft for his attention – something that made his stomach churn with nausea – but, try as he did, Akan simply couldn't see what it was that Bili was showing him.

After that, there were only vapours of his brother in his recollections. Mere glimpses, they offered Akan nothing that helped with the mystery of his being here, and it made his heart ache to imagine just how they came to actually be separated.

Akan's own injuries had been severe enough that if he'd remained in the wild he almost certainly would have died. On a leg that couldn't support his weight, with ribs that made movement unbearably painful – and with a head wound so bad it had changed his actual appearance – he stood no chance of taking care of himself. But what kind of suffering had his brother endured? It must have been so truly awful that it had killed him, for if he'd survived it, would he too not be right here now in the ground-men's simulation of the natural world?

With the fretful land-orangs now done with their sweeping, Akan, cheered by the return of his brother to his life, went to join the others. Ari and Riz were a degree more aloof around Akan since he'd told them of the lightning. Their reaction to the account, however, gave him a feeling of satisfaction, and as the sunlight dulled into the radiant tones of evening, he span more reports of imagined incidents from his life.

There was the time he'd found the biggest jackfruit ever seen in the basin and hauled it back to share with the other youngsters and his aunties. Then there was the occasion when he saw a lizard so large it could swallow a full-grown male in a single bite. He'd won contests, was commended for his bravery, was widely regarded as the smartest forest person in the whole basin.

But none of that seemed to appeal very much to Ari and Riz, so he dreamt up something more dramatic.

'In the basin, there was a big orang called Iki,' he told them. 'Iki was mean to all of us juveniles. He shooed us away from the figs, and took all the rambutans for himself, and chased around our mothers even though we were still young and they weren't yet ready to grow another child. One day, Iki issued his long call, warning the rest of us males to spread ourselves wide through the forest. Well, the others all quickly took off, but not me. I stayed right where I was.'

'Didn't Iki make himself clear enough?'

'Oh, he made himself clear alright. We were *not* to be here when he arrived. But I didn't agree to that, so I kept on chewing figs by my mother's side. Iki came trudging along the forest bed on his knuckles, and as soon as he looked up and saw me, he leapt up into the ironwood. But I was ready for the chase, and I led him all the way over to the limestone hills where there was a scary cave, and he followed me into the scary cave, and when he got inside I jumped on his back, and using just these' – Akan held aloft his fingers – 'I took Iki's life.'

Ari and Riz looked at each other. 'What do you mean? You took his life using just your fingers? But how?'

Akan smiled, pleased that his account had piqued their interest. But he felt it better to say no more now. This way, they'd want to stay friendly with him.

Ari reached out and brushed Akan's side, on his hairless patches. 'I got burned once,' he said.

Riz's eyes widened. 'You did?'

'Yeah. I saw something in the undergrowth. At first I thought it was just a firefly—'

Firefly?

'—but then I noticed it wasn't moving at all, and that smoke was rising up from it, and I realised a land-orang had dropped it. I wanted to know how it felt, so I slowly reached out my hand.' Ari held out his finger and let it journey downwards through the air, causing Akan's head to jolt to one side. 'But the moment I touched it I got hurt. I'll never try to touch a firefly again.'

Akan became suddenly animated. 'I just remembered! The thing in the cave my brother was holding up – I can see it now! It was a finger!'

'A finger? But, whose?'

Akan's brow furrowed.

'It was... It belonged to... my *bapa*.'

~

The next morning, Akan awoke with a pain in his head.

His wound hadn't bothered him too much, but ever since last evening, when he remembered an adult male with wide cheek pads called Dama, his mood had darkened and the fibrous web of scar tissue on the right side of his face began to needle.

None of the others were up yet, so he made his way off his pretend nest and left the wooden hut. Alone in the pretend forest, he waited for the fruit to arrive.

The birds were calling, and the gibbons too, and for the first time Akan regarded the netting around him with hatred. He didn't want to be enclosed. He wanted to be out there, watching for flashes of iridescence on the wings of kingfishers and sneaking up on cicadas as they clicked their deafening groans, to crunch them up between his teeth.

Out there were trees. And in the trees was strength.

Trees had built him up from a helpless infant into a thing that used to soar. There were lessons still to learn – and trees, as his teachers, would have shown him all he needed to know.

Yet in here there was nothing. The ironwoods, such as they were, may once have towered in the deep forest, but in their old age they'd been denied their last monsoons and stood now as dead posts, uncrowned by any canopy at all, fit for monitor lizards to sleep in or, at best, roosting hornbills.

The only thing of any interest was the swinging black circle, and that was out of bounds to any orang who didn't much fancy getting their face clawed and their ribs smashed.

He looked down at the pebbles Riz had arranged yesterday. Bili always loved to make things with scavenged materials; without exception, Akan found each one to be marvellous. There were animals, and waterfalls, and the whole basin. And there were faces, too.

Three of them.

Like a blade of light entering into shadow, a scene was becoming visible in Akan's inner vision. There'd been a clifftop. And a very odd kind of forest, where the trees were spires of brittle stone. They'd found him – Dama, was his name – in the canopy, where he'd let out his long call. Bili wanted to give their bapa a gift, to entice him back to the basin.

No.

Bili had *already* given him a gift. It was a picture. But Dama didn't like it, so he meant to give him another one.

Bili had been angry. Akan remembered carelessly hurling a stone. It landed in the centre of the picture, and Bili was cross because he thought it was ruined, and Dama went away again so all their journeying had been for nothing. They'd failed to entice their bapa back to the basin.

But they'd found Dama again, and Bili had figured out another gift for him, but this time Akan himself thought of something that would impress their bapa even more. Something so beautiful – but dangerous in a way few things can ever be.

He'd gone to fetch a firefly. Down the cliff, in a clearing used by land-orangs, there were pretty boxes that gave light. Inside were tiny points of flame. He took one; as carefully as he could, he carried it up a pathway tree to a plateau at the cliff's top.

Bili was already there with their bapa. The sight of them together made his heart feel ruptured.

He'd called his father to look at the gift. But Dama merely turned away because Bili had manipulated their father to care only for him.

In his temper, Akan had thrown the box, which

narrowly missed Dama, and that was when a burning rock struck his head, and the only thing he could remember happening after that was what Bili did.

His own brother, with whom Akan had shared every one of his days on earth, kicked him off the ledge.

There was a rush of branches. Flaming shards of stone cascading all around him. Then there was nothing.

His brother and his bapa had planned it all out. They wanted to rid the forest of him.

Bitter tears now streamed in Akan's eyes at the memory of it, and he lifted his hand to the scaly wound that made his head throb with pressure.

From inside the wooden hut, a sudden hooting struck up, jolting Akan back to the present. The other captive orangs had awoken.

He turned to face the limb jutting out from the central tree. The black circle was perfectly still at the end of its rope.

Akan's face, and the pain in his temple, felt unusual. It was his cheeks again. They felt tingly. Compressed, somehow.

No, not compressed.

Stretched.

It was as though his cheeks were beginning to grow.

A mirthless smile spread across Akan's lips. Then, without wasting another second, he made his way to the lifeless tree – and climbed right inside the circle.

12

A FOREST WITH NO SOUL

BILI'S newest picture lay on the forest floor, set aglow by a magnificent white beam that pierced the canopy. He knew he ought to be putting in a bit more effort, but the radiance of that illuminated column was so very entrancing that it had stolen Bili's focus. It was like a half-felled ironwood made of pure light.

Through this bright shaft, all manner of creatures were flitting. There were butterflies with triangles of iridescent green on their bird-like wings, and, fleetingly, a flycatcher, whose long tail streamers cascaded like water off a rocky shelf. It was business that Bili understood.

Conversely, the affairs of the ground-men were incomprehensible to him. As he sat against a buttress root, watching the grieving party readying to journey off into the trees, he felt theirs to be a behaviour that was entirely alien. The females were marching off with their salvaged belongings strapped onto their backs, calling to Bili's mind a gang of river turtles. The males, meanwhile, carried on as though they were a single body. Upon rectangles of fabric they knelt, each facing the same direction, their foreheads pressed to the ground. They murmured words in unison, then, when their curious speech was concluded, they rose, shouldered what was left of the possessions, and followed behind the females.

Bili expected the child to run after the adults, but the little land-orang stayed as he was, nestled into his fur, studying the composition of twigs and leaves arranged on the forest bed. Bili had taken care to make this picture quietly, so as not to attract the attention of the bigger people and end up with a length of rope around his own neck like poor Oli. Yet, in spite of how slowly he worked, the boy had sat beside him the whole time, equally determined, it seemed, to keep their friendship a secret.

The boy's eyes flickered from side to side beneath a brow furrowed with confusion. It was as though, to him, the picture were nothing more than detritus gathered from the forest and jumbled in a random heap. But how could he not see it? It was so simple!

At the left of the picture, Bili had placed several twigs vertically in a row, with green leaves over their tops. On the right he'd arranged something similar, except here he'd used dry and crumpled leaves – and these he set at the foot of the twigs. The meaning couldn't be any more obvious: west, along the river, the ground-men would find healthy forest. But if they proceeded east, only horrid, choking fires awaited them.

When the boy did indeed rise to follow the others, Bili gave a quiet hoot and reached out for his hand. But in spite of the delicate pull he gave, the child remained on the spot, his dark eyes blazing with curiosity as he struggled to work out what Bili wanted.

'The sanctuary is this way!' Bili said. 'Don't you want another home?'

A female voice called out. 'Rahimi! Stop dawdling!'

The boy, taking off at a sprint, went and caught up to the others. Bili slumped: what else could he do? These were creatures with their own free will. If they wished to choose hardship over security, it was up to them.

The female yelled again. 'No, Rahimi – leave the pet in his basket! Rahimi? Where are you taking him now?'

The boy came back and stood before Bili, clutching Oli's tether tightly. 'Tell my pet,' he whispered.

Little Oli wrapped his fingers around Bili's thumb, and gave it a squeeze. His wide eyes were fixed upon him, expectantly.

'Those land-orangs,' said Bili to Oli, 'are going the wrong way. If they follow the river, as I am, they'll find a place for forest dwellers who are hurt or who have lost their homes. I think my brother's there.'

Oli hopped back to the boy, and he and Bili took a hand each. Together, they pulled him towards them.

The boy yelled, so explosively Bili rushed up the nearest bough. 'Mama! Mama! We must go this way!'

'What, Rahimi?'

'This way, mama.'

'No, Rahimi. The town is that way. It's not safe for us there.'

'But mama,' wailed the child, his eyes now dampened. 'We must. It's safer.'

'How would you know, Rahimi? You've never been either way before.'

The oldest member of the party stepped forward, he who had argued with the bald-headed man back at the burning village. 'The river is to the west,' he said, the deep creases in his face twitching as he spoke. 'Perhaps the child is right, Nadia. In open forest we can be attacked from all sides. At least the river provides one line of defence.'

'Those devils are hunting us like they do their boar. They'll get us whichever way we go.'

'If that is God's will, so be it. But let's not make poor judgments just because we're grieving.'

The female began weeping loudly again. 'He was only seventeen, Haji!'

Bili shifted on the branch. The mournful squall

coming from below was so like another he'd once heard, when some aunties learned that a juvenile had fallen to his death from out of the canopy, and in this sad moment he supposed the grief of all mothers – no matter their kind – was equal.

The old man lay his hand on the shoulder of the female. 'Luqman lived a devoted life. He lives now in paradise. But come, Nadia. We have a duty to those who survived the barbarism of those thugs. We must shepherd them to safety.'

The elderly individual issued a shrill whistle. The rest of the group halted, then awkwardly shifted their encumbered bodies around, and Bili's mouth curved up into a wide smile.

The entire party of homeless land-orangs was coming with him, west along the bank of the river.

The sun beat down without mercy as the day stretched on into afternoon.

From out of the canopy, Bili surveyed an immense slope of forest. It was quite possible the trees went on and on for days to come, but the corruption in the air caused by burning haze meant it was impossible to be sure. Not even the eyes of the great war-kite, Lang, would be able to penetrate a barrier like that.

With rain remaining as elusive as the forest elephant and her calf, the fires showed no sign of dwindling. Bili, making his way noiselessly along the mid-trees, wondered whether flame could simply keep burning forever. It was like a creature whose stomach never filled. Even the fat-nosed monkeys, who could eat all day long, eventually grew satisfied. This stuff, though, went on gobbling down everything it touched: the hardwoods' canopy and its narrower limbs; the new growth and underbrush; the fronds of palms; the spiky fruits bulging beneath boughs. If it carried on this way, the wildfire would simply run out of food to consume, and then the forest would be no more, the greenery of foliage and the rainbow of fruit just a layer of grey ash.

What would Akan make of so much flame, if he were here? Surely he wouldn't still swoon over its beauty – not when it stung your eyes and burned your throat and made you cough and rasp and blow dirt out of your nose? Even the land-orangs seemed to be suffering: morning, noon and night, they spluttered and spat and gasped for clean air.

As he journeyed, Bili ensured he could always see the bright hair of Oli down on the ground. He noticed the tiny orang looking up into the trees for him, too, and it seemed to be the case that Oli always looked behind Bili, as though fascinated by some shadow that travelled with him.

That poor creature weighed heavily on Bili's mind. The sand-coloured rims of Oli's eyes had turned a shade of purplish red like the skin of fig fruits, yet he voiced no discomfort. In fact, he seemed comfortable in the company of the ground-men. orangs weren't built for the ground, though, and Bili worried that, as the infant grew first into an older child, and then into a full adult, he would do so with a changed nature. It was hard to imagine he'd be able to tolerate a knot around his neck when his cheeks had grown into splendid wide pads. But what other life would Oli know once he reached such an age?

Bili's shoulders slumped as a truth was revealed to him. These anxieties weren't for Oli at all: this was worry about his own brother. The hope of finding Akan kept Bili going, but hope was like a tongue of dancing flame: it flickered out of reach and wouldn't be held.

Though he thought always of Akan, there was no fixed vision of his brother's current state. One moment, he pictured him happy and healthy, surrounded by trees, his hands occupied and his mouth full of mangosteen. The next, he imagined him wanting for fruits and nuts, and lacking the space to leap and roll as he so loved to do. All Bili could hope for, really, was to find a creature who was able to think and feel and want, a creature who – if it wasn't too whimsical to entertain – simply recognised that he still had a brother who loved him.

As the sun blazed into the high branches through the afternoon, Bili did his best to ignore the troubling thoughts. He put all his focus on where he placed his hands and feet, and travelled at a steady pace until the shadows grew longer. It was then, at the emergence of evening, when he suddenly heard, from his left side where the river meandered, a faint hum. He paused: this was a noise he'd not heard since the day Akan was taken away.

The hum rose – a persistent, steady raspberry of a sound. Then a boat appeared.

Filled with riders, the individual at the front of the boat was calling up into the treetops: 'Budi! We know you're hiding in there somewhere, you scoundrel!'

The folk on the forest bed below crouched until they were completely concealed. But the little land-orang stayed on his feet, lost in some thought.

'Rahimi!' yelled the weepy female. 'Get down at once!'

The young boy stooped onto his hands and feet. Bili smiled: he looked almost like a tree-man.

The humming disappeared upriver, and the group emerged from out of their hiding place, chittering with obvious angst. Bili was crestfallen at the sight of them. Over the course of the day, they'd managed to bend to the forest, to fall into its rhythms. It wasn't that the weight of their possessions grew any lighter, or that the lines of their brows softened, but the towering trees had given these people comfort and strength – and now that strength was gone again.

Up ahead was a break in the rainforest. Bili sent a warning squeak back for Oli, but as it was lost to the screeching of the cicadas from this height, he hurried on and went to ground.

Emerging on all fours out of the last of the ironwoods, Bili proceeded into a clearing unlike any he'd encountered before. What was this peculiar place? Everywhere, the trees were short. And there was something else very odd about them: they were all *exactly* the same.

Vaguely palm-like, their trunks were fibrous and flared at the base. They were equal in height, as though they'd all grown from seedlings at precisely the same time, which was a preposterous notion, since every orang knew that forests were in a constant state of flux. Where the fronds fanned out from the trunks' tops, clusters of purplish fruitlets sat like bulbous growths.

Bili was delighted, at first, to see the fruit. But this excitement melted away the moment he tasted it: the flesh of the kernels was so oily he could barely stand to swallow a single one.

So uniformly were the palms spaced from one another, that at any one spot it was possible to look down long corridors, each one extending further than his eye could see. There was something unreal about the place, as though it were a mere impression of a forest, like one of his pictures. About the only positive thing he could say about it was that at least no fires danced here.

Longing to be back in real trees again, Bili kept to the outermost row of the oil-fruit palms, trudging on ahead of the others. But so lost was he in thoughts of Akan, he almost walked straight out into the path of a second group which was making its way towards Oli's party.

He drew to a halt, his stomach fluttering with anxiety. Who were *these*? Did they mean harm, as the bald-headed man's gang did? Crouching low behind a palm, Bili observed the bearded face of the new group's leader, which, thankfully, opened into a smile. When the two parties combined into a single larger one, and it was apparent to Bili they were friends, he continued on his way.

On and on, the palm rows stretched. How odd it was, to be in a forest devoid of life and soul. Where were the birds with their ceaseless gossip? The cicadas who groaned all day long for the heat? It was as though this vast tract of cleared rainforest existed only for these spiritless palms. There weren't even any termite trails to be found, or giant ants dancing this way and that on their mad business.

Finally, just when Bili was feeling he could take no more of this place, the oil-palms came to an end. He'd been longing for this moment, but now it had come he regretted his wish.

Beyond the palm forest was land-orang territory.

And this one was no mere village.

⚓

The journeying group of ground-men seemed every bit as nervous as Bili to have reached civilisation.

Adorning the edge of the oil-fruit forest was a collection of squat huts, lit beneath harsh, unnatural lights. While Bili concealed himself behind one of these huts, Oli's group congregated at the front, and muttered in whispered tones with the bushy-beard man.

Filling the air was a most unusual sound. Song-like, but sad, it drifted over the buildings that stood beyond the fields. The males of Oli's party let their possessions down onto the dusty ground, and proceeded towards the source of the song. But no sooner did they set off than a loud commotion sounded.

Appearing on the road, on wheeled machines, was a third group of land-orangs. 'Thought you could outrun us, did you?'

The voice was familiar. Bili, straining his neck around the side of the hut in order to see, recognised at once the piercing eyes of the bald-headed man and his gang of angry-faced individuals. In their hands were tools like those they'd used to hurt the villagers last night.

The man with the bushy beard stepped forward and positioned himself between Oli's group and the angry arrivals. 'What's the problem here, Yahya?'

'The problem? I suppose you heard that Patrick Congo was stabbed yesterday morning by Budi, that Madurese dog?'

'Yes, we heard he was killed,' said the bearded man. 'Patrick was a strong figure in our community. He will be sadly missed.'

The bald-headed male snorted a cruel laugh. 'Never mind missed! He'll be avenged! Now step aside and let us finish our business.'

The bearded man's group banded tighter together, forming a barrier behind which Oli's party cowered.

'I understand you feel put-out by the policies of the government,' said the man with the beard. 'I am a Dayak too, and I understand many of these frustrations. But we are better than this, Yahya. Savaging men on their way to prayer? That is not the Dayak way.'

The bald-headed male spat on the ground and stared at the individual before him, his eyes glowering with naked hatred.

Bili scanned around for the child, who was clutching the legs of the female.

'Boy,' he hooed, quietly.

The child failed to hear it.

'Boy!' he said again, this time a little louder, and now the child twisted his head around to meet his eye. 'Come here.'

The little land-orang broke away from the adults, and joined Bili around the corner of the hut, where he held his body tight in to him.

Yet another group of land-orangs then appeared, these ones in a long machine that flashed bright with red and blue. They stepped out onto the hard ground in fabric dappled like the forest, and instantly rounded on the smooth-head and his gang.

'What the hell do you think you're doing, Yahya?' said the widest of the new men.

'These are the scum who hit Patrick Congo. We're going to rough them up a bit.'

'Is that what you're calling it? "Roughing them up"? We've spent all day dealing with a bloodbath in a jungle settlement. Four corpses! Did I miss the memo that said it's alright for vigilantes to go around murdering now?'

The bald-headed male smiled darkly.

'What do you know about that, Yayah?'

'Nothing to do with us, captain. Isn't that right, Madura pigs?' barked the smooth head.

The adults of Oli's group looked at the ground and said nothing.

The wide man in the forest fabric addressed Oli's party. 'Where are you going now?'

'Our brothers at the mosque are sure to take us in,' replied the elderly individual. 'At least until we can raise the money to resettle in the countryside.'

'Best if we escort you. Yayah!' yelled the wide man, turning now to the glowering posse. 'Go shoot some pool at the bar and calm yourselves. And if I were you, I'd think seriously about taking a trip someplace.'

With scowls contorting their faces, the smooth head and his friends stepped aside, and the terror-stricken travellers began to move off behind the machine with its flashing lights.

The boy's mother called out. 'Come, Rahimi!'

The child brushed Bili's face with his fingertips. 'I've got to go,' he said, and though he smiled, Bili could see through his eyes into a heart that was anything but happy. 'Thank you.'

Bili took hold of the leash around Oli's neck, and pulled at the knot. The rope slipped to the ground.

'Rahimi! Come on!'

The boy looked sadly at the infant orang. 'Up to you, pet,' he said.

Oli's head turned to Bili, and for a moment he thought the tiny orang was coming to him. But he then picked his tether from off the floor, and hopped away after the little land-man. He'd made his choice.

After so much commotion, the deepening dusk seemed quiet; even the words of the land-orangs who'd lingered behind were uttered softly.

'Looks like we're going to have to split for a while,' said the bald-headed one. 'But we'll give them something to remember us by, huh?'

'Yeah!' chanted his friends. 'Let's burn this hellhole to the ground!'

13

SEIZING THE MOMENT

AT MID-MORNING, just after the mangos were brought to the enclosure, the ground-men became jumpy.

Amid air thick with the haze of scorched forest, Akan's throat was dry and prickly. His eyes streamed with tears, and his red-brown hair, which had grown shaggier since he first came here, was now heavy with the scent of smoking foliage.

But the physical discomfort the haze brought was easier to bear than the mental anguish. What was it about this smell that made him so very surly? There was something so maddening about the way it followed him around to each corner of the enclosure. Not even biting sandflies were as persistent as this. For as long as that woody aroma clung to him, he couldn't help but think about his father and his brother: this acrid odour was the very scent of their betrayal.

Near the nesting hut, the ground-men were talking. A fretful energy was coming from them, and they checked over their shoulders repeatedly, as though they were afraid a snake was sneaking up on them. One man spoke into a little black box and waited for it to speak back to him; each time it did, his anguish grew deeper.

'*All* of them? Are you sure? OK, we'll get ready. Over.'

The concerned male turned to his companions. 'You get that? We're evacuating to the visitor centre. You two, bring the crates over. Su-su, I need you to get this lot back into the bedroom.'

'Why only me?' snapped the girl, whose dark eyes simmered.

The male frowned. 'Why do you have to be difficult, Su-su? Fine, I'll call somebody to help you.'

What happened next was perplexing. From the corner, Akan watched as Ari and Riz suddenly appeared *on the other side* of the netting. Though they were confined to wooden boxes barely big enough to contain them, they showed no sign of distress.

One by one, the other residents of the enclosure began to appear on the walkway, too, until only Mali, perched on the bough above the black circle, remained. But Mali wasn't giving up this treasured spot easily, not after Akan's brazen display.

Akan had expected the big male to react with fury. But when Mali emerged from the nesting hut at dawn to see Akan casually swinging away, he gave a dismissive flick of the head and went instead to the climbing frame in the back corner. It was only when Akan grew bored of the circle and dropped down onto the ground that the adult sauntered on over to it.

In the time since, Mali hadn't once vacated the central tree, not even for mangoes, and now no amount of enticing from the banana-wielding ground-men could convince him to surrender it.

'Akan,' yelled Ari from his box. 'Go into the hut.'

'Why should I?'

'Because,' said Riz, 'if you don't, they'll put you to sleep.'

At that moment, a male land-orang came by clutching a tool. It was metal, and cylindrical in shape, and the sight of it caused a panicked Mali to swiftly drop down from the long bough and take off for the hut.

That was enough for Akan. These orangs knew things he didn't, and learning things the hard way was something he could do without.

The land-orangs sealed Mali and Akan into their own boxes, then set them down on the walkway beside the others. Smoke now drifted across the area in thick, grey clouds, transporting Akan once again to the clifftop where he'd thrown the flame onto Bili's picture.

At the memory of it, he slumped. If only his aim had been more precise and he'd hit Dama in the face. Where would Bili have been then? One thing was sure: he wouldn't have tried to take Akan by himself. Ever since they were small, his brother always lost in their play fights. Bili may have had an edge when it came to solving problems, but Akan was always the stronger of the pair.

Why couldn't he have taken Dama out with that box of flame? Then it would have been Bili who went over the ledge. Who spent endless days behind walls of blocks. Who was beaten and clawed at by a brute. Whose torso ached any time he moved. Whose face was marked with an angry web of scars. Who sat now in a wooden case, choked and blinded.

The man spoke into his black machine again – 'Standing by!' – and a few seconds later a thing on wheels approached.

Ari and Riz became excited. 'We're going on the train! They're taking us to the hall! Count how many animals you can see this time!'

The ground-men began lifting the boxed orangs into the empty cart the wheeled thing pulled. Akan was distressed when it jolted into motion, but was soon so transfixed by what surrounded him that he forgot to pay any attention.

Peering through the bars of his box as it wound its way around the area, he was amazed by the many creatures dwelling in the other enclosures. For every one that was familiar, there was something novel, too.

Elephants lived beside an absurdly tall kind of yellow deer whose neck reached up to the very canopy; a wall separated crocodiles from chubby little upright birds whose wings were too short to be of any use; sunbears occupied the netted enclosure beside a type of pangolin that was completely covered in black and white spines.

And what were these things?! There was a cat the size of a young rhinoceros, its fur gold like the sun and a ring of bushy hair around its terrifyingly wide face. Then there was a kind of deer that stood only on its hind legs, great powerful things that protruded either side of a tail twice as long as its body.

With each new exhibit, Akan's excitement grew ever more dizzying. Around a sharp bend they went, until they came to a section of the park where the birds were housed. Akan watched as hornbills passed by, and a long-legged upright creature with a blue head and bright red neck and a claw that could open up an orang as easily as it could a banana.

But then, as though he'd plunged into a pool on a hot afternoon, his excitement was instantly cooled.

Sat on a perch, in a very tiny cage, was the kite.

They had captured Lang, the mighty spirit of war!

∗

The hall, like some vast, cold cavern, was terrifying.

To help control his nerves, Akan listened as Ari and Riz chattered away.

'When was your first time in the hall?'

'Not long after they rescued me. It was flooding, that time.'

'I remember that! It was monsoon. The water came all the way up to the floor of our hut.'

'Two nights, they kept us here. That was how long it took for the water to go down.'

'I thought I was going to freeze in here that time.'

'Me too.'

'Are you cold now, Akan?'

Akan wrapped his arms tighter around his body and gave a nod of his head. The hairs on his forearms stood erect upon chill bumps.

Because of the position of Riz's crate, Akan's view of the other animals was almost completely obscured. Annoyed, he had to make do with watching the groundmen instead, who were huddled in the corner, their faces darkened with unease.

One in particular, a young female whose head was wrapped in fabric, seemed especially distressed, and was currently addressing her companions.

'But there's plenty more space in here!'

'Look around you, Su-su. What are we going to do with a giraffe?'

'Of course we can't bring the big mammals in. But I'm not talking about those. What about the smaller animals? Why leave them out there to burn when we can easily fit them in the hall?'

'It's not up to me! It's park policy. There's a priority list.'

The young female scowled. 'What does that even *mean*?'

'It means,' sighed the older male with whom she was conversing, 'that, in the event of emergency, certain species are prioritised for evacuation.'

'How's that decided?'

'Well, there's a range of criteria. If they're highly endangered. Or if they're participants in breeding programmes. Or they might be what we call "ambassador species" – the ones that bring in paying visitors.'

The female stomped her foot angrily against the shiny floor and balled her fingers into tight fists. 'So, some lives are worth more than others. That's all it boils down to. Why does this sound so familiar?'

'Su-su,' said a shorter female in a soft voice. 'Not everything is about politics, you know.'

'Why don't you tell that to your daddy? Maybe then him and his friends will stop squeezing every drop out of my family!' With that, she stamped away to another corner of the hall, leaving the shorter one to lean into her companion.

'That's what you call "speaking their minds", huh? Well, I think the Madurese are just plain rude.'

Just then, the hall filled up with the sound of laughter, and the ground-men clapped their hands together with glee. 'Wind direction has changed!' they cheered, and proceeded at once to carry the boxed animals back to the train.

Land-orangs walked alongside them as the train made its way back through the park. Now evening, the air was still hazy, but the thick, choking smoke was, thankfully, gone.

'Lucky break,' said a male.

His companion smiled. 'Very! Did you see the edge of the park? It was just beginning to catch.'

'Management is sending a couple of cases over to the fire department. They deserve a cold one after a day like today.'

The train neared the bird enclosures again, and Akan felt his chest tighten. From the corner of his eye, a deep red-brown appeared, and soon he was looking directly into the face of the kite.

It was – *almost* – more than he could bear. The eye of Lang blazed into him with an unyielding intensity, as though the Bird-King were searching for something he felt lurked deep within him, where the darkness was gloomiest. Akan brought his fingers up to cover his eyes, but still he peered through them to hold the stare of the kite, until, finally – mercifully – the train twisted away.

How had this happened? Inside that bird was the very spirit of the war god. It was said that Lang's call was enough to turn the trees of the forest against one another. Yet there he was, confined to a dwelling so small he couldn't even spread his wings.

What did it mean to the wider world, that the kite had been captured? Akan slumped in his box, desperately wishing he had a mother or a father – or even a sibling – who could answer that question for him. But in the absence of any family, he forced himself to take comfort in the fact such an unfathomable power had been safely contained.

The train arrived back at the enclosure, and the ground-men hauled the boxes down from it, setting them on the walkway beside the netted front. Positioned in a line, Akan was one away from the end – only Mali was further – meaning he was going to be one of the last in, and therefore late to the pile of chopped-up watermelon.

One by one, Akan watched as the others were released from their boxes. They hopped into the nesting hut, then charged out of its back side onto the open expanse of dry earth, clearly thrilled to be able to move "freely" once again.

It was now Akan's own turn. With his hands tucked under his armpits in a gesture of coldness towards the ground-men, he lumbered into the hut. Winding through the nests that lay upon the floor, he climbed out into the main enclosure. But rather than take off into any of the dead trees, he remained near the entrance hole, keeping his body discreetly concealed.

And when Mali emerged, Akan sank both hands into the soft flesh around his neck, and squeezed with all his strength until the adult male dropped like a stone onto the ground.

Akan stood above Mali, observing as though in a dream. But he was brought crashing back to reality when the adult's eyes suddenly sprang open. He was supposed to be dead already! Wasn't he? Was that not how this worked?

Akan leapt over to the enclosure's waterless pond and wrenched up as big a stone from its edge as he could carry. Then, with Mali still down and dazed, Akan slammed the rock into his knee, and the adult's leg buckled into an angle it oughtn't have. Mali's head flopped backward onto the ground, and he began to snore.

Calmly, assuredly, Akan then went and climbed into the central tree, to watch out over a territory that was now his own.

✈

Over the days that followed, the land-orangs maintained a constant presence on the walkway outside the netting.

Although Mali's injuries occurred so near their train, they didn't notice the actual incident at the time. It was only the next morning, when he failed to show up for his breakfast, that they began to investigate.

With Ari and Riz either side of him, Akan had watched from the central tree as a ground-man's face came poking out from the hole in the sleeping hut. The individual's mouth fell open on sighting Mali coiled up in pain and sorrow, the blood pooled around his leg appearing black beneath the blanket of flies that had moved in.

Within minutes, more land-orangs had come to take the injured Mali out, and Akan could do nothing to stop the smile rising on his mouth. It was the adult's turn now to spend dawn after dawn recovering behind the blocky walls.

Others came to clean up. When it was done, they stood around, jaws agape, and watched each of the orangs intently. Akan may have only imagined it, but it seemed that their eyes lingered more on him than upon any of the others.

Ari and Riz were aloof, to begin with. But the moment

Akan invited them up into the central tree with him, they soon relaxed, eventually coming to enjoy themselves in a way Akan hadn't previously seen.

Of course, sharing the circle was as much a benefit to him as it was to them. So long as he took care not to be seen in it alone, the clever brains of the ground-men wouldn't work out that it was he who was to blame for Mali's terrible injuries. Besides, sooner or later Akan intended to get out of this enclosure, and a pair of allies in the wild would help him accomplish what he knew he must.

It was on this point that Akan had waited to speak to the boys, and now that the ground-men had ceased watching over them all, he felt it was time to share his sad history.

As Akan's tale unfolded, Ari and Riz listened attentively. The pain of it lived in Akan's heart at all times, yet speaking it aloud to his new friends made his lip quiver with emotion.

'Why would your own bapa and brother want to get rid of you?' asked Ari.

Akan had no answer, but Riz proposed a theory. 'Perhaps they felt the forest would be too dense with three of you.'

'Maybe,' said Ari. 'But his bapa could have just commanded him to leave. Us orangs don't *kill* for territory. It's not in our nature.'

The pair went on quizzing Akan until the light of day faded, and he answered each one of their enquiries, even though he hurt to relive it over again.

Finally, Ari voiced the most important question. 'What will you do if you see them again?'

Akan nodded his head, gently. Once again, the familiar, bothersome tingle had returned to his cheeks, promising another night of discomfort. 'We just couldn't see it before, Bili and I. Perhaps we were too immature. But knowing what I know about my bapa, I have a gift that would win him over for sure now. I'd show him how alike we truly are.' With that, Akan held his fingers up and gave them a wriggle, and Ari and Riz, who'd seen how he'd laid them around Mali's throat, turned away.

The time was fast approaching to retire into the hut. Ari and Riz had a final swing in the circle, and went to ground. But Akan had one more thing he wished to discuss, and called them back up. 'Twice, you've been taken to the hall now. Correct?'

The boys nodded.

'The first time, you said it was because the monsoon flooded the enclosure. And the last time, because the trees beyond the park were burning.'

Ari swatted a fly off his eyebrow. 'Yes. So?'

'So, I want out of here.'

The pair looked at each other. '*Out?*'

'My home is the forest, and I want to be back in it. I have business out there, and you boys are going to help me with it.'

'But we can't get out, Akan. You haven't been here long enough yet, so you don't understand. But the more time passes, the more you just sort of accept that this is your home now.'

'There might be a way.'

Ari and Riz glared at Akan with expressions closer to fear than curiosity.

'All we need is a reason for land-orangs to put us on the train again. When we're on the walkway, I think we can break out of the boxes. Then we can make a run for it. Did you see the elephant? If we could get into its enclosure, we could climb into the trees on the far side of it. And we'd be out.'

Ari's head dipped. 'Maybe. But we can't influence what happens outside the enclosure. How are we supposed to give the land-orangs a reason to take us out again?'

Akan blew air out of his nostrils while he considered

it. 'There's nothing we can do about rain, that's for sure. But I've held flame in my own hands before. If we could only get them to bring that stuff here, I could cause trouble with it. Then they'd be forced to bring the train to us.'

He sat back for a moment and watched his companions' expressions – and wasn't at all happy when Ari and Riz simply rolled their eyes away dismissively and climbed down from the tree.

14

THE GROUND-MEN'S WORLD

ALONE AGAIN, Bili held his breath as he readied to make a run for it.

With Oli and the child now gone, he ached for his brother's company. How strange a thing it was, to pine for a thing that may no longer exist. All his hopes had been focussed on finding the world of the land-orangs, yet now he was here, the fear Akan was not among its residents needled Bili's neck like a creeping rash.

Keeping himself concealed behind the hut at the edge of the oil-palm fields, Bili went over the plan. This was easy! All he had to do was reach the river via the two separate tree clusters on the other side of the road.

With no more hesitation, he broke cover, and stepped out into the dark. But halfway into the road, a vehicle approached, its lights flashing red and blue, sending Bili scuttling back behind the hut with a whimper.

When it went quiet again, he made a second attempt. But the very moment he walked out, a pair of land-orangs came by, running for what seemed like no other reason than the enjoyment of movement. The pair pointed and laughed as they passed. 'An escapee!' one of them said, and they trotted on, back into the uninviting world of the city into which Oli and the child had vanished.

Bili chided himself. He'd been as good as across that time! It had taken longer to get back to the hut than it would have to get up into the nearest cluster; now, for his cowardice, he was going to have to try a third time.

The mournful song he'd heard earlier came drifting through the air again. Still as a stone, Bili waited for it to stop. Behind him, in the palms, a rustling sounded, as though something were gently skulking among the foliage. He turned, desperate as always to catch this shadow in the act of stalking him, but the moment he did, his ear was attracted back to the city, where, on a light breeze, he thought he heard the hooting of gibbons – followed an instant later by the long call of an orang. That was it, then. His brain had descended into madness. With no rainforest here, such noises were impossible.

When the song came to an end, Bili peeked around the edge of the hut, noting the absence of any threat. A big intake of air steadied his nerves: there would be no fourth attempt.

He hopped out. Crouching low, he knuckle-walked ahead, wincing each time the bones of his hand struck the road. The gibbons, which weren't really there, began calling again, faintly present alongside the drumming of Bili's heart which thumped inside his ears. Though he was on the verge of panic, he remained committed to the task and, after a slight stumble at the halfway point, he bounded the rest of the way, across at last.

To be in the trees again was immediately soothing, even if they were only the low kind. For a moment, Bili considered fracturing a few branches back on themselves to form a nest, but he let the idea go. He couldn't squander the advantage of darkness, not unless he wanted to be trapped in this corner of the ground-men's territory even longer. He had to push on to the river.

Swinging along the boughs, the cluster soon came to

an end. But with the other standing nearby, Bili wasted no time climbing down the trunk. He checked to his left and his right, then tottered up to a wide stone basin in the middle of the clearing, just in time for a jet of water to shoot out from it, high into the air.

The familiar, loathsome scent of burning came wafting across from where the city was denser. Bili's shoulders went taught: his throat was going to feel scratchy again, his lungs heavy and tired. He plunged his hand into the basin and scooped out a couple of palmfuls of water while he had the chance; it tasted filthy.

Quickly making it to some shrubby bushes, he got into the next set of trees, where the barbed stems of sweet-scented flowers scratched him as he climbed. He advanced through the low canopy until he came to its edge; the sense lingered that he was still on the outskirts of the habitation, though it was clear by the noise that he had now reached a deeper point within it.

Wheeled machines rolled by, one after the other. Across the road, distantly twinkling beneath the dots of yellow light, was the river. Bili's heart swelled with gladness at the sight of it, but this melted away the moment he saw that no trees ran alongside its inviting banks.

Squinting his eyes to see better in the darkness of late evening, he understood at once that the only way he was going to be able to proceed was by keeping low behind the hedges which bordered the riverside's walkway. As it stood, no ground-men were ambling along it – but there was every chance he'd find it packed with them further along.

He descended to the bushes, and rested for an instant. In the distance, a distinctive roar rose up into the humid night sky; this time, there was no question of its being real. A thunderous blast of air, this was the unmistakable call of an elephant. Wrapping his head in his hands, Bili bucked with confusion. The gibbons weren't just his imagination – nor the orangs. There was more to this territory than had first appeared.

Hurrying out from the bushes, he scuttled upright across the road's hard surface. Then, when he'd just reached the middle of it, an awful din, like a mechanical scream, startled him half out of his skin. But he'd learnt already not to turn back at a time like this, so he proceeded the rest of the way until he came to the hedge, where he plopped down onto the grass and covered his ears.

The deafening scream accompanied the red and blue lights of an approaching machine. It grew even louder for a moment – so loud Bili thought his head might burst – then, when the wheeled thing sped by, it became quieter, and his heart gradually calmed.

Although he could glimpse no trees ahead of him, Bili had the walkway to himself, so moved along the river as quickly as he could. As he bounded along the low verge in a crouch, the horrid smell of smoke grew stronger, and more mechanical wails sounded in all directions. Some kind of trouble was happening in the world of the ground-men, but he knew better than to let it distract him.

He pushed onward until the riverside walkway met an intersecting bridge. With a decision now necessary, Bili considered his options. To his right was a brightly-lit building. Sat upon its top, like a very odd kind of mushroom, was a shiny dome, with two tall spires, sharpened into points, either side of it. Land-orangs were congregating outside, among them Oli's group. Turtle-shells of possessions were heaped beside them; it was clear in the intensity of their expressions that they were discussing something important.

To Bili's left, beyond the bridge, was a road. Bordered by a high wall, a wide swathe of forest canopy stood on the other side of it. Within the treetops was the pulsating orange glimmer of flame – perhaps this accounted for all this strife among the ground-men? The lure of the trees was strong; just a quick nap in them, and he could carry on in search of the sanctuary. But sleeping amid fire was no option at all. Aunt Ivie had always been clear on that point.

Catching his ear now were the sobs of the little land-orang. He turned back to the lit-up building. The ground-men were moving away from it now, but something had saddened Oli's young master.

'But why, mama?' he was wailing. 'Why can't I keep my pet?'

'Because, Rahimi, we're going to be guests in this kind man's home. And his family doesn't keep animals.'

'But he's only small! He won't cause any trouble!'

'I'm sorry. Once we get back to the forest we can get you another one. I promise.'

'But what will we do with him, mama?'

Bili watched as a tall male with a circular head covering put his arm around the boy's shoulder. 'See that wall across the bridge? That's the outer perimeter of the zoo. They're a rescue centre, too – they take in orang-utans from the forest all the time. Let's go now, and see if they can help.'

'Thank you, Haji,' said the boy's mother. 'You see, Rahimi? He'll be just fine.'

'Come now, young man. We can walk there together.'

✦

Akan thought of nothing else but escape.

Each new day passed the same as the one before. Dawn came with the hooting of gibbons, as it used to in the basin. But the song they sang in the adjoining enclosure was a mirthless one, as arms that were built for swinging remained limply at their sides. The fastest creatures in the entire forest had just two trees to leap between; it was a wonder they found a voice at all.

By first light, fruit would be dumped at the nesting hut. The rainforest offered an embarrassment of riches, yet now Akan's diet consisted of the same food: always bananas, some days mangoes with watermelon and, very occasionally, something spiky like a tarap or a handful of rambutans. He longed for a fig – not only to taste it, but to choose it on the tree, to squeeze it for just the right stage of ripeness, to feel how the branch snapped back when the fruit came loose from its stalk.

It was always the female land-orangs who brought breakfast. They liked the captive tree-men, and lingered beside them while they ate, either chatting to them or each other; there was never silence. Later, a pair of males would arrive to clean out the enclosure. These tended to get on with the task in silence. Then, with dusk bruising in the west, a second pair of females would come with snacks, and beckon them into the nesting hut to beds that were never quite comfortable.

The faces, however, began to change. This morning, only one of the usual females had appeared; her companion was a stranger. Akan, who didn't like to eat with the others, was off to the side, working his way through his banana pile, but even from here it was obvious that the pair were upset: the eyes of the regular female were damp with tears, and her voice had gone squeaky.

'It's honestly not my fault that Su-su got fired. I only said she'd taken her break already because Mr Tan asked when I had mine and I said, "At 10.30, with Su-su." How was I supposed to know she'd been taking extra breaks?'

'You weren't. Listen, Mr Tan has wanted to get rid of her since she started. It's got nothing to do with you.'

'That's not what Su-su is saying!' A sob spilled out from the young female's mouth. 'She's going around town telling everyone I got her fired!'

Akan paid little interest to this pair; it was the males whose presence excited him, and he was preoccupied all through the day by their visit. Of course, it wasn't them that excited him as much as the glowing sticks they always rested between their lips. The other orangs were repelled by the strong stench of the blue smoke that curled up from the ends of those sticks, but to Akan, this was potential: the ground-men brought actual points of flame right into the enclosure.

The moment they arrived this afternoon, Akan went and sat by them while they wielded their tools.

'Who cares what happens to Su-su?' one was saying. 'She's only a Madurese. They can get work anywhere.'

'Her boyfriend cares, that's who.'

'That creep Budi? He thinks he's so tough because he races water buffalo.'

'He's on his way here now.'

'Seriously?'

'Yep. He's going to sort Mr Tan out.'

'I'd like to see him try. Mr Tan is a well-connected man. You knew Patrick Congo, right?'

'*Every*one knew Patrick Congo.'

'Yeah, well he was Mr Tan's brother-in-law.'

As they spoke, the flaming sticks bobbed up and down in their mouths. Oddly, these glowing things were shrinking all the time. Even while he watched, Akan wasn't sure if it actually was flame, or simply a kind of light.

Akan went and climbed into the central tree, and dangled from its lone bough. Ari and Riz hadn't been back in the circle since he'd spoken of getting out, but another pair had been only too happy to take their place.

Amay and Inda, brothers who'd been brought into the enclosure when their mother was killed by a dog, had spent the full day in the swinging circle, unable to believe their good fortune. How lucky they were to have a friend like Akan!

Watching them at play, Akan simmered with emotion. He'd had a brother once, he told them. A half-brother, actually; until recently, he never really understood what that meant. But as they grew together, he came to realise something: the part of their personalities that their mothers gave them was more significant than either of them had thought. His own mother, he asserted, knew nothing of treachery and tricks. But Bili's mother – his Aunt Effie – had put strange notions into his brother's head when they lay together in their nest at night. She told Bili that he was better, that their bapa loved him more. Wasn't that a truly despicable thing to do?

The young brothers, giddy with laughter as the circle rocked this way and that, were having far too much fun to take any notice. Still, though, Akan went on. It *was* despicable. And it proved something he never would have guessed about life: that you never really *knew* anybody. He hooked his forefinger over his lower lip and cast his eyes absently down at his belly. 'That's the trouble,' he grumbled. 'You only know what they show you.'

A mechanical roar came from beyond the park's perimeter wall, in the world of the land-orangs. Some of the park's residents were upset by this commotion: langurs screeched; a hornbill barked; a mystery creature produced a musical whistle – and Lang issued a blood-chilling shriek.

Nearby, glass shattered, and angry voices began to bellow. Then some female land-orangs screamed.

Akan let his head dip over the long limb beneath him. Upside-down while he watched them play, he posed a question which made Amay and Inda turn to him in confusion. 'Which one is the brother who makes things?'

They stared, blankly.

'Come on!' squeaked Akan. 'Is it you, Amay?'

'No, Akan.'

'Then it's you, Inda.' He became agitated by the lingering silence. 'Why aren't you answering me?'

'We don't know what you're talking about, Akan.'

Akan let his body fall off the limb. Catching it when his arms were fully extended, he dropped the rest of the way to the ground. 'Follow me.'

The pair trailed him as he walked upright to the front side of the netting, where a pile of pebbles lay scattered in the corner. 'Make me a picture.'

The pair looked at the pebbles with indifference.

'I don't care which one of you does it, just make me a picture!'

'A picture of what?'

Akan struck out with his open palm and caught Inda on his cheek. 'I don't care what! A rambutan. Or a basin filled with forest. No, a family. Three tree people together. The older one in the middle and two younger ones on either side.'

By now, the rest of the enclosure's orangs were aware of the tension, and came crowding around. Ari and Riz looked on, their eyes bright with fear.

Inda gathered the pebbles into his fist. 'You want me to make… a picture?'

Akan gave a firm nod.

'Of a family.'

Nod.

'And I'm to use the pebbles.'

Nod.

Inda scattered a cluster of stones out onto the dirt, which landed in a random jumble. He repeated the act twice, then studied what lay in front of him. Then, with a trepidation that was obvious to all onlookers, he brought his eyes up.

'Seems like you don't want to be my friend, after all,' said Akan, exhaling audibly out of his nostrils. 'Well, that's fine with me. Just make sure I never catch you swinging in my circle ever again.'

The sky went dusky, then dark, but still the pair of males with their smoking sticks failed to return.

Remaining in the central tree long after the others had retired to the hut for sleep, Akan stared out onto the walkway with anticipation. Hopefully, they were just running late today. Something must have held them up on their usual route – perhaps it had to with all that smashing and yelling?

The papery sticks were an obsession for Akan now; he was certain that the red tip was flame. Things that burned gave a beautiful light, and from that light came smoke – and so did it stream in a grey-blue line from off the ends of those cylinders.

Less obvious, however, was how he might use such a tiny point of flame to bring the necessary chaos. He scratched his head as he worked through the logic of it. Trees burned – he could smell that some were on fire right now. Trees were made of wood. The nesting hut was made of wood. Thus, the nesting hut would burn!

How, though? Would the hut ignite the moment he pressed the tip to it, the way the bite of an ant causes an immediate shock to the skin? Or did heat take time to move from one thing to another, like how contact with ivy leaves only became apparent later on, when the rash flared up? It may be that the hut was simply too large a target for such a small dot of flame.

But what if he lit something smaller first, like a twig, then wielded that? Or, even better, if he ignited many twigs gathered in a pile.

Many twigs gathered together in a pile.

A nest.

The hint of a smile rose on Akan's lips as he mentally worked through the sequence.

First, he would steal the flaming stick out of the man's mouth. Next, he'd flee with it into the hut, and drop it right into the heart of one of the nests! The flame would find its way to the other nests, and the hut itself would become engulfed, then the ground-men would bring their train with its boxes, and he could make a run for it over to the elephant enclosure and up into real forest!

It was a plan that couldn't be bettered. And it might have worked, too. But what happened next meant he'd never find out:

A new group of land-orangs had come.

And they'd brought mayhem with them on a scale Akan couldn't ever have imagined.

SANCTUARY OF CHAOS

BILI'S HEART thumped with nervous excitement as he followed the little land-orang across the bridge. Faintly detectable through the burning haze was the odour of animals. Was he at last nearing the sanctuary?

Earthen and dusty, Bili had picked up the scent back on the other side of the river, but his attention then was focussed on trailing Oli's small party as discreetly as he could. Closer now to the swathe of forest, however, he was sure of it: there were things close by that wouldn't typically be anywhere near a place like this. It was the scent of creatures who dwelt in hidden places, as far from the world of the ground-men as it was possible to be.

But odour wasn't the only thing on the air. The land-orangs who carried Oli were emitting an intense sort of worry. It was as though a terrible event had been set in motion someplace else, and now it was only a matter of time before it caught them up. Perhaps it was that they were heading to some hostile place, one where confrontation awaited. Perhaps it would end up like the last time, with bodies strewn over the ground, their heads no longer attached.

Piercing yells made the land-orangs jumpy, and as

they advanced along the road, Bili kept as close to them as he dared, holding himself tight against the wall, afraid that the light from the metal trees was going to illuminate his red hair and give him away.

As tall as a palm, and stretching ahead as far as his eye could see, the wall was all that separated Bili from a patch of forest he longed to sleep in. If Oli's group kept on going much further, he'd do just that: rest before finally finding Akan's sanctuary home. But for now it was enough to stalk them, listening to their fretful chatter as they advanced down the road.

'Why do the Dayaks hate us so much, Haji?' the little land-orang was saying, as he clutched Oli close to his chest.

'There are millions of Dayaks, child,' said the tall man with the round hat. 'Some of them are upset that your people were allowed to settle on Borneo. But most of them understand you've done nothing wrong besides seek more fertile land to grow your crops. The ones you've encountered are the worst of the worst. But they are a tiny minority. Don't forget that.'

'Yahya took my brother's head, Haji. They're going to take Budi's too when they find him, aren't they?'

The boy's tall companion sighed. 'As you know, our book holds that murder is the most atrocious act. But murder is a fact of life, as it has been since the days of Adam's sons. Your brother's killers will face eternal torment for what they did to an innocent man – a faithful young man whose life had barely even started.'

'Why, Haji? Why did they do it?'

The adult sighed again. 'Who knows why people do what they do? Perhaps these rogue Dayaks inherited blood from their ancestors, the headhunters who dwelt all over Borneo until very recently? Or maybe it's more simple than that, and life just twisted these thugs all out of shape.'

The land-orangs went on this way all down the path, but Bili tuned out from their patter when an unmistakable noise sounded on the other side of the wall. This familiar alarm was made only by gibbons: something had riled them.

But the gibbon song sounded only a fraction ahead of the next commotion. Now, a multitude of creatures were screaming, their very lives quite obviously imperilled.

Bili hadn't even begun to process the cacophony before more chaos broke out up ahead, where a pair of wheeled machines came thundering out from a gap in the wall.

He flung himself to the ground, and turned to see what the others were doing: the adults, without delay, had shielded Oli and the boy.

The machines slowed to a crawl as they passed. Seated on the frontmost one was the bald-headed male, his mean eyes lingering over the party intensely.

The boy's tall companion called across the road. 'Just what business do you have at the zoo at this hour, Yahya?'

Laughter roared out. 'Friday nights were always so boring in this garbage town. We thought we'd liven things up a bit for you.'

To Bili's complete bewilderment, there now emerged from out of the gap up ahead an actual *elephant*. And behind that was a creature that defied belief, something so improbable that he doubted his very sanity: its legs went up to the elephant's eyes, and its neck – standing out at an angle like a tree blown askance in a mighty wind – dwarfed it by half.

'Consider it our parting gift.'

'They've let the animals out!' exclaimed the tall male as the machine screeched away. 'God help us! Run! Pick up the orang-utan, child, and get to the bridge as fast as your legs can carry you!'

Bili, still on the ground, jolted. What was happening? The ground-men were now heading back the way they'd come! He rose to his feet, wondering if he should follow. But the moment he got upright, he heard the cry of battle.

'Whoo-haw! Haw-haw! Hook! Hook!'

It was the first long call he'd heard since his father's, all those dawns ago.

The nature of it was meant to ward him off, but Bili was so excited to be back near real forest again, he ignored the impulse to retreat. No matter that it was an adult male, he *had* to see another of his kind again.

He *had* to go to it.

But how? Ahead of him was an elephant readying to charge, beside a beast that made chill bumps break out across his neck just to look at – something which, for all he knew, could sprout wings from out of its back any moment and fly over to swallow him whole.

He looked up at the wall. It was simply too tall to be scaled. Unless…?

Bili darted out to the other side of the road, into the soilless clearing. Sharp shards, like jagged green stones, made the going rough, but he scanned the wasteland until he found a wooden post. It would have to do.

Scuttling upright back to the wall, Bili jammed the post into the soil. With his left hand and his left foot, he steadied himself against the wall, and with his right extremities he clutched hold of the wood. Carefully, he shimmied higher, but before he could reach its full height, the post toppled over, sending him right back to where he started, on the dry soil.

More noises arrived to distract him. First, heavy footfall sounded from the road: the elephant was now in full charge. Then, from the direction of the bridge, there emerged a mechanical wail. Flashing machines were zig-zagging this way and that, coming to a stop as Oli's group reached them. Bili strained his eyes to see the tall man herding Oli and the little land-orang inside one of the machines, which rolled away again, back over the bridge.

Again, Bili jammed the post into the ground, pushing down as hard as he could. He jumped and splayed open his legs, making a solid purchase between the wall and the wood, and, as he pulled his body higher with his hands, he made sure that each upthrust was buttressed by his feet.

Had the elephant wished to trample him, it would already have been over; as it was, the huge animal hurtled right past. But the gangly giant was advancing now too, seemingly startled by the thing behind it, an animal that looked like a clouded leopard, only significantly – *horrifyingly* – heftier.

Now steady at the top of the pole, Bili gave his arms as firm a push as he could manage. He threw out his hands, extending his fingers – and caught hold of the wall's ledge. He was up.

Sitting a moment on the wall's top, he gazed over a scene of untold strangeness. The world of the land-orangs was truly an enigma. But it was their world, and they could do with it as they wished. Now, all he desired was to get into these trees.

Wasting no more time, Bili ascended into the canopy. A voice began yelling from inside the walls: 'Whoo-haw! Haw-haw! Hook! Hook!'

It was another long call!

The acrid stench of burning immediately dulled Bili's excitement, however. He knew he must stay clear, but the temptation to glimpse the mature tree-man, even for a moment, was too great.

Into an orchid-filled fork he dropped. He cast his eyes across a wide, enclosed space. And then he saw, there in the mid-trees across from him, a number of tree-men. They looked confused, almost frightened, by their surroundings, as though they were somehow out of place, but Bili was nevertheless delighted to be so near his own kind again.

✦

The other orangs looked to Akan to help make sense of this commotion, but he was every bit as clueless as the rest of them, and simply sat, watching it unfold with panic and confusion dulling his senses.

The ground-men had come into the park with a roar of machinery. On two wheels and on four, the land-orangs, led by a man whose hairless head reflected the light, tore across the site with no regard for nighttime's peace, causing animals who never spoke during the dark hours to squawk and holler as though the sun had come up.

The land-orangs came on foot, too. A whole gang of them, cackling and calling, swigging drink from green bottles which they tossed onto the hard ground with bursts of shattering shards.

In a row, Akan and the others sat along the front side of the netting, gawping out through it in the hopes of glimpsing anything that might make sense of this pandemonium. A fog of acrid smoke drifted in front of Akan's nose, causing a ripple of frantic energy to course through him; if wildfire was here, he was going to end up with even more hairless patches across his body.

A sudden growl sounded to his left side, unlike any he'd ever heard in nature. The depth of it told him it had come from out of a very large throat. He turned to a see an animal of incomprehensible size: striding freely along the walkway, its head held proudly aloft, was one of the golden cats.

In unison, every orang scurried to the middle of the enclosure and ascended the bare ironwood. The terrifying cat, however, paid them no heed, and simply carried on its way.

In the sky above, there then sounded a strident bark

and the unmistakable beating of large wings: a pair of wrinkle-beaked hornbills had taken flight.

'How can this be?' said Riz. 'Why are the animals *outside*?'

Ari swung apprehensively around the fractured trunk's top. 'The forest is burning again. They must be evacuating the enclosures. But they're not doing a very good job of it!'

'Where's the train for us?' asked Riz. 'They wouldn't let us burn, would they?'

Just at that moment, the shiny-headed man came tramping along the walkway with a long, sharp object in his hand. Though he only glanced at the orangs, it was enough to reveal to Akan a meanness he had never observed in their kind, a look so cruel it made his cheeks tingle with blood.

The hairless man ran his metal over the net as he strode past, and a straight gap appeared along its width. A two-wheeled machine juddered up behind him, which he climbed onto, then a deafening blast of noise exploded from its back side as it speedily carried the man away.

Akan regarded the slit in the net with disbelief. 'You two,' he said to Amay and Inda. 'Get down there and see what he did.'

The pair shimmied down the dead tree's trunk and knuckle walked up to the enclosure's front. From the branch, Akan watched as they sat in front of it, side by side. They tentatively held out their hands – which passed into the outside – then they pulled themselves through the slit.

The other orangs hooed with gleeful astonishment.

Akan eyed each of them in the line. 'Go.'

'What?'

'Go.'

'But we don't know the outside. We want to stay with you.'

'Fine,' said Akan. 'But go ahead of me. Just remember.

Leap into the elephant enclosure from the walkway. Cross the field and go into the trees. You can wait for me there.'

'But what about, you, Akan? You've spent so long talking about this.'

'I'll be right behind you, boys. There's something I need to do first.'

Still the prickling sensation needled Akan's cheeks. Lifting up his fingers, he felt the beginning of two unusual pads protruding from each side of his face, and in that moment an urgent cry appeared in his throat which he sent up into the still air of the night:

'Whoo-haw! Haw-haw! Hook! Hook!'

He descended the tree, and walked to the open net, then stepped right through it.

'Whoo-haw!' he called again. Then, as quickly as his legs could take him, he went across to the bird enclosures.

Several of the boxes already stood open, their residents gone – but not the one he was here for. In front of him, perched unhappily on a bar of metal, was the Bird-King, his feathers the very same shade of red-brown as Akan's own hair.

His heart throbbed with such force that he felt it as physical pain. Too completely terrified this time to look into the eye of the mighty spirit of war, Akan stared at the shiny mark upon the cage's bars, where somebody had recently struck it.

Akan gripped the mesh in his fingers, and pulled. The door swung open with a loud creak, and the kite dipped his white head.

'I give you your freedom, mighty Lang,' said Akan, stepping to the side. 'All I ask in return is that you assist me in my own war.'

The kite hopped onto the metal bar on which the door had sat, balancing upon his clawed yellow feet. He dipped his head once more, and then he leapt, spreading out his wide wings, and took off onto the branch of the nearest tree.

Anguished lang-orangs began calling out in a pleading tone. 'Please stop this! It's not safe for the animals to be let free like this!'

Startled by a loud smash, Akan ran back to the walkway as the two-wheeled machine came thundering up behind him. Its riders laughed cruelly as they passed him, and the male on the back threw a green bottle in his direction, but already he'd come to the low wall of the elephant enclosure, and was over it before the hurled object shattered against the ground.

Without once stopping, Akan scurried across the field, hauling himself up a low-hanging branch on its far side and into the safety of the trees. Immediately, he felt their strength radiate into him.

Ari and Riz and Amay and Inda whooped at the sight of him. 'It was as you said! The elephant enclosure led us to safety!'

Akan felt the edges of his mouth creep up. This was indeed a cause for celebration; it may not have happened the way he wanted it to, but the only thing that mattered was that he had found freedom.

'What now?' said Inda.

It was a thought that hadn't really occurred to Akan, so preoccupied had he been with simply getting out. 'Now… now you choose. Your lives are your own. You can learn to live as wild orangs. Or you can stay with me, and I will teach you. But if you wish to come with me, I expect you to help me take care of something very important.'

'What? Help you with what, Akan?'

He readied to answer, but before he could open his mouth a familiar voice called out from down in the elephant's enclosure, a voice so improbable in these surroundings Akan felt it must be in his imagination.

Yet it continued.

And it was calling him by name.
'Akan! Brother!'

Nestled among the orchids in the fork of a mangowood, Bili was mystified by the behaviour of the young orangs across from him. Why hadn't they scattered in response to the long call? They ought to be nowhere near that male.

He peered through the foliage to a vast netted enclosure. This surrounded a few unnaturally positioned trees, from which an odd black circle was swaying. The net had been slashed along its front side, and a lone male was making his way through the opening. 'Whoo-haw!' he barked, as he went bounding along a walkway.

Bili followed the individual with his eyes as he went across to a cage. A creaking of metal sounded, and a large bird swooped away unseen, but just then land-orangs appeared on the walkway on their wheeled machines, and the lone male went running over to a low wall bordering a field. He leapt up onto this, then jumped into the trees on its other side, joining the other orangs who were gathered there.

Bili could see that the male had the appearance of an adult with the first sign of cheek pads widening his face, and that the side of his head was marked with a spidery scar. Glowering, the male sat beside the others, scanning the environment, and that was when Bili's heart skipped a beat: when the orang looked his way, he recognised him.

'Brother!' hooed Bili, running out into a clearing that smelled strongly of elephant. 'Akan! Brother! I've finally find you! It's me, brother! It's Bili!'

Bili saw Akan leap back in shock for just a moment, and his eyes narrow. Then he heard a squeal come from his mouth.

'That's him, boys! Get him! If you want me to show you how to survive in the wild, you'll help me kill that nasty little orang!'

16

CROSSING THE RIVER

AKAN HAD DREAMT of this moment, yet his first free steps were anything but joyous.

Dropping onto the road from the low-hanging boughs that cascaded over the sanctuary's outer walls, he was met with pandemonium; the land-orangs' world was entirely too bewildering for the victory to be savoured.

In the street, males were fighting males. There were bloodied noses and knocked out teeth, and lights which wailed as they flashed red and blue. The heavier men with shiny caps on their heads drove clubs of wood into the scrapping gangs, leading certain individuals away with their arms tied firmly behind their backs.

'Why are you taking *us*?!' spat one tied man. 'They caused this when they killed Budi!'

Yet all this mayhem proved lucky for Akan: with most of the violence unfolding to the right, Bili would have fled to the left.

Akan's enclosure mates dropped down beside him, immediately balking at the scenes surrounding them, but Akan was quick to focus them on the task at hand. 'Keep up!' he shrieked. 'My brother won't have got far!'

Galloping on his knuckles, along a road thronging with activity, Akan led his friends to a bridge over a wide river, where three directions stood before him. Straight ahead was a brightly-lit, domed building: the kind of place no forest-man would ever wilfully approach. The left route was the quietest, and dark too, which would have appealed to Bili. But a long hedgerow that skirted the riverbank to the right was tall enough to conceal a crouching orang, and the clusters of trees standing tall at the end of the hedges would have been hard for Bili to resist.

Akan held his gaze on those far-off trees long enough to see, only faintly visible in the darkness, a clambering dot of red-brown.

'That's him!' barked Akan. 'Stay close!'

He led his party along the hedgerows, trying not to be distracted by the many odd sights and sounds. In the sky, an eagle passed over, a chubby wingless bird clasped in its talons, while on the road one of the wheeled machines crawled slowly by, a distorted voice blaring out from its top.

'Please remain in your homes! Dangerous animals are roaming the streets!'

Where the hedges ended, Akan went straight up the first palm in the cluster. His heart thumped with the anxiety of losing sight of his brother, yet still he had the capacity to appreciate being in real trees again, and leapt through them with exhilaration, paying no mind to the possibility of a fall. All that mattered was keeping on Bili's trail.

Back on ground again, Akan flicked his head from side to side until – there! – he saw another patch of trees across the road. But the moment he stepped out, the two-wheeled machines appeared with a cacophony of growling, and he was forced to wait while its grimacing riders went past.

Reaching the soft grass of the verge, Akan led his gang up into the next cluster, and raced to clear it. He came to ground once more, and, looking ahead across the next road, he gave a startled hoot: Bili was simply standing there.

'Is that him?' asked Riz, when the others caught up. 'What's he doing?'

Akan swatted a fly away from his eye, noticing Lang's wide wings in the hazy sky above. 'He knows he can't escape me.'

He balled his hands into fists. A great wrong was about to be righted. The next phase of his life – a happier, more just one – was soon to begin. But right as he stepped out, his companions grabbed him back.

Akan protested fiercely, but then quietened when he saw, standing to his left, upon four incomprehensibly huge paws, the golden cat. Close enough that even in the dark of night the wrinkles in its nose were clearly visible, it held open a jaw full of the most terrifying teeth Akan had ever seen.

The others turned to run, but Akan gave a hushed command. 'Don't.'

On the right was one of the animals from the park, the two-legged creature with the tiny hands and the formidable tail. Its back to the cat, it was nibbling the berries in the shrubs. 'It's got that weird deer in its sights,' whispered Akan. 'If we attract the cat's attention now, we'll become its prey.'

The cat dropped its head and stuck its behind up, its shoulders bouncing up and down alternately. Then, with the foraging creature still oblivious, it pounced.

By the time the prey spotted the predator, it was too late. The cat took the neck of the deer-thing in its horrid mouth and held it to the ground, negotiating his body away from the kicks it issued as it futilely fought for its life. One final thrust of the deer-thing's feet concluded its struggle, and the tension in the cat's absurd torso relaxed, and it dropped to the grass to began licking at the blood that trickled out from the punctured neck.

So absolutely horrifying was the ordeal that Akan

couldn't take his eyes off it, and when he eventually did, it was only because Bili was making a run for it, escaping into a forest whose trees appeared all oddly alike.

Panicked, Akan ran out, and slapped his palms against the ground in naked rage. 'We've lost him!'

His four companions remained at a distance. Ari and Riz knew better than to look Akan in the eye at such a time as this, but Amay and Inda, that bit younger, made the mistake of glaring directly into his face, and for the imposition nearly earned themselves some fresh scratches. But before Akan could strike, more machines came screeching to a halt in front of them, and a group of wide-eyed ground-men piled out.

'They want to take us back to the enclosure!' yelled Amay.

Akan looked in every direction for an escape route, but they'd left themselves in the wide open. However, an unusual thing then happened. The ground-men formed a line, and ushered the five orangs across the road, into the peculiar forest.

'Go on!' said one of the them. 'Go back to your home.'

Akan didn't see his brother again for days.

Only after two dawns had passed did he even get a sense of his Bili's intention, but he was sure now that he was heading east, in the direction of his beloved basin.

He left behind no clues. Akan knew, the moment Bili had vanished into the endless stretch of oil-fruit palms, that he would do everything in his power to remain invisible, which made surveying the forest for nests pointless. Time spent looking for his brother's bed would only allow Bili to widen the distance.

Instead, Akan had to rely on intuition. He went up to the canopy often, stretching his head out beyond its tallest leaf to read the landscape ahead of him. In all directions, long lines of smoke billowed where wildfire consumed the treetops. It was a grim spectacle to behold, but it wasn't all bad: Bili was obligated to travel according to the flames. After all, what tree-man would venture where the forest burned?

Avoiding any section where the inferno risked closing in on them, Akan led the others along a winding course, until they eventually came to a river. Bili would like this; he could just hear him, arguing in favour of journeying along it. 'It's our one safe boundary from the threat of flame,' he'd say. And he'd be right: fire could leap on a breeze at any time to trap any creature. But it couldn't leap into water.

So, for mile after mile, Akan pushed through the sub-canopy along the river's edge, nesting where the boughs of the ironwoods forked just right. With every branch he gripped, Akan felt the power of the trees radiating into him, and though the memory of that awful enclosure would never leave him, it did at least begin to dim.

Then, disaster. Up ahead, blocking their path, was a wall of flames, towering to the very height of the treetops.

Ari and Riz slumped glumly. 'We have to go back.'

Inda and Amay took a different view. 'Or we could go around it.'

But Akan dismissed both ideas. 'Look,' he said, tipping his chin towards the other side of the river.

'What are we supposed to be seeing, Akan,' said Ari. 'There's nothing there.'

'Exactly. The fire is only on this side.'

Riz shrugged his shoulders and held his hands out wide. 'But how does that help us?'

'Because,' said Akan, 'we're going to cross it.'

The four juveniles began hollering – 'It's too wide! It's too fast! We'll never make it!' – but Akan ignored their pleas, and climbed down to the bank to get a better look at the centre of the river.

A torrent of brown water was splashing up, with white spray at its fiercest points. Nothing at all made him want to attempt to cross it, save for a single thing:

On the other side, making his way up into the high boughs, was Bili.

He'd already made it across.

A low groan came from Akan's throat. In moments, his brother was about to lose himself in a vast tract of open rainforest which, if the absence of smoke was anything to go by, was clear of wildfire.

The groan grew. 'Whoo-haw!' it went. 'Haw-haw!' Then, bellowing what he now understood was his own signature long call, he voiced the full cry. 'Whoo-haw! Haw-haw! Hook! Hook!'

The long call drifted across the river, causing Bili to turn back and lock eyes with him. The fleeing brother's shoulders heaved with the labour of crossing the water, but since he knew he was in no immediate danger, he took his time with his ascent.

Akan then, to the surprise of the others, began to laugh. He'd so desperately needed to catch this glimpse of his brother, which proved his intuition had been right all along.

Eventually, he *was* going to catch Bili.

Inda, far more excited than he ought to be, was whooping, too. 'How did he do it? How did he do it?'

'He must have jumped,' suggested Amay.

Ari and Riz gave hoots of laughter. 'Jumped! What do you think he is, a gliding squirrel?'

'Well,' protested Amay, 'he didn't swim it, that's for sure. If you're all so clever, why don't you tell me how he did it.'

'He must have gone around.'

'A hornbill carried him.'

'The river must have stopped flowing for a moment.'

But Akan ignored their squabbles, and simply

watched as his brother vanished into the canopy, uttering, after a time, a single word. 'Bamboo.'

The others fell silent.

'He worked this out a long time ago. We must have only had four or five monsoons behind us. He decided he wanted to get across our basin's river. He made us wait where the water was shallow, until a long stalk of bamboo came floating past. I had to hold onto the roots in the bank, while he held onto my hand. Then he waded out, and grabbed the bamboo stalk. We threw it up onto the bank, then waited for a second one. At first, I thought he was going to push them across like a bridge, but they were far too short.'

'So what did he do?'

Akan let his lips form the faintest of smiles. 'Help me get some stalks and I'll show you.'

In no doubt this was going to take a while – after all, Bili had only just got across himself, and he'd had a significant head start – Akan patiently directed the others down into the water, and soon they'd formed a chain extending a third of the way into its width.

They made quicker work of it than Akan had expected. *This* was why he wanted others with him on his pursuit of Bili. What had taken his brother a long time, had taken them mere minutes.

'Imagine these stalks as extensions of my legs,' said Akan, standing beside the pile that now littered the bank.

Inda and Amay rasped with delight. 'Nice to meet you, stalky legs!'

Akan silenced them with the back of his hand.

'Listen! It's just like pulling yourself up into the canopy on a pair of vines: get each one firmly in a hand and a foot, and hoist. The trick is to make sure they're firm in the river's bottom. If the water's too deep, we'll have to wait until we can get longer stalks. But so long as your head and shoulders are above the surface, you can walk your bamboo legs across the river's width, one at a time. Be warned, though, this will tire you out. Who wants to go first?'

Ari and Riz looked at each other. 'We'll go. But we want to do it together.'

'As you wish,' said Akan, and while the pair lowered themselves back onto the pebbles and waded into the shallow edge, he felt his breath constricting with anxiety.

Sensibly, Ari and Riz practiced balancing on the bamboo poles before they went in. They held themselves in the air without an issue, and soon were striding along in the shallows. But now the time had come to make the crossing, would they find it quite so effortless?

Out they went, one pole at a time, until their legs vanished – then their bottoms, then their bellies. The water was rushing against them, but they held firm, making sure with each new step that the poles were sunk deep into the soil, just as Akan had instructed. They then proceeded through the central torrent, and marched out onto the pebbles on the other side, hooting with victory.

Akan, alone, went next. Initially impressed with how well the pair had coped, he could feel in the bed of the river the perfect grounding: the poles took purchase the instant they were set down, allowing him to cover the rest of the distance with ease.

Now only the younger pair needed to come across, and Akan could resume the chase. Not since the incident with the big cat had he been so near to his villainous brother, and a frisson of excitement tingled in his spine.

But when they reached the middle of the river, Amay and Inda got stuck. Smaller than the other three, they lacked the strength to hoist out their stalks, so remained where they were, neither coming nor going.

'What do we do now?' they yelled, but what was Akan supposed to tell them? They were in the same trouble whichever way they went.

'Look,' Akan called out. 'Here's another bamboo stalk

coming. Reach out and grab it, then see if you can walk on that one.'

Amay, who was nearest to the approaching pole, twisted his body around to maximise his reach.

'Ready?' yelled Akan. 'Now!'

Amay threw out his arm, but the stalk was wider than any of the original ones, and he failed to clasp his hand around it. Instead of letting go of it, though, he quickly tossed out his other arm – which shifted his weight away from his legs. At once, the extensions toppled over, and Amay was sent straight into the torrent.

Inda gave a whimper of shock. Just what he hoped to achieve with his next move was unclear, but Inda suddenly jumped out for Amay, abandoning his own supports.

Now the pair of them were under, and, in barely the blink of an eye, they were washed downriver. Only their reaching hands were visible as they battled to save themselves, and, to Akan's horror, it didn't take long for those to sink as well.

※

It would be as many days again until Akan next saw Bili – but it wasn't with his eyes that he detected him.

By now, a new odour had arrived in the forest. There was little variation in the way things smelled in these parts – smoke clung to surfaces like moss to rocks – but every once in a while, on some limb or other where branches bulged with figs, there was now an animal smell. Vaguely musky, with undertones of sweat, this was undoubtedly being left by an orang who wasn't aware quite how quickly he was growing up.

The party of three advanced in silence, as they'd done ever since the loss of the younger boys, while Akan sniffed at conspicuous crevices and feeding spots. But catching a scent of things was getting difficult, not only because of the sooty smell of burned foliage on everything, but because there now seemed to be a lot more wildlife around.

Why was forest life so dense here all of a sudden? In every tree, there was something: a slow loris crammed into a cavity; a frog clasping to the underside of a leaf. Different varieties of hornbill, which often squabbled in each other's company, now shared boughs agreeably. In one mangowood there was a sad-eyed bearcat; in another, a python. Even the bulbous-nosed mangrove monkeys had moved into the vicinity, knowing full well they'd have to abandon the food they so cherished.

It was as though something were attracting them all here.

No.

Not attracting.

Repelling.

Akan darted up into the canopy as quickly as he could, to be met with a startling sight.

The entire north and south horizons were awash with a thick grey-white wall of smoke.

Once again, the forest he found himself in had been reduced to a mere corridor.

Akan hooked his fingers over his lower lip, unsure of how to feel about this revelation. A corridor narrowed the parameters of Bili's escape route, which improved his chances of catching him. But the encroaching wildfire made the way significantly more dangerous for them both.

17

STALKER

WHERE THE FOREST met the river, in an eroded nook overhung by the earth, Bili awoke.

Nesting on the ground was safer than in the trees, with things as they were. There were ants, of course, and spiders — to say nothing of the scorpions and snakes and clouded leopards and civet cats who seemed suddenly to occupy this part of the forest. But the alternative was much, much worse, because an orang called Akan was hunting him, and that clever boy had form in tracking a tree-man by his nests.

To think how impressed Bili had once been with his brother's skills! The sharpness of Akan's eye was what had led them to their bapa, many dawns after they set out from the basin. But that same talent was now the very thing that put Bili's life in danger, making it imperative that he remain down from the boughs at day's end.

The discovery of the riverbank nooks, therefore, was a rare bit of good fortune for Bili, and he'd awoken this morning feeling unusually well-rested. Quite by chance he'd spied this one, when he went to the water's edge yesterday to pluck away an orchid for inclusion in his latest picture. A coolness had been coming up from below him, and when he dropped onto his belly to dangle his head over the bank, he was greeted by a hollow as deep as a palm frond, and he knew at once that an *underground* shelter was the perfect solution to his problem for as long as Akan stalked him back to the basin.

Emerging from out of that hollow now, into the blanket of pure white morning mist hanging over the river, Bili smiled at the thought he'd just spent the night sleeping on a cloud. But his amusement was fleeting, because the moment he pulled himself up onto the soil, a bright red missile hit him on the head.

Panicked, Bili scrambled to the first bough of the nearest tree, certain Akan had found him. He threw a fearful glance down, noticing something furry flapping on the ground — and the tautness of his body loosened. It wasn't an ambush at all, just a clumsy old moth that had clattered into him.

Halfway up the trunk, Bili found branches drooping with figs. He ate his breakfast amid a chorus of waking insects, and let the pretty song of flycatchers drift into him. Closing his eyes, it was easy to imagine he was right back in the basin, this whole horrid period of his life just a feverish nightmare.

Yet the smog of burning haze brought him right back to the here and now, and a deep sigh depressed his chest and shoulders. This ordeal was far from over.

Ready for another day on the run, Bili was about to make his first swing along the corridor of trees when the moth's scarlet stripes caught his eye again. Pausing to observe its strange convulsing, Bili wondered whether the wildfire fumes had got inside the thing. It was a worrisome thought. He coughed a lot himself these days; all this smoke didn't do a living thing much good.

The moth took to the sky. It approached Bili's tree in a disorientated, zig-zagging manner, like a pot-bellied mangrove monkey filled up with too many leaves. Up and up the moth came, right into the canopy, moving now as though in a state of distress, until it abruptly clamped onto a branch with its soft mouth parts. Its furry wings, ablaze with a red so bright as to appear almost unnatural, twitched and flickered. It arched violently inwards, then out, and then it was dead.

Bili threw out a hand to pluck it away for a snack. But just as his fingers went to clasp its fat body, he pulled them away again, repulsed by what was suddenly happening.

Poking its way out from the moth's head, right in front of Bili's eyes, was an odd kind of stalk with a bulbous tip. Like a leech questing from a sapling, it was extending slowly outwards, only stopping when it had reached the approximate length of his thumb.

Bili lay against the branch, entranced. Smoke hadn't done this to the moth: it was the work of a forest fungus.

He fixed his eyes on the bulging ball at the stem's end, ready to witness the exciting next stage of the fungus's lifecycle, and, right on cue, the tip exploded with a puff, sending a cloud of spores drifting down to the forest floor. They vanished as they dispersed, but Bili climbed down to where he imagined them landing, coming to ground just in time to see another scarlet-winged moth feasting at a hibiscus flower.

Unknown to this second insect, an unseen rain was presently falling upon it, finding its way into its tiny organs, setting in motion a macabre chain of events. Within hours, a new fungus would begin growing, and as it thrived, so the host would weary. The moth's brain, sickened by the parasite, would urge it to fly up to a high place, before compelling the creature to clamp onto a twig with its soft mouth parts – and the whole, terrible, cycle would repeat again.

Bili turned to face the dense undergrowth of the onward route, and his brow furrowed. He wasn't sure why, but this tragic pair of moths reminded him of his bapa and his brother.

Setting off now on his day's journeying, Bili pushed

on along a corridor of ironwoods, desperately racing to keep ahead of Akan and his gang while wildfires raged all around. The sun's heat grew in intensity, then grew some more, then, as the sky came awash with colour, its anger dimmed, signalling the arrival of evening. The time to seek a nook in the riverbank had come.

All his thoughts were concentrated on what bed he might find, and Bili dropped down to the forest floor hastened by excitement. But what was waiting ahead brought him to an abrupt halt.

He let out a yell of despair.

The wildfire that had raged all day had consumed trees on his left side, across the river, and on his right, in the south; now it was apparent the two fronts had closed. The way ahead was impassable.

Bili had reached the corridor's end, and the scene before him was truly nauseating. The last of the greenery bordered an endless landscape of deep black. What was meant to be rainforest was now just scorched stumps and half-fallen trunks standing from spongy clumps of ash, out of which foul-smelling smoke billowed.

He wasn't sure which was worse: that this beautiful tract of rainforest was incinerated, or that he'd spent the day venturing ever closer to a dead end.

Tentatively, he waded out into a devastated wasteland of fire-ravaged forest. The debris was still warm underfoot – these trees had burned recently – but even if he'd been able to bear the temperature, there was no way he could have tolerated the fine dust that swirled into the air each time his toes disturbed it.

Bili ached for the loss. Every one of these trees had been a thing with life, and every one had allowed other life to thrive. They had weathered countless downpours, provided untold generations of animals with a home, and sought nothing in return but to be allowed to bask in the rays of the sun they adored so very much. And now, like so many of the trees he'd encountered outside the basin, they'd melted away to nothing.

How long were these dreadful wildfires going to go on? Just one day, that was all he longed for, a single day with eyes that weren't sore and a throat that wasn't coated with soot. The few rain showers that had fallen had done nothing to douse the inferno; it seemed likely now that the flames were going to dance forever, until the forest was nothing but a charred blanket of ash and stench.

With a groan of sorrow, Bili turned back, facing once again the city he'd been so relieved to flee, that awful place with its ferocious beasts and its chaos of brawling. He leapt up, onto branches his feet already knew, and cried as he ventured westward.

Back at the riverside, he found the air even smokier than it had been before. He had to strain to see across the flowing water to the clearing, which was barely visible. The smattering of flimsy dwellings over there reminded him of the nests he put together after first leaving the basin: hastily built, and without much care. Bili thought of Oli's party — could this forest camp be theirs?

Ground-men suddenly appeared on the clearing, and Bili was disappointed to see neither Oli or the little land-orang among them. Yet though they were a different set of individuals, their angst was familiar.

There was no joy to be found on any of their faces, and their eyes blazed with a complex emotion Bili couldn't properly discern: a mix of sadness and anger and fear. Scrambling to gather their things, it seemed their plans – like his own – had been disrupted by the converged walls of wildfire.

With urgency, the small group formed a line, and marched off along the river, looking around themselves in every direction as though expecting something to jump out at them any moment. Indeed, a sound did then rise up out of the trees, but while it did not faze the people, it sent a wave of panic through Bili, for it was a long call, and it belonged to Akan.

Without hesitation, Bili descended to the forest bed and got himself nestled into the tall buttress root of an ironwood. The moment he knew must come had arrived: with his backtracking, it was inevitable he'd run into his brother.

He waited, perfectly still. Thankfully, with the sun low in the west, dusk's shadows were long, keeping Bili well concealed from Akan and his gang, who would be passing above any moment, perfectly oblivious to the scorched barrier awaiting for them up ahead.

Branches rustled, hastening the rate of Bili's breathing, and he looked up to see a flash of red-brown swinging through the trees. He held his body tight into the trunk of the hardwood, allowing one eye to peer around, just in time to see Akan's boys.

And then he saw Akan himself, the scar on his head angry and vibrant. But why was he sniffing the air like that? He was expecting flame, perhaps. And he was going to find it, too – or its aftermath, at least – when he made it to the blackened debris at the end of this corridor.

Bili swallowed hard, and took a steadying breath in through his nostrils. There was no need to panic. Though Akan was heading to a dead-end, it would be dark by the time he knew that, and he was certain to halt the pursuit. All Bili had to do was let them carry on as they were and he could skulk away into the banks of the river for the night, and they'd be none the wiser.

Above, Akan was suspended from a bough, like a very strange fruit. He held his face close to the ironwood as he caressed the bark, as though some information resided there that might help him on his way. He then dropped to a lower bough, and continued his sniffing, and as Bili craned his neck up to better see what his brother was up to, Akan tilted his head downwards and looked directly his way.

Bili ducked back. To make it around to the concealed side of the wide trunk, he was going to have to go up and over the neighbouring buttress root, so, as discreetly as he could, he manoeuvred onto it, then dangled off the other side.

But how careless! He hadn't even thought to check first, and now found his lower body fully immersed in the mature stems of a rattan plant. Rows of sharp teeth bit at him, tearing the flesh of his legs and bottom. The pain was intense enough to bring a squeal of pain to his throat, but since he'd be heard for sure, Bili clenched his teeth tight and let himself drop, falling the rest of the way to the soil and landing awkwardly on his hip.

He gave his sore hip a quick rub, then sat up and readied to snuggle in tight to the root. In the trees above, all was silent. Akan was still up there, waiting.

He sat up, and readied to snuggle in tight to the root. Inching back, Bili rested his palm on a stump, using it to pull himself the rest of the way into the nook. But it was weakened by rot, and the moment he put his weight down on it, his hand went straight through the brittle bark.

Akan shifted. But Bili remained exactly as he was, still as stone, while a soggy, crawling sensation moved over his hand where it lay inside the decrepit piece of trunk.

He let his eyes wander down to his hand, which was deep in a writhing ball of leeches.

With a wave of chill bumps standing up on his neck, Bili noiselessly brought his hand out. The leeches that had not yet taken purchase fell away, but many had attached, and a plump one was beginning to swell on the back of his hand.

He buried his face in his armpit, driven by the need to stifle the scream of horror. There may have been no elephant to scare away this time, but lingering in the branches above was a tree-man who wanted to kill him.

From further along the corridor, an unfamiliar voice suddenly called out. 'Have you found something, Akan? Do you want us to come back?'

'No, Ari,' said Akan. 'Stay where you are with Riz. We're on him, for sure.'

A limb creaked, and dry leaves rustled.

At last, Akan was advancing on.

Wasting no time, Bili shunted the leeches off his fingers. The fat one was on tight, however; when he plucked it away, it left an open wound, from which dark blood poured freely.

His hip hurt as he put weight down upon it, and the slashes of the rattan's barbs stung, but Bili remained on the ground as he scuttled to the river, throwing himself onto his belly when he came to its banks to peer down from the overhang.

Into a perfect hollow, Bili lowered his injured body, and as he dangled to swing himself into it, he caught a whiff of the scent he'd picked up while he was stifling his scream in his armpit. It was his own scent! When had this happened? He smelled like an adult! *This* was how Akan was tracking him!

On the damp, earthy soil, Bili lay on his side. For the first time, he was aware he had reached maturity. Yet he felt as though he were a little child, and – just like one – he cried himself to sleep.

❧

The blaze was intense enough that Akan – along with every other creature of the forest – was forced into the narrow band of trees skirting the river.

A knot of angst had resided in his belly all day, as he worried about the changing direction of the wildfires. He'd done well to lead his two companions where no flames leapt, but with dusk now bruising the sky, he had no cause to celebrate, for a new – and formidable – barrier was ahead of them.

Not even the very longest stalks of bamboo would help them across this one.

The trees here had suddenly gone to ash. Blackened stumps, billowing smoke, were all that remained of what once was pristine rainforest. It was a maddening sight, that made his heart instantly sick.

But so too did it make Akan's cheeks needle with anger, for it meant that somewhere in this corridor, in this last vestige of greenery for miles around, the young orang who'd so nearly killed him was at this very moment hiding.

Desperation overcame Akan in his need to locate Bili, but after backtracking a fair distance, and with the light of day now all but gone, he was eventually forced to a halt. 'It's no good,' he hooed. 'It's way too dark to get him now. Go up and make nests.'

Ari gave a groan of complaint, and made a show of gathering up the leafiest branches he could find. 'But you know we prefer the ground, Akan!'

'Then nest on the ground. But keep your eyes sharp. There's snakes around.'

Riz rolled his head as he looked nervously through the branches. 'Do you still think your brother is here?'

Hooking his fingers over his lower lip, Akan grumbled. 'He hasn't passed us, has he?'

'No.'

'Then he must be.'

'He could be watching us right now.'

Akan bristled. Well, Bili could watch all he liked. He ought to make the most of it, though, because soon his eyes would be closing for good, and it would be less than he deserved for the injustice he'd inflicted upon his own flesh and blood.

'Get some sleep,' instructed Akan. 'When the sun

comes up, we're going to have to find a way around the inferno.'

Akan hastily assembled a nest, and settled into it, and after rubbing the soot out of the corners of his sore eyes, he went straight to sleep.

But his night was not free of disturbance.

In the darkest hours, when the forest was at its quietest, a sound roused him, somewhere between a squeal of protest and a hoot of shock. Was it Bili? No, it was coming from Riz, down on the ground. For a fraction of a section, Akan considered investigating. But since no more noises followed, he drifted right back off to sleep.

His eyes opened again when the day was dawning. With a stretch of his long arms, he let out a yawn, then clambered over the edge of his nest. 'I've got a good feeling about today,' he said to himself as he descended.

Far below, Akan could just about see Ari sitting slumped beside Riz's ground nest. With his chin resting upon his fists, the young orang appeared somehow dejected.

When Akan made it down, Ari greeted him with a simple question.

'Why did you do it?'

Akan yawned a second time, and scratched the itch between his shoulder blades. 'Do what?'

Ari kept his distance, and avoided Akan's gaze.

Now wondering whether something serious had occurred, Akan walked nervously over to the nest, and his eyes widened with horror at the sight before him.

It was Riz. He lay stiffly, his dead eyes open wide.

Akan let up an anguished hoot, which drifted through the trees into a region now completely encircled by wildfire.

Not long after the stars had come out, Bili awoke with a start.

Akan and his gang, as expected, were on their way back from the impassable scorch zone, and were beginning to nest.

Momentarily wondering whether he should flee, Bili soon closed his eyes again. He had nothing to worry about. Not with this hiding place.

But later on, deep in the dead of night, he woke up again when, on the ground directly over him, footfall began to shake the soil. An animal was stalking up there.

A big one.

Bili held his breath, and listened intently. A kiss-squeak sounded — the type only made by his own kind — and his suspicion was confirmed: it was a tree-man, standing just an arm's length above the crown of his head. And Bili had a strong sense of just which tree-man it was.

His heft was impressive. Had Akan really grown so much? His face had certainly developed; now it seemed his body had matured too.

But as the seeker came, so did he quickly go, and finally, Bili was able to breathe again.

He went back to sleep, and the next thing he knew, the cicadas were whirring into life, ecstatically greeting the coming of day. Bili longed to climb out and stretch his sore leg, but he knew he must stay where he was until he'd heard his pursuers move off.

He heard more than that, though. Blatantly, Akan let his distinctive call ring out through the trees. Screeching and wailing, it was as though he were being crushed with pain. A crashing of branches followed — quick movement — and that was that: Akan's boys had pushed off in front.

When Bili eventually clambered out from the riverbank hollow, he stalled, savouring the fact that for the first time since he'd found his brother, it was once again the case that Bili was following Akan.

As he prowled the forest bed, the desire struck him to make a picture. But as he surveyed the area, he spied something odd: a nest on the ground, concealing a mound of red-brown hair, just like his own.

Startled, Bili gave a hoo. But the orang inside the nest didn't wake.

In fact, the individual wasn't moving at all.

Not even to breathe.

Step by wary step, Bili edged closer, until he saw something that elicited a wail of sorrow. The occupant of the nest was dead. Around the young orang's throat was a jumble of fingermarks.

Akan had obviously choked the life out of him.

Overcome with emotion, Bili scuttled away, slumping down in a soft bed of orchids growing out of a bole on the trunk. From this vantage point, he noticed a flitting blaze of red below, almost unnatural in its scarlet tone. It was another moth. And it was very clearly unwell.

Bili brought his head up to his hands, a harsh truth now revealed to him.

The parasitic fungus in that poor insect's brain was forcing it to act against its nature.

It was just like his father and his brother: something that wasn't meant to be there had infiltrated Dama's brain. And from that brain was borne the very thing that manipulated Akan's.

What his kin were doing was against their nature as peaceful men of the forest. And unless they learned to restrain themselves, they would end up much the same as these sorry little moths.

18

THE SKY OF BLOOD

WHEN BILI WAS LITTLE, at the age where he and Akan could just be trusted to climb into the canopy unsupervised, his mother gave an account of something that had never happened.

As she'd told it, it was a time of wildfires. Ground-men had moved into the rainforest from their towns, and had razed a whole horizon's worth of trees. It was old-growth forest, so ancient than no living orang had seen it in a state of immaturity.

The ground-men grew plants in the clearings they cut, and the crops yielded food. But when the harvest was over, they set fire to what was left of the stalks, and the flame blew up into the canopy, and the rainforest began to burn.

Yet even after the trees had crumbled away into dust, the fires kept burning. Somehow, the ground itself was fuelling the inferno.

On and on the swampy soil burned, until the moon went from plump to shy to plump again and every living creature was tormented by the smoke's choking haze.

And then, one day, the whole sky went red.

Bili had looked at Akan when she said that, and the brothers laughed. It was the one part of her story that asked too much of their imagination, and they went off to climb rather than listen to any more of it.

As far as untrue accounts went, hers wasn't a bad one.

But, Bili realised now, it was no mere story:

Above him, the entire sky was *actually* red.

It was as though the whole world had turned into an open wound. In its flatness, the red sky made everything look the same, but the river appeared especially ominous, for it was like a rushing torrent of blood.

Yet even in spite of the eerie atmosphere of the waterway, the thought of straying from the river provoked a feeling of desolation inside him. The river was his route back to the basin.

In order to deaden the sound he made, Bili journeyed as low as he could, barely above the height of the coconut palms. At the earliest opportunity, he would need to head south, where, with any luck, a route around the wildfires could be found. But for now his only concern was escaping this narrowing corridor without being detected.

Catching his eye on the forest floor was a fallen branch, heavy with berries. This was too good an opportunity to waste – many animals were now using this band of trees as a refuge, and food was growing scarce – so Bili swung down on a strangler vine to get it.

Despondently, he ate his meal. Beneath a sky of such startling strangeness, the flavour of the berries was not a thing to be savoured.

As was usual, he arranged the stalks into a picture. This morning, it was another go at the extraordinary creature from the sanctuary, with the long legs and even longer neck. He would have liked to spend more time working on the piece, but even he wasn't foolish enough to risk his life for the sake of one of his creations, so he hoisted himself back up onto the first tier of boughs and carried on his way, pleased to be journeying at last without being pursued.

Yet after a few moments, Bili began to prickle with a sensation he knew all too well.

Never had he been able to catch a glimpse of the thing he felt was behind him. Just as before, when he'd laboured alone in search of the sanctuary, a suspicion existed that his own shadow had a life of its own, and that it was playing games with him. It moved as silently as he did, rested when he rested; it used the same route through the trees, placing its feet and hands on the very wood he himself clutched. But very occasionally, it stepped where it oughtn't have, bending back a twig or shivering some leaves, then ducked aside right before Bili turned.

He was letting his imagination get the better of him, that was all this was.

'*Ackha! Ackha!*'

Bili froze.

That was a cough! The cough of an adult orang!

This was *not* all in his mind.

Calmly, Bili twisted his head around. Bathed in flat red light, on the ground where he'd eaten the fallen berries, was the unmistakable shape of a large male.

Relieved, a slow trickle of breath seeped from Bili's nostrils. But he soon went still again, for the adult then shifted onto his knuckles to more closely examine the picture left on the ground, and when he did, Bili identified the individual

It was bapa!

A rush of thoughts dizzied him, foremost among them whether or not this was a chance encounter. So long had it been since he last saw his bapa, it was conceivable they'd simply run into each other on their respective journeys. Yet it didn't take long to work out that Dama had followed him from the clifftop plateau all the way to the sanctuary.

And how easy Bili had made it for him! Each and every morning on his journey to find his brother, he'd left a picture in the undergrowth: a bird here, a flower there; Akan and Aunt Ivie cuddling in their nest. Dama had simply kept pace behind him, taking pains to conceal himself every step of the way.

Bili shut his eyes tightly. Why was bapa doing this? The last time they met, Bili had jabbed a burning branch into his side to spare Akan being killed by his father's hands.

So why hadn't Dama clasped his nine powerful fingers around Bili's own throat?

⭑

'It wasn't me!' barked Akan, scrambling to catch up.

Ari, saying nothing, simply carried on along the corridor, hoots of heartbreak spilling out on his breath.

'Please, just listen. I didn't kill Riz. I didn't even leave my nest.'

'I saw you, Akan! With my own eyes. I thought you were just discussing your plans with him. I wondered why you ran away when I called out, and now I know. You put your hands around his throat, didn't you? Just like you did with Mali.'

'No, Riz! I mean, yes – I did put my hands on Mali's neck. And I did squeeze. But it didn't work. That's why I hit him on the knee with the stone. Why would I do that to Riz when I knew it didn't work?'

Ari leapt down onto the bough of a mangowood, and quickly scurried along it before grabbing hold of a clump of branches and swinging onto the next tree.

Akan called out after him. 'The orang you saw was my bapa! Bili will tell you, if we can ever catch him. Dama hates me even more than Bili does. It's me he wants.'

'I don't believe you, Akan! You didn't get hit by lightning trying to protect your mama, and you didn't find the biggest jackfruit in the forest! The only thing you told us that's true is that you killed Iki with your fingers!'

'No!' hollered Akan. 'I only said that because I was scared!'

But in spite of his protests, it was no good; where they needed to drop south in pursuit of Bili, Ari simply carried straight on, leaving Akan no choice but to set off alone around the wildfires.

Requiring a read of the trees ahead, Akan clambered higher, and as he ascended, the chase weighed heavily on his mind. Bili could now be far in front of him. If he'd made it into open forest, he was as good as gone.

But when Akan's head broke through the canopy, it wasn't the expanse of trees that chilled his heart. Although every part of the sky was the most appalling shade of red, he was able to see now that the great walls of smoke were even closer. The inferno was tightening its grasp around the corridor – and it was doing so at a speed that was astonishing to behold.

Driven by urgency, Akan pushed south, and eventually came to land-orangs, who were busying themselves around their makeshift dwellings. From a high limb above their clearing, he peered down and scanned for the safest route through. But he didn't need to plan at all; the ground-men were hurrying to get away. 'The swamps have gone up!' one of them was groaning. 'The peat will burn for months! May God help us, and every living thing that dwells in this forest!'

Their clearing stood empty within moments, and Akan went down. Bounding across it on his knuckles, he found on the other side a small heath grove. But how peculiar! In the sandy soil, there were no footprints. Bili *had* to have been through this way! Either the fire had already got him, or...

Clever Bili! He'd covered his tracks! His brother had simply swept away the impressions from his feet with a palm frond!

Akan rushed through the heath grove and up into a jungly patch, noticing just how much hotter the air suddenly seemed to be. Nearby, voices were calling out. 'Come on! Quickly! Get on the boat!'

The breeze that blew was unlike any he'd felt in his life: it made Akan's face even warmer. Upon the air, embers were dancing like fireflies. He watched the sparks as they drifted up, igniting the dry leaves the instant they touched them.

And with this, the flames had finally caught him.

Scrambling through the palms and shrubs of the scruffy jungle, Akan paid no heed to the quality of the branches supporting him, and before he even knew what had happened, he was on his back, on the ground. He span, and pushed himself onto all fours, knuckle-walking as quickly as he could, barely outrunning the advance of the leaping flames.

The sound of running water ahead made him yelp with panic. There was no way he could get over a river!

As he ran, the memory of the last crossing played in his mind. The sight of little Amay losing grip and vanishing beneath the surface was sickening, but what happened after was now a scar on Akan's spirit. Inda, seeing his brother in trouble, didn't hesitate to help. With no thought for his own safety, he'd simply reached out into the water as far as he could to lend Amay a hand, and was dragged under, ensuring that neither of them got to see another dawn.

It was the bravest, stupidest thing Akan had ever seen, and it made him ache. How cruel, that one should be born into the world with kin who'd give up their very lives for their brother, while another should be shown no love, or compassion, or mercy.

Emerging now from out of the jungly patch, Akan saw the land-orangs heading off on a boat, which gave its familiar roar. The water they travelled on was barely deep enough to support it, though; baked into a mere sliver beneath the fierce heat of the sun, most of the riverbed was exposed.

The meandering river was shallow. An image of crocodiles momentarily flashed in his mind, but he gave this little heed, since fearing something which *may* give harm was silly when an actual threat was burning white hot right behind him.

With noisy splashes, Akan waded across the meander, and soon found himself on a sandy oval of beach on the other side.

And that was when he realised his mistake.

He had just cornered himself.

Towering into the sky above him was a sheer face of limestone. He was trapped against the biggest obstacle conceivable: a slab of rock so tall it was doubtful even the Bird-King himself could fly above it.

This was where it was going to end for him. Watching the edge of the tree line burn, Akan felt the heat prickling his skin. He was ash.

With his eyes scrunched tight, he pressed himself into the wall. Though the stone scraped painfully along his back as he inched blindly along the limestone, it was better than what his front side was having to endure: the flames across the river were now so formidable that they whipped at him.

But then the face of the rock behind him was suddenly not there, and he fell *through* the limestone, crashing onto his back in a befuddled heap.

He hopped up onto his feet, overawed to realise he was now standing in the entrance of a tunnel which led to a vast cave. Perhaps Bili had found his way in here, too?

He took a single step deeper in, not daring to hope his life may just have been saved. But then, in the river behind him, a frantic splashing sounded, and he turned to discover his brother hadn't been in front of him at all.

There in the water, rolling to put out the embers burning across his hair, was Bili.

✦

The corridor was now a tunnel of fire.

With smoke sullying the red sky all around, Bili raced through the low trees, certain he was being followed by his father. Though the muscles in his arms groaned for rest, the fear that the tunnel's flame walls were going to converge up ahead kept him swinging hastily onward.

With disgusting haze choking his throat, Bili detected a flash of colour in the trees to his left: distantly approaching was an orang a few monsoons younger than him. Down on the ground, his eye was then drawn to a host of other animals: a tapir charging among a herd of boars; deer skittering in the saplings. Flying lizards were clattering into winged squirrels as they both glided with urgency from trunk to trunk.

He shot a glance back — the tunnel had closed! – and gave a call to the fleeing tree-man. But in his distraction, he slipped from an ironwood's limb, and suddenly found himself folded over a lower bough, the wind knocked out of him as his arms and legs dangled down.

This moment of stillness turned out to be lucky, however: over the terrifying crackle of wildfire, he heard the growl of a boat.

A boat! That meant water!

Breathlessly, Bili hoisted himself up. He scrambled along to the next branch, which whipped him through the air to another one, and with his rhythm reestablished, he advanced towards the mechanical noise.

With no thought of the land-orangs who may dwell upon it, Bili darted straight out into the open tract he came to, finding on its other side a heath grove. A single trail of footprints were impressed upon the sand there;

these he followed as best he could, until they eventually became mixed up in a jumble of others.

Entering a new swathe of forest, he squealed with terror to discover the trees here were completely engulfed. Keeping his head low as he rushed into it – the air seemed a touch more breathable at the ground – he noticed steam drifting up from the pitcher plants: the liquid inside their bowls was beginning to boil.

The heat on Bili's back was so intense that smoke was coming off his own hair. Knowing that if he stopped, even for a moment, he would be incinerated in the firestorm, he scrambled as wildly as he could until he finally broke out of the trees and toppled onto a riverbank.

Although the water he found was shallow, it brought instant relief to the searing pain across his back. He submerged himself in the river, then dragged himself up onto his feet on the other side – yet before he even managed to wipe his eyes dry, an almighty shove sent him back to the ground, and a sudden flurry of blows was striking him on his face.

Akan had him pinned, and was calling out: 'Do you see, bapa? Do you see which one of us is worthy of your love?'

'Akan!' cried Bili, shielding his face. 'Why are you doing this? I only came to help you!'

'I know you're here, bapa! I saw what you did to Riz! But I can do it, too! Are you watching, bapa? Let me show you your gift!'

Bili felt Akan's hands working their way up his neck, and he shoved him off his body to twist away. But he was free from Akan's clutch for only an instant; the moment he was back underneath his brother, he felt his fingers suddenly tighten around his throat. He thrashed his arms and kicked his legs, but the effect was almost immediate.

Unable to catch a breath, his senses dimmed.

The terrible red sky faded to darkness.

The crazed screams of his brother grew silent.

Even the noxious, dirty odour of tree smoke failed to disturb his nostrils.

And then, quite suddenly, his senses returned to him.

Dazed, Bili span his body onto all fours, overwhelmed by the sudden chaos. What was happening here?

Legs stood on the sand to his right side – and there were four of them. He lifted his head to see the wide body of an adult covered by scars: the very ones he had himself put there the day he thrust the burning branch into his bapa's side.

Dama had arrived, and, with an almighty shove, sent Akan hurtling onto his back.

'Do it, bapa!' Akan hollered, as Dama grappled to get on top of him. 'Finish what you and Bili started!'

Bili's dizzied state deepened. 'No, Akan!' he shouted. 'You've got it all wrong! I tried to save you that day! It was *him* who had his hands around your neck. Don't you remember? Look at his scars!'

Dama now had Akan pinned, and was biting him and clawing at his eyes and nose. Bili tottered up onto his feet, becoming upright just in time to see the young orang from earlier leaping through the air and landing on the giant male's back.

Dama gave a yell of shock, and twisted away from Akan.

'Ari!' squealed Akan. 'Be careful! He's extremely—'

'You killed my friend!' hooed Ari. 'You killed my friend!' He then sank his teeth into Dama's back, dropping the adult to the ground with a roar of pain.

As the pair flailed upon the earth in a violent tussle, Bili felt his brother's eyes on him, and he turned. Akan's eyes were blazing with rage, and his shoulders heaved with a pain and fatigue which clearly overwhelmed him. He was on the very cusp of springing forwards for Bili when a dreadful cry from the young orang stole both their attention.

The little tree-man was in a bad way. His eye was glued shut with blood, and from the edge of his mouth foamy sputum bubbled. But that was the last of his worries, since Dama had by now managed to embed his fingers into the poor orang's neck.

Bili took several paces across to the left of the beach. The trees across the river were now saturated beneath a wave of white flame, their canopies falling onto the ground with loud explosions. He turned back to the limestone, looking up to see if there was any way to scale it, edging further along until his feet were almost in the water where the cliff rounded the meander – and then he felt a distinct pocket of cool air.

Right beside him, a cavernous hollow sat in the rock. The briefest of glimpses revealed that multiple smaller cavities lay within it – and that one deeper in opened out to a great yawn of a cave entrance.

Bili dropped low, ready to scramble to safety. But before he took off, he looked back at his brother. 'Bapa!' he was shrieking. 'Please leave Ari alone!'

But it was obvious to Bili in the way the young orang's tongue lolloped in his mouth that the life had already left him.

Dama's head whipped round to face Akan, and in his crazed eyes, Bili saw disease. If anything healthy dwelt inside this ruined creature, it was no more substantial or luminous than a single firefly.

Dama lunged, but Akan jumped quickly back to the cavity bored into the cliff face.

And within an instant, both Bili and Akan were retreating into the limestone, their bloodthirsty father fast behind them.

19

A LIGHT IN THE DARK

WAITING in the cave was a darkness comparable to nothing. A night spent low in the ironwoods, with a moon too shy to show even a sliver of itself, was a dazzling noon when viewed against this.

It was like journeying into a beast of unfathomable scale, and, as Bili tunnelled ever further, he supposed he must at last be reaching that creature's innermost core.

Hours now since he'd shaken off the crazed Dama, he wasn't willing to rest for even a moment, so he pushed ever onwards, deeper and deeper down the cave's echoey arteries. But in his frantic effort to get away, he forgot to pay attention to his route, and was now lost in a hidden world as alien to a man of the forest as the canopy was to a fish.

Weaving and dipping as the terrain demanded, he felt his way ahead with outstretched hands. Then, just as he was on the brink of abandoning all hope, he saw, like a single star in the night sky, a dot of light hovering in the distance.

The path to it was rough. The passageway's slickness caused him frequent tumbles, and much effort was needed to first climb, then descend, each of the many barriers that stood between him and the illuminated speck. Every time he felt he was getting closer, the blue-white glow seemed to edge further away, but gradually he found he was becoming lit by it; then, after at least half the day in total blackness, he could make out his fingers grasping in front of himself.

On he went, ever lower into this gargantuan beast's belly. And then, around one final corner, he saw, far, far up in the cave's domed lid, an ear-shaped hole. It appeared tiny to Bili, yet he suspected it was at least as wide as an ironwood was tall, and through this opening, a radiant shaft of pure light streamed into a cavern that was utterly wondrous in both its size and its beauty.

So entrancing a sight was it that Bili's lip began to quiver with emotion. Swallows and bats flitted distantly through the light, whose brilliance made it apparent that the inner walls of these caves were far from the colourless sheets of rock he'd imagined them to be. Marbled with yellows and reds, and a purple like the stains on his fingers left by mangosteens, there was as much vibrance in here as there was in the world outside. Even the cave bed was carpeted in greenery!

Stepping out from the tunnel and into the vast chamber, Bili was startled to realise just how high in it he was. He wondered for a brief moment just how he was going to get down to its floor, but as his eyes adjusted to the dim light, they picked out a natural pathway winding along the rock.

On the long trek down, the magnitude of his surroundings entranced him. The thought that he might be the first ever forest-man to set eyes upon this secret world was a giddying one. At every stage of his journey lower, he passed beautiful stone spikes that stood upright from the rock. Like softer versions of the brittle spires they found on that accursed clifftop long ago, these odd pillars were of every height and shape, and it seemed that for every one that grew upwards, a counterpart was to be found dangling down from the ceilings.

To think that these things were always here! The way they stood – in some places by themselves, in others grouped in clusters – made him feel less lonely, as though they were residents of this hidden place. Taken all together, the spires formed a kind of audience. But what was it they watched, if not for the still, silent emptiness? A smile spread on Bili's face; the creatures of the caves might say the same about his basin, when to him it was more beautiful than any place his mind could conjure.

A jumble of emotions overcame him at the memory of the slopes of the beloved basin. How very much he'd love to return there, to know it hadn't suffered the same devastating fate as the incinerated forests that loomed far and wide in this part of the world.

Such unimaginable destruction to the forest habitat – it was starved of rain, levelled by machines, burned by the mysterious hands of the land-orangs – provoked in him such terrible worry. But with a happy hoot, he dismissed his fear. The basin was there. It would always be there. And he would always be one of its children.

Coming at last to the floor, Bili's spirits brightened. Awestruck, he made his way towards the two enormous columns of stone standing at the cavern's centre, a pair of towers which seemed to reach the very roof. But so entranced was he by them, that he paid no attention to where he was placing his feet – and promptly fell through the floor.

His fall was broken by his ribs. With his arms splayed upon the cavern bed, Bili realised his entire bottom half was over a shelf, dangling away into a lightless chasm. Heaving himself out of the hole, he lay a while on his back while the drumming of his heart calmed, in no doubt that he'd just cheated certain death.

Dizzied, he rose to his feet, observing now how the entire floor was pitted with hundreds of these terrifying craters. He flicked a pebble inside the neighbouring hole, which ricocheted off its sides for an age before crashing on the bottom. Had his own crater been sheer instead of sloped, that pebble would have been him.

With extreme care, he progressed along the chamber's bottom. In a dry section, to his great surprise, he located a cluster of plump green pitcher plants. But his eye was attracted away from them by the many spires of soft, gold-brown rock – especially to the three that stood in a row all by themselves.

At roughly shoulder height, this trio of stone fingers magnetised him. They stood level, with the middle one just slightly taller than the others, and were less tapered at their top than many of the others here. Directly behind them, a circle of absolute darkness lay flat upon the rock: a cavity whose depth was sickening to imagine.

He looked again at the pitcher plants, and the hint of a smile lifted his lips. He gave a mirthful hoot, which echoed in the cavern's infinity. 'Of course!' he said to himself, then excitedly scrambled around for a pointy rock.

He carried his rock across him to the trio of spires, and struck the taller of them near its top, sending a chunk of it toppling to the ground.

Bili's brow furrowed with concentration as he struck it again. With only two hits, the middle spire had taken on the approximate form of a head.

A rush of blood made him swell with joy. This was it! This was his chance to make the picture he'd dreamt about!

Back when he'd first envisioned it, after their father responded with blankness to the image Akan had ruined, Bili knew more could be accomplished with dimension. Pictures didn't need to be flat: they could be shaped like real things.

Yet the stone shards at his disposal on the clifftop then had proven inadequate. He simply couldn't build them up into the shapes he desired, since each time he balanced the pieces, they immediately toppled again.

The material in front of him now, however, was *already* built up. Now, it needed only to be shaped.

This was how they were going to finally deal with the menace of Dama.

But he wouldn't be able to pull it off without his brother's help.

❧

No beams blazed, and nothing green grew, and the only sound was the echo of drips and a bat's sporadic shrieks. Yet even here, deep in the interior of the cave, the air was tainted with the noxious haze of a million scorched trees.

A place sealed off from the outside world, Akan could conceive of nowhere better to hide. As he lay aching, curled up in a hollow set in a tunnel of ludicrous depth, he supposed this was how a pangolin or a stink badger experienced the world, their home a complex of connected shafts, pits and passageways. But he was a forest-man, not a burrowing creature. Eventually, he was going to have to find his way outside to face his doom.

By now, his cuts had begun to crust over. The taste of blood had gone too, washed away with a rinse of bitter water scooped out of the puddles that sat atop the many mysterious spires. His neck, however, felt bruised – even turning his head from side to side was difficult – and his hands had swollen from the effort of defending himself against Dama's frenzied assault.

He reached up to his face. Beneath his fingertips was a veined web of scarring to which, he supposed, his father had just added some extra threads. Yet more would have joined them, too, if he hadn't been able to lose Dama in the cave's enormous entrance chamber earlier.

Bili had done well, coming in, and Akan knew he was lucky to have been so close behind him to benefit from his quick thinking. Running for his own life rather than to take his brother's, Akan had followed him around the chamber's main path; when Bili pulled himself up onto a higher trail via an overhanging ledge, Akan had done the same.

At the edge of that elevated path, within the chamber wall, small tunnels led into the darker regions of the cave. Bili had already vanished into one by the time Akan himself scrambled up, but it was enough then to remain where he was, since an oblivious Dama was charging onwards to the rear of the entrance, still on the lower path.

Bili had probably saved him with that piece of shrewdness, and as Akan lay wearied and bruised now on the smooth curve of rock, he found he couldn't get his brother off his mind. He longed for sleep, hoping that it might dull the soreness of his pains, yet a nagging echo of the recent attack kept his thoughts busy.

He recalled being pinned by Dama to the ground, and Bili calling something out. In the heat of violence, those words had simply drifted into his ears, then right back out again.

Bili was cheering Dama on, that was it. Urging him to rid the world of the nuisance that was Akan, once and for all.

Wasn't he?

While Akan's eyes darted from side to side, he forced himself to catch hold of the cries his brother had made back there.

"Look at his scars…"

Was that it? Dama *did* have scars: hairless, coarse patches on his father's flank, so like his own.

"Don't you remember?"

Remember *what*, Bili? All Akan could recall was the fiery clifftop overlooking the ground-men's clearing, and a horrid pair ganging up to destroy him.

"You've got it wrong…"

No! It was just clever Bili tricking him! That was all this was!

"It was him *who had his hands around your neck…"*

Akan ran his touch below his chin. The pain burning in the skin and muscles of his throat now was the same as it had been then – because it was caused by the same nine fingers!

Another of his brother's cries then materialised – and as it did, tears welled in Akan's eyes.

"I tried to save you that day…"

Suddenly back on the clifftop, the memory Akan had tried so desperately to reclaim was now playing in his mind.

It was a memory of being shaken violently by the shoulders, and of his brother, screaming out.

'Please don't hurt him!'

Of bapa, overcome with some kind of unnatural rage, stretching his fingers into points and moving closer, clasping him around the neck and squeezing, squeezing, squeezing until the light dimmed and the colours – the green of the canopy, the flickering orange of flame – faded.

'Cover your throat!'

On and on, the memories flowed, of Bili, stepping forward with a burning branch in his hand, thrusting it into bapa's side to prompt a squeal of pain, then crying out as he dropped the flame-covered branch to reveal a pair of hands gone red with blisters. But still Bili was seeking a way out of that horrifying situation.

They were just about to make a go of getting down the flaming trunk, of fleeing the savage brute, when, with terrible abruptness, a great force then shunted him from the back…

Akan snapped back to the present moment, and his eyes, dampened with anguish, came open.

It had nothing to do with his brother.

It was – *all of it* – his father's doing.

It was Dama who threw the flaming rock that struck him on the head. Who starved him of air. Whose kick had sent him hurtling down the length of the pathway tree and smashing into the ground like one of the many boughs burnt away from its trunk.

The rush of emotion that suddenly poured into his heart was more powerful than the torrent that washed away poor Amay and Inda – and Akan, physically unable to bear it, passed into unconsciousness.

🐦

'Brother!'

The voice came in a whisper, but was enough to rouse Akan from a tortured sleep.

He opened his eyes, but in the darkness of his hidden nook, this made no difference at all.

Tripping off the limestone in a streak of quiet echoes, the voice sounded again. 'Brother! Where are you?'

Akan gave a groan. 'Bili?'

'Brother! Help me find you!'

Akan sat up, aware now of his hair's dampness where a trickle of water had run beneath him. 'I'm here!'

'Sshhh! Quietly.'

'Here. Bili, is that really you?'

A soft shuffling sounded on Akan's left side, and he suddenly felt the warmth of hands on either side of his face, where his cheek pads were emerging. It immediately calmed the fluttery rush of anguish in his belly.

'Are you alright?'

'I don't know,' wheezed Akan. 'Maybe not. My throat —', he swallowed hard, '—it hurts. I'm weak.'

'Then just listen. Dama wants you, and he's not going to give up until he's killed you. I wish that wasn't the truth, but it is. I might have come up with a plan, though.'

'Why?'

'Why what?'

In a strained voice, Akan spoke slowly. 'Why *me*? What did I do? Why not you?'

'I don't know, for sure. But I think something happened to him when we were just babies. I think bapa saw a ground-men use his hands to kill. And it was like he caught some kind of horrible disease that damaged his mind, and now, anything he sees as a threat, he feels compelled to destroy.'

Akan coughed. 'He's not threatened by you, though.'

'You were always the stronger one, brother. Besides, I think he *is* threatened by me. But something about the pictures I make seem to bring him back to himself. It's like medicine. That's the only reason he didn't kill me, and why he followed me all the way as I came for you. Something inside him wants to go back to how he was before.'

'You came for me,' rasped Akan.

'Of course I did. You're my brother. I love you.'

Akan let out a pained moan. 'But how can you?'

'Love is forever, brother.'

'I don't deserve it.'

'All things deserve love.'

Akan reached up and took Bili's hands in his own. He caressed them with tenderness, feeling the fibrous scars. 'You were hurt trying to save me. And when you tried to save me again, I nearly killed you.'

'It's not your fault. The disease that's in bapa is now in you, too. And it's in me. But we have a choice, Akan. I saw a land-orang do a terrible thing to one of his kind, but I'm not going to allow their disease to alter my mind the way it has bapa's. Don't torment yourself with what happened. You thought you needed his love. We both did. But we were wrong. We don't need anything from Dama. Our mothers taught us to look after ourselves, and that's what we must do now.'

'But how, Bili? How are we possibly going to get him to stop?'

A certain vitality was present in Bili's words now, and it may have been the case – in darkness this absolute, Akan couldn't know for sure – that his brother was smiling. 'We're going to give him a choice.'

'What does that mean, Bili?'

'Don't worry about that now. Just do as I ask, will you?'

'Of course, Bili. I'll do anything you want me to do.'

'I need you to lure him to me.'

'But how will I find you?'

'I've found a place that's going to help us. When I start my work, you're going to hear knocking. Follow the sound until you see a speck of light far away. Keep going – deep, deep into the tunnels – and you'll eventually see me in a cavern below you. Come down to me, but only when the knocking has stopped. That's very important. Be warned: the going is hard.'

'I don't mind, Bili. I'll do whatever it takes. I promise I won't let you down.'

'Good. Listen to me, Akan. You need to watch every step. There are pits in the cavern floor that seem to have no bottom. If you fall, it will be the end of you.'

'I'll be careful, Bili,' said Akan, and although his desire was to keep hold of his brother's hands forever, he released them from his clutches and listened sadly as Bili shuffled off into the depths of the caves.

20

THE CHOICE

A LONG TIME passed before Bili's knocking commenced. Or, it didn't; it was impossible to know for sure in a place where the sun's passage was invisible.

Fumbling blindly as he crawled through the tunnel, Akan focussed only on moving forwards. He pulled his body over cratered mounds, and crammed it beneath low ceilings, until, eventually, he discovered he could stand straight again.

Being upright brought him no joy. What a truly unpleasant place these caves were! Things were scuttling around his feet where he tentatively edged ahead, and his mind tormented him with a ceaseless cascade of scary thoughts: he was about to walk into an orb-weaver's web; there was a pit viper coiled near his foot; Dama was waiting around the next corner with his nine terrible fingers.

And then there was the smell.

Somewhere nearby, below bats in their million, was a mountain of their noxious poo – a sharp, musty stink almost unnatural in its intensity. These creatures could dwell anywhere they wished – in the very clouds if the fancy took them – yet they chose to make these caves their home, and that made no sense to him at all.

There was a reason these endless dark chambers stood empty. Life was meant to be lived where there was light, where lessons could be learned from the visible environment. Anything that spent its life in a cave would be half-mad, its mind as still as the finger-like spires that grasped up from the floor and down from the ceiling.

A faint whimper spilled from Akan's tender throat. Who was he to remark on the minds of other beings, when his own had become so twisted?

As he pushed onward towards the approximate location of the knocking, it was a question that endured. How had it happened, this corruption of innocence? Some of it, he supposed, was down to his fall. His memory was as pitted with holes as the limestone beneath his knuckles, and in his confusion he'd built a version of history that simply didn't match with reality.

But, no. The bitterness had dwelt in him to begin with. He'd put himself back together using only what pieces were already there. So lost had he been in his own envy and insecurity, he couldn't even see when his brother was trying to help him. It truly *was* as though he'd been touched by some kind of disease.

The darkness of the cave served to amplify Akan's misery, and he went on, step after step, torturing himself with remorse. Eventually, however, he rounded a corner, and in that moment, the knocking grew clearer, and a small band of light could be glimpsed up ahead.

His torment subsided. *That* was the place! It was there that Bili wanted their bapa.

He turned back to face the void, and took a huge breath into his lungs. Then, as loudly as he could, he issued a call into the blackness. 'Bapa!'

The echo bounced an unbelievable distance; Dama *had* to have heard it. But Akan was taking no chances.

'Bapa! I give up! You hear me? Come and put an end to this!'

Every few steps, Akan repeated the call, listening

intently for a sign it had been received. None came, but he knew he'd done all he could for now; pushing on along the arduous path towards the knocking, he just had to trust it had worked.

Finally, Akan emerged into a glow bright enough to make his red-brown pelt visible. He'd come out of a passageway high up in a chamber whose sheer scale was breathtakingly vast. Every creature he'd ever met in the forest could dwell in a cavern of this size – and all the land-orangs from the city, probably.

The chamber's floor seemed as far away again as the entire distance he'd already covered, but thankfully the pathway down the cavern's edge was easy going. On his descent, he was struck by how wrong he'd been in his impression of the cave. This place wasn't ugly at all – it was quite possibly the most beautiful space he'd ever seen.

When he drew nearer to the bed, Akan began to wonder just what Bili was so very busy with. The knocking had been ceaseless: a chip, chip, chipping that preceded the sound of debris landing upon the ground. Whatever it was, there was no doubt in his mind that it was important, and he wished to follow Bili's instruction exactly.

Akan cast a glance over the ground he now stood on, seeing at once why Bili had been so clear about walking with care. A single misstep down here would mean the difference between life and death.

Faintly visible in the low light, Bili was on the chamber's far side. Akan wanted nothing more than to be near his brother now, but with the knocking of stone against stone still echoing across the walls, he knew he wasn't yet permitted, so he slumped against a spire, and watched.

High above, in the passageway that had brought him here, a speck of red moved.

It had worked.

Dama had come for them.

Akan jolted, then sent a hoot of alarm across to Bili. Carefully avoiding the holes in the ground, he leapt out into the open, and journeyed around the two massive towers of rock standing in the chamber's centre as he made his way over to where Bili was working.

'Akan?'

'I know you're still working, brother, but bapa is here.'

'It's alright. I'm as good as done. Come!'

The moment Akan saw what his brother had made, his mouth fell open.

It was *them*!

Standing in front of a very deep pit were three spires, whose tops were rounded into the shape of heads. The taller one – Dama – was in the middle, with Bili on the right and Akan on the left. Gouged out from the front side of each head was a pair of circles: eyes. There was a line too along the lower half, curved slightly up: these were smiling mouths. And on two of the heads, Bili had left a pair of curved, protruding disks: the cheek pads.

On the left spire – the stone Akan – a fracture line ran around the neck, and for some reason Bili had dug out the foot so it stood balanced on a narrow base. To Akan, this looked extremely precarious: barely a twig supported the entire structure. But he trusted his brother knew what he was doing.

Bili looked shyly at his feet. 'What do you think?'

Akan took hold of his brother's hands, studying them momentarily. What incredible power his brother held in these nimble fingers.

'You need to hide now,' said Bili, 'before bapa sees you. He'll be down soon.'

'But what are you going to do, Bili?'

The sound of gravel spilling along the pathway indicated that Dama was on his way.

'I'm not going to do anything. What happens next is up to him. Now hide.'

Akan's eyes glistened with tears. 'Bili. I know I'm not as smart as you. In fact, I think you might be better than me in every way. That's why I behaved like I did. I'm so sorry.'

'I know you are. I knew it the moment we fled from that burning beach. But you needn't be. Now hide. He's coming. Oh, and Akan – I'm not better than you in any way, brother.'

Akan hopped around the rims of the craters, and lowered himself behind a chunk of stone. From beyond the ear-shaped hole in the chamber's top high above, a dreadful shriek rang out from a mere speck of red-brown in the sky.

It was the Bird-King.

Akan's heart began to beat violently. What was Lang doing here now? He wasn't needed anymore!

Heavy footsteps sounded on the cave bed, then drew to a halt. Akan peeked around to see that Dama had arrived. In his eyes was rage, in addition to an obvious sense of curiosity.

'Come closer, bapa,' said Bili. 'Come and see the gift I've made for you.'

Dama walked on his knuckles to the three carved spires. His eyes settled first on the one on the right.

'That's me,' said Bili.

Dama gave a snort and held out his hand, which he let rest, just for a moment, around what was meant to be the neck.

'And this is you in the middle. Ignore the mark on the side of the head. That was just an accident I made with my tool.'

Akan watched, his breath held deep within his lungs, as Bili began to step cautiously nearer to the pit on the rear side of the spires.

'Do you like it bapa? It's us.'

Dama sat blankly, his eyes blazing upon the strange structures in front of him.

'And look, bapa,' said Bili, reaching out to the figure on the left. 'Here's Akan, too.'

Immediately, Dama reared up. He wrapped his large hands around the statue's neck, whose fracture line saw to it that the head rolled backwards off the body, and it rolled down into the pit. The many seconds of silence which preceded the thunderous smash told Akan that the hole was twice as deep – maybe three times – as the pathway tree whose length he had himself plunged.

The attack, however, wasn't enough for their bapa, and he continued to push the stone Akan as though he wished to see that toppled into the hole as well. Taking a run up at it, Dama hurtled his body into the rocky figure – but so delicately was it balanced upon the weak base Bili had carved, it stood no chance of resisting such force, and toppled backwards. And Dama, his arms clutched violently around it as it rolled towards the edge, staggered with it.

With only two figures now standing, Akan slapped his hands against the ground and hooed with laughter as he realised what Bili had done.

It was a pitcher plant! Bili had lured their father with something he couldn't resist, right to the very lip of oblivion!

Akan ran out just in time to see the spire drop into the hole, and with it, Dama.

'Bili!' he called out. 'You really *did* give him the choice!'

Bili looked back at him with the strangest expression: in his eyes was a sense of peace like Akan had never before seen. It was as though he knew a thing must now happen, and had chosen to meet it with bravery. Then his eyes opened wide, and he vanished into the hole.

Dama had taken Bili by the ankles on his way down.

And now Bili was gone.

A crash sounded: the stone Akan had finally hit the bottom, where it shattered into pieces.

Akan raced to the rim of the pit, only to find Bili clutching hold of a brittle ledge, his fingers slipping back quickly.

But he didn't appear in the least bit frightened. 'Brother!' he smiled, half enveloped by the cavity's darkness. 'Promise me you'll go back to our basin. Do it for me!'

And with that, those incredible fingers of his lost their grip, and Bili followed Dama into the very bowels of the earth.

Akan jumped onto his stomach and slid along the dirt until his own head was looking down into the lightless abyss, and for a moment he saw in his mind young Amay and Inda, and he considered jumping in after his brother.

But instead, he waited for what he knew must come.

After a sickening delay, a crashing thud told Akan his father's fall had been broken.

Then, an instant later, another crash followed behind it, as his brother hit the bottom.

Akan thrashed his fists upon the rock, bitter tears spilling into the chasm. He rolled over and lay on his back, delirious with grief, sobbing and pleading into the depths of the cave.

Yet there with nobody to hear him but the swiftlets and the bats – and a great red kite, circling in the blood-red sky above.

⁂

Time moved in a surreal series of jumps, its passage marked only by the movement of the bright shaft of sunlight spilling in from the opening far above, which seemed to be here one moment, and way over there the next. Eventually, this brilliant beam of light found its way directly onto Bili's creation, and only then did Akan get up.

Lit this way, completely bathed in golden light, Akan was compelled to approach it. With his own figure now gone, he saw only his father and brother, standing beside one another.

A familiar sting of bitterness cut into him.

But then he reached out and let his palms settle on the statues a while, and when he pulled his hands away again he noticed something upon the side of the left head he hadn't spotted before.

Bili had told their father to ignore it. *An accident*, he'd called it.

Yet it was shaped, very deliberately, like a web-shaped scar.

It wasn't Akan's brother and father who stood side by side in this chamber of unmatched beauty.

It was he and Bili: brothers, solidified in rock, who would stand here together for all of time.

21

CLIMBING FROM SHADOWS

IN THE DAYS after Bili fell, Akan didn't once venture from the very spot of the tragedy. Curled up in the space between the two stone figures, he waited, his ear trained upon the dreadful pit for any kind of call. But it never – no matter how desperately he wished for it – came.

After a while, nature got the better of him. Driven by hunger and thirst, he began to wander around the chamber, deriving a certain pleasure in its enchanting beauty. His weak legs struggled to carry him as he ascended the various pathways, but after he slaked his parched throat with a pool's cool water, he felt some of his old strength return, and dared to venture higher up the walls, where he pilfered eggs from out of a swift's nest.

But the sight of Bili's creation down on the cavern bed – it stood as a mere speck from up here – cost him his renewed vigour, and he hurriedly descended again to be beside it.

He sickened. Cramps in his abdomen and feverish chills kept him flat on the floor for days, and all he could do in that wretched state was look at whatever the bright beams illuminated as they spilled down from the ear-shaped hole, and at the two almighty columns of rock that towered in the centre of the chamber.

As he began to recover from the stomach sickness, these towers became an obsession. The shorter one was as high as any tree he'd ever climbed, but the larger one standing behind it was almost half as tall again, its head so very far from its foot that it couldn't properly be seen. Though the heights of these rocky trunks were endlessly interesting to Akan, what was especially alluring was the patch of greenery crowning their tops. Amid the gloom of the lower chamber, these two splotches of foliage stood out like stars in the night sky, and he imagined how soothing it might be to once again feel softness like that beneath him in place of the unyielding solidity of rock.

One evening, just as the shaft of sunlight had turned golden and was about to settle upon the pair of stone brothers, Akan had a startling revelation. For hours, he'd done nothing but yearn to be amid that foliage. But even though the shorter tower was climbable, there was no way he was going to leave his brother in the cave. Except, the tower was *in* the cave! There was a way he could stay with Bili, *and* experience the sensation of being back in his native habitat!

So, the next morning, he climbed it.

Though he was exhausted when he reached the top, it was worth it for the fresh air alone: a reprieve from the constant funk of bat droppings. But there were berries too, ripe on the emergent trees, fruit which brought energy to his muscles and just a trace of a smile to his lips.

Yet by far the biggest benefit of climbing it was the view it afforded him of the neighbouring column. The taller one was actually *connected* to the world outside – it was a pathway tower! And, what was more, he could see that outside the chamber, growing above the roof, was actual *forest*.

So tantalising was the sight of it, he knew at once he

was going to have to scale the other column, so this morning, after a big scoop of water from the pool and an egg swiped from a swift's nest, he began the ascent.

At the top, he collapsed in the shade of the bushes. After so long in shadow, the glare of the afternoon sun made his eyes stream with tears, so he scrunched them shut and promptly fell asleep. But now, upon waking, he was ready to explore.

He clambered up the final slope of rock which led to the chamber's roof, and found himself at last outside the vast network of caves.

Standing atop limestone hills that offered a vista of such immensity, he forgot momentarily to breathe. The hills into which they'd fled, he quickly understood, acted as a barrier to the encroaching wall of flame.

To the left side of these cliffs was a heartbreaking expanse of charred forest, stretching all the way on to the distant land-orang clearings where lines of smoke were still, after all this time, billowing. Down there was where Akan had pursued Bili. The corridor that had given them safe passage to the river was now nothing but blackened stalks rising out from a bed of ash.

To the right, however, on the other side of the cliffs, was a wilderness that stood in total contrast: sweeping endlessly on as far as his eyes could see was green canopy, banks of low mist hanging where it dipped here and there into valleys.

The moment he saw it, he knew the time had come to honour his brother's final request. But he wanted one final night in the chamber with Bili – and to accomplish something that was, in all likelihood, doomed to fail.

He got to it at once. The first stage of the task required nothing more taxing than tearing away palm fronds, but even this took time; the clear blue sky was just so very distracting. There was so much life out here! Swooping nearby was a pair of hornbills, their bushy white crowns fluttering as they went into the canopy to perch. Cicadas whirred, and swallows trilled and, distantly, gibbons sang their playful songs.

An embarrassed smile rose faintly at the sides of Akan's mouth as his pile of fronds grew higher. How very silly he'd been, to keep himself hidden away down there for all this time!

Since he'd last been in open air, the moon had fattened to a circle and slimmed to nothing at all. He'd made a point, at the beginning, of counting each new dawn on one of his digits, but after the sum exceeded his available fingers and toes he gave up. What difference did it make, how much time had passed since Bili fell? All that mattered was that he had, and by doing so he'd condemned Akan to dwell inside the caves like some scuttling cricket or white-eyed salamander.

Day upon day, Akan had skulked in shadow, never once leaving the vast chamber. He'd decided early on that this was where he lived now, a suitable home for a creature whose heart had gone so dark not even the very deepest nooks of this forgotten world could compete, and though he missed fruit, and the texture of wood in his hands and feet, he wished only to deprive himself of all that was verdant and fresh.

But that wasn't what Bili wanted for him.

Bili, as always, had known better.

Confident now that he'd stripped away the longest of the palm fronds, Akan dragged his pile back with him to the slope, and stood at the apex of the taller tower. One by one, he let the fronds sail down into the gloom of the lower cave, then, very cautiously, he climbed after them.

By the time he reached the ground, the brightness of day had softened, and the enormous beam of light that found its way in through the cavern's opening was glowing with a warm radiance. Knowing that soon the light would be upon the stone figures, Akan set to work right away.

First, he gathered the fronds together, heaping them at

the side of the cleared space in front of Bili's creation. But then, as though a waterfall's cold cascade had suddenly landed upon him, he froze on the spot.

He hooked two fingers over his lower lip. What was he supposed to do now? Bili made it look so very easy!

He grabbed up four fronds. Bending each in its centre, he laid them down so that they formed a circle. But the shape that appeared was too round, so he snatched up the top and bottom branches and made their bends shallower, before laying them back in place. Now the circle was flattened: less like a coconut, and more like a mango.

Time was running out – very soon, the chamber would grow as dark as midnight – so he quickly placed two more fronds, bent delicately, at each of the rings' squashed ends so that they sloped away from the main shape.

It would have to do.

With urgency, Akan then began to peel off the leaves from the central stems of the leftover fronds, which he scattered beneath the circle to fill up the space between the two slopes.

He looked up: the edge of the beam had now found the stone Akan and his stone brother, Bili.

The final task was to scoop up handfuls of pebbles; these he tossed on top of the ring as neatly as he could, positioning the bigger ones where his memory told him was most appropriate.

And that was it. Time was up. The glowing beam of soft red light was now upon the messy arrangement of banana fronds which lay before the two stone heads.

Akan plopped onto the ground and pulled his knees up beneath his elbows. 'If only I could have been like you were,' he said to the stone Bili. 'All you ever wanted was what you already had.'

He began to weep.

'I tried my best. But you probably hate it, don't you,

brother? I just thought that, in the evening when the sun shines here for a minute or two, you might like to look upon our basin.'

✦

The trees were strength.

With every thrust of his legs from off some high bough, Akan could feel these living giants toughening him. Every clamber, every swing. From the fragrant, papery leaves in the lowland heaths to lone palms buckling with bananas, from the spindliest of saplings to the ironwoods of the rainforest, within each and every vine and branch was a power: there for any creature who had the will to accept it.

And Akan accepted all of it, gladly.

Yet theirs was a strength not quite as formidable as he'd known it once to be, for the rains, it seemed, had still failed to arrive.

Back in those days when he dwelt in the cave, he'd see it come in every now and then. Thunder clapped in the clouds above the ear-shaped hole, amplified ominously by the lightless tunnels snaking all through that secret world. The sight of a torrent as it spilled into the chamber, visible only where the dim rays permitted it, gave Akan hope that the monsoon had come at last. But each downpour was a mere shower, and the forests beyond, so very parched amid the choking haze that lingered upon every horizon, were forced to endure yet more hardship.

Still, simply being back in the canopy was a thing to be savoured. Akan, physically altered and shattered emotionally, felt almost like his old self again some days. The wound inside him was raw – a fresh pit in the bed of the limestone chamber – but it was increasingly becoming the case that the pain of it was not so great that he couldn't enjoy the serenity of a jungle stream, the sweetness of a mangosteen, the soothing cooing of a pair of doves.

As he journeyed on, it seemed he saw things among the trees that he'd never really noticed before. The unique shade of green on a birdwing butterfly had always been that colour, yet in the past he thought nothing of it; now, though, he hoped every morning when he rose in his nest that he'd get the chance to look more closely at one for a moment. It must have been the cave that had done this to him; when things were bathed in shadow for so long, it made everything seem that bit more vivid.

One morning, while he was keeping his eyes alert for a glimpse of some pretty bird or other, Akan saw a glowing in the corner of his vision, and he recoiled. Unwilling to even look at the hovering firefly, he turned the other way, and his ears picked up voices.

These were the first ground-men Akan had come across since the ones who fled on their boat. Oddly, no clearings scarred this part of the forest; the land-orangs were actually *journeying* beneath the canopy.

Cautiously, Akan followed the sound. From his vantage point in the mid-trees, he looked down to find a small group. A female was tending to a youngster whose foot was wet with blood. 'Be still, Rahimi!' she was saying. 'You've got to let me clean it!' She proceeded to pour liquid on the foot; the injured young male gave a scream that made Akan's stomach turn.

Thankfully, the anguish died down, but the chattering among the group continued.

'We can't live like this.'

'It won't be forever, Nadia. Once we make it to the port we'll be safe.'

'But we've never even *seen* Madura. This has always been our home. Why were our grandparents' generation encouraged to come if we're not really wanted?'

Another pair of young males appeared from out of a fabric dwelling then, and Akan was struck by the scarring that marked one of their heads. Their faces were dirty and their coverings torn, and in their eyes was a weariness that spoke of deep pain.

'Perhaps it will all be brought under control soon, and we can return to our village.'

'There's nothing wrong with having hope, son. But we have to be realistic. It's likely their attacks on us haven't even begun yet. They're not going to stop now. The best we can hope for is to make it onto the boat before they find us. And in the meantime, Rahimi, we'll just have to take extra special care where we put our feet, won't we?'

Just then, the firefly caught up to Akan, forcing him to look at it as it drifted through the undergrowth beneath him. And as he watched the glowing creature gliding through the bushes, it made his heart sicken with shame.

A second group of land-orangs appeared a short time later. Again curious as to why they were so deep in the rainforest, Akan approached from the canopy to check them out.

Like the first lot, they appeared afflicted with a weariness, and in the tattiness of their coverings it was clear they too were suffering. In fact, the closer Akan went to the small band of ground people, the more their anguish became acute. The females were sobbing – one more so than the rest – and a small girl was letting out howls of distress as she clung to the legs of what he supposed was her mother. Then the sombre energy shifted into one of terror. 'Run!' they yelled. 'They've found us!'

It was rare for land-orangs to move so stealthily, so Akan was surprised when a third group of ground-men came bursting out of the undergrowth, sending the others scattering away. Akan shifted his body around the side of the trunk to avoid being seen, but when agonised calls drifted up into the mid-trees, he craned his neck down to see exactly what the arrivals were up to.

By the time Akan's focus snapped on the figure laying below him, it was apparent that the individual was already dead. No others, from either party, remained here now; faint yelling indicated they'd already moved on.

Akan dropped down on the boughs of the fig tree, then negotiated the high buttress roots until he made it to ground. The land-orang lay face up with his eyes open wide to the canopy. From his neck, blood oozed, and the only thing that went through Akan's mind while he looked blankly down at the body was Dama.

On the day he fell, Bili speculated that it was an incident just like this one that gave their bapa his sickness. Dama, he'd reckoned, had seen something it wasn't common for a forest-man to see, and it had troubled him in ways Akan would likely never understand.

Perhaps Bili was right, and the pictures may have helped to bring Dama back to who he was before. The magnificent shapes Bili had sculpted in that vast chamber ought to have been all the medicine their father could possibly need. Yet, rather than let that marvellous creation cleanse him, he chose to destroy himself, and its creator.

Leaving the body on the ground, Akan went back into the treetops. Pushing his head through the canopy to scan the horizon, a sight up ahead took his breath away: as though it were floating on a hazy bed of mist, a hill with a plateaued top sat distantly in the east.

Buoyed by the sight of it, he swung at arm's length in its direction. But in his mind, he was still reeling from witnessing yet another act of violence.

He himself was infected with the mysterious sickness of the land-orangs. A remedy existed though – dear Bili had shown him this. From now on, he would do everything in his power to ensure he cleansed himself as often as he could, so that the disease passed out from him forever.

He held his hands up in front of his face, and studied them as never before. A wide smile lifted the edges of his mouth. Such amazing tools!

They could be used to destroy.

Or they could be used to create.

The ground-men had made their choice.

And he had made his.

22

A SILLY LITTLE BIRD

LOVE IS FOREVER.

Bili said that, and there hadn't been a single day on his journey back that Akan didn't ponder it.

Finding his way to the basin wasn't difficult at all, in the end, which made all those nights spent worrying in his nests a complete waste of time. He wasn't lost, and never had been; since he couldn't travel where land-orangs had hacked down the trees, nor where the trees had crumbled to soot, the route was all but decided for him – and, luckily, it had led him exactly where he wished to go.

So much forest had burned in the time since he'd set out with his brother. It was an odd sensation: somehow, the rainforest seemed to have *shrunk*. Of course, there was still plenty of it – enough, at least, that days went by without sight of another orang. Yet Akan, who had come to know of such matters, carried within him a vague sense of its parameters, as though the *whole thing* were now merely a corridor, and not the endless expanse he'd always imagined it to be.

But unlike the last corridor he'd traversed, this one met no dead end: directly ahead of him, atop an incline of canopy, was a circular ridge of rocky cliffs. The basin, spared from the inferno's dreadful appetite, appeared just as they'd left it.

At the sight of the towering rim, Akan's eyes welled. He could almost see his brother's reaction. Bili always got silly when he was excited: he'd be dangling upside down, clambering up onto Akan's shoulders, jumping circles on the spot while he hooed and squeaked and blew raspberries.

In his absence, Akan could manage only a sad smile. He sat in a high branch awhile, and simply looked on at the rising slopes, wondering if the residents within that vast bowl even knew of the chaos and anguish that existed this side of it.

Up ahead, a flash of colour suddenly drew his attention away. At the sight of wisps of red hair, Akan's head drooped, and he stared sadly at his bellybutton.

Not a single one of the tree-men he'd encountered since he left the caves had tolerated him. All he wanted was to simply sit awhile with his own kind, but something about his presence compelled them to move away.

He lifted his fingers up to the side of his head and delicately brushed the scarred threads of his web-like wound. Others probably assumed no good could come of mixing with a creature as battle-ravaged as him, even for a minute or two. Although he meant no harm to any of them, they saw in him only what they wanted to see.

Perhaps that was his punishment? He wore his history upon himself. Scarred as he was, he would never be allowed to forget any of it.

Then again, he didn't *want* to forget. His history was who he was. Yes, there was shame in some of it. But a life without shame was a life without learning, and any creature who failed to learn failed to truly grow.

Akan looked up to discover that the orang – a recently-matured female – had actually come closer.

Opening his mouth to say hello, he was surprised to hear something else altogether emerge from it.

'Hook! Hook! Whoo-haw!'

Why had he done that?! Embarrassed, he slapped himself on the face, noticing that his cheek pads had grown even rounder.

But the female wasn't deterred, and came and sat directly beside him.

'I'm Iza.'

'Hello, Iza. I'm Akan.'

'You're sad.'

'Yes,' said Akan, turning away. 'I am.'

'Somebody hurt you.'

He brought his hand up to his scar, though more to cover it than because of any physical discomfort.

'Yes,' he said. 'Actually, I sort of hurt myself.'

'What did you do?'

How to even answer that! His shoulders slumped, then his fingers hooked over his lip as he searched for the right way to respond. 'I suppose I let the things that don't really matter to me become more important than the things that do.'

'Oh,' said Iza. 'All of us do that.'

A quiet moment passed while Akan built up the courage to utter something he'd not yet had the chance to say out loud. 'My brother died.'

Iza turned to face him. His eyes met hers for only an instant, but it was enough to see she'd felt the weight of his words. 'I lost my sister.'

'You did? How?'

'She fell, Akan. We were climbing in forest where flame had once been. A branch gave way beneath her. And she was gone.'

'When did it happen?'

'A couple of monsoons ago.'

'Do you still miss her?'

'Of course. But she's still here, really. In my heart.'

'Do you ever wonder why it was her who fell, and not you?'

'I do. But that doesn't achieve anything.'

'Maybe not,' said Akan. 'I can't let it go, though. Ever since I lost Bili, I feel this great pressure. Sometimes it feels so heavy I'm not sure I can bear it.'

'What kind of pressure?'

'Like I'm supposed to, I don't know, make more of myself. Like it's not enough to just *be* here now. Like I've got to prove I count for something because I get to sit here, breathing the forest air, listening to the whistling cicadas and talking with you, and he doesn't.'

'Do you think he would want you to torment yourself like that?'

'Bili? No! He was far too kind to think that way.'

'Then the pressure is coming from inside *you*, Akan.'

Just then, a deep clap of thunder rolled through the dark clouds above, and a wind – uncommonly cool for these endlessly humid times – shivered the canopy. He looked up again to the rocky escarpment, then rose to his feet. 'I have to go now,' he said. 'I enjoyed talking though.'

'So soon?' replied Iza. An unfamiliar kind of playfulness in her eyes made his stomach oddly queasy. 'I thought you might want to hang around with me for a few days.'

Akan gave a shy smile. 'Some other time, maybe. I have a promise to keep first.'

And with that, he swung off eastwards into the neighbouring tree, the wind now so blustery that some of the spindlier branches were sent hurtling down to the forest bed.

✣

When Akan made it up to the basin's western rim, it was still the middle of the day. Yet the sky was as dark as dusk.

Lightning whipped across the face of the clouds in ropes of blinding light, a ceaseless mayhem of violence that made his brow dip fretfully. The gusts were so strong that, during his climb up, he'd avoided straying out on limbs; the last thing he wanted after finally arriving was to join the hornbills struggling in the sky above.

He was standing on rocks where, many dawns ago, Bili had sat dangling his feet into the pool, stroking the tail of a bearcat. Almost against his will, Akan's eyes tracked away from the empty river bed and along to where Bili had later laid pebbles into circles, and his heart fluttered to see the three rambutans still there.

Rambutans! How cross his brother had been with him to discover that his carefully positioned circles had been rearranged. But how was Akan supposed to know what smart little Bili was thinking?

Blankly starting at the three pebble smiles, a pit-patter of rain specks began to fall upon the sun-baked verges of the escarpment, stirring up a scent that was at once soothing. The specks then became globs; the wind howled up the inner slopes of the basin – then, with a suddenness that was alarming, a sheet of rain fell from the dark clouds.

And it didn't stop.

Akan held out his arms and let the torrent wash him clean of the dust and the smoke and the blood and the tears of a journey that had brought him to maturity.

The monsoon, at last, had arrived.

Making a shield above his eyes with his flattened hand, Akan looked down over the vast bowl of rainforest as steam began to rise from out of it. The river bed was already filling, sending white water cascading down all seven tiers of the waterfall to nourish the basin below.

Soaked to the bones, Akan lowered himself from the

verge and into the cover of the forest. On careful swings, he went to the ironwoods that bordered a stretch of fast flowing water. Then, just as he took shelter within the nook of a fig's buttress roots, a shrill shriek sounded and a blaze of reddish-brown came swooping in above him.

It was Lang, the Bird-King. The spirit of war had returned.

Without thinking, Akan picked up a large stone and immediately hurled it in the bird's direction. 'Go, silly thing!' he yelled, and the kite took flight over the ridge, and as it vanished down the outer slope, Akan saw that it had never been anything more than that: just some silly little bird.

He settled back into the protruding roots, and watched with awe as the rain pelted the surface of the river to create a million ripples, and as he did, he thought of Iza and her sister.

'She's still here… in my heart,' she said.

It was true then.

Bili, as always, was right:

Love really is forever.

Akan lifted a branch from the sodden earth, and smiled sadly. His heart needled with pain, but so too was it gladdened to know that Bili's life and his own were forever bound together by a love that was as permanent as a couple of stone statues in some faraway cave.

The intensity of the rain calmed just a little, and the magnificence of his surroundings was suddenly revealed.

This was why Bili wanted him to come back: so that he knew to never, ever take for granted again what it meant to dwell in the majesty of their basin.

From off the tip of the leaf beside him, drips steadily cascaded into a puddle. The *glop-glop-glop* was satisfying; more so when he drummed his stick against the buttress root in the space between the splashes.

Glop. *Tik.*

Glop. *Tik.*

Then he added the *swish-swosh* of a nearby leaf to the arrangement, and when it too fell into rhythm, Akan gave a hoot of laughter and toppled to his side, slapping his hands onto the earth of a forest once again blessed by rain.

THE END

HISTORICAL NOTE

In 1997, one of history's worst megafires broke out on the tropical paradise of Borneo.

The blaze was prompted by the lethal combination of a natural weather phenomenon and a style of farming known as "slash and burn". Since Borneo was suffering a prolonged drought at the time, the deliberate burning of crop fields spelled trouble for the wider Asian region.

The inferno's impact, however, was soon felt globally when the peat swamp forests subsequently caught on fire. Peat swamps are formed where rain and floodwaters prevent organic matter from fully decomposing, leaving soil permanently wet. Like a giant sponge, this layer of peat captures thousands of tonnes of harmful carbon dioxide per hectare. As a result of the Borneo wildfires, so much CO_2 was released back into the atmosphere that the biggest ever annual jump in harmful emissions was recorded.

The effect of the wildfires was devastating. Lingering burning haze caused widespread damage to respiratory health across eight countries, with an area of rainforest roughly the size of Germany incinerated. For an endangered animal like an *orang-utan* (from the Malay "person" + "forest"), loss of habitat on this scale is catastrophic.

Wildfire only tells part of the story of Borneo's shrinking canopy, however. Ancient and pristine rainforest is increasingly being replaced by row upon row, million upon million, of oil palm trees. Currently estimated to be worth just under $100 billion, the palm oil industry continues to grow. It's estimated that every person on Earth gets through an average of 8kg of this versatile oil every year. It's in our chocolate, our peanut butter, our ice-cream, our soaps and shampoos, our lipstick – and a miscellany of other products.

Shrinking forest can house fewer animals, thus numbers of wild orang-utans have plummeted by over a half in just one decade. By 2025, it is estimated that only 47,000 orang-utans – the most intelligent primate, bar humans – will exist on Borneo. This is around the average attendance of a single Premier League soccer match.

✦

Violence between the Dayak and Madurese ethnic groups has existed in some degree on Borneo since the 1950s.

The tension stemmed from the Indonesian government's "transmigration" policy, which sought to redistribute people from overpopulated centres to the nation's sparsely inhabited outer islands. As well as easing the pressure of urban crowding, it was also hoped that the policy would help tackle poverty, since landless farmers could now grow valuable crops on earth hastily cleared of its forest.

The people of Madura – a crowded, poverty-stricken island with infertile soil and limited economic opportunities – made the most of their government's scheme. Hundreds of thousands of Madurese islanders uprooted, with many heading east to settle on the beautiful, rainforest-blanketed island of Borneo.

The influx of migrants caused immediate unease in sections of the local population, who felt the Madurese people to be arrogant, rude and inclined towards criminal activity. The Dayak people, a large ethnic group historically renowned for the practice of headhunting, saw themselves as suddenly disadvantaged by the arrivals who, they claimed, were in part responsible for the worsening of their own living conditions.

It wasn't until the late 1990s, however, that the rivalry between the competing groups turned into something altogether more deadly. Between 1996 and 2002, bloodshed – predominantly Madurese – became commonplace at locations across Indonesian Borneo, with the resulting atrocities shocking the nation and onlookers around the world. Of the approximately 1000 Madurese fatalities, over 300 were reportedly beheaded – many publicly – with villages looted and burned and fleeing refugees hunted in the jungles by raiding Dayak parties.

By the time the violence was finally concluded, around 70,000 Madurese settlers had been driven from their homes.

In recent times, ethnic tension has calmed. It is interesting to consider, however, the possible effects of a proposed future transmigration: Indonesia's current President has declared that the nation's capital, Jakarta – a vast city of 10 million people – will be moved later this decade to the interior of Borneo.

ABOUT THE AUTHOR

Welsh author Justin Morgan was lucky enough to have lived on the island of Borneo for five years.

He cherished his time in the rainforest, where he could often be found with his camera and binoculars hoping to spot one of the many living creatures residing there.

Now living back in the UK with his wife, Charlotte, he dreams of returning to the forest one day, and hopes to find its spectacular beauty in at least as pristine a condition as when he last laid eyes on it.

Get the FREE BOOK "Malchik of the Metro" by visiting
http://subscribepage.io/justinmorganauthor

ACKNOWLEDGMENTS

My five years of residence on Borneo (in its smallest nation, Brunei) were greatly enriched by the staff and pupils of SM Tanjong Maya, SM Sayyidinah Othman and SR AHMY Kati Mahar; my colleagues within Education Development Trust/Ministry of Education, especially Deputy Permanent Secretary Awang Aliuddin bin Haji Abdul Rahman; the Brunei Nature Society, in particular its president, Professor Ulmar Grafe, and secretary, Professor David Deterding; animal welfare champion Bud Chapman, and the indomitable Shavez Cheema, whose 1StopBorneo Wildlife conservation group does such valuable work.

As always, I'd like to acknowledge the support and assistance of my wife, Charlotte, without whom the production of my books would be a lot more difficult than it already is. Thanks too to all my friends and family, who are always so kind with their encouragement.

I would also like to acknowledge my mother and father, Gillian and Peter, who so bravely shouldered the grief of losing their nine-month old son while still so young themselves.

My final acknowledgement is reserved for Peter Lee Morgan. Although we never got to meet, you've influenced my life in more ways than you could know, and I'm very proud that we'll always be brothers.